On the planet Barious, war has become a national pass time. During one of these conflicts Taralin Zarco, Queen of Barious, was abducted by the Barion's mortal enemies the Locheds. When our story starts the war has ended, the Barions have won, and the queen has just been found on a distant planet.

Enter Drewcilia Qwah a ruff and tumble salvager, who drinks to much, smokes to much, and has a mouth you wouldn't kiss your mother with. Drewcilia (Drew) and her partner, a huge hair covered alien named Van Gar, have been hired by the kings emissaries to take the confused queen to meet her husband.

Only two real problems with this plan:

Drewcilia hates royalty.

The queen has no memory of being queen or of her husband.

Meet a strange world filled with, palace intrigue, rebel plots, assassination attempts, civil unrest, economic depression, trash, and the unscrupulous salvager who wants to change it all to suit her own needs.

Praise for Selina Rosen's
Queen of Denial

"Down-home science fiction? Redneck interstellar adventure? A full-throttle journey through the rural spaceways? Hey, it can happen and happen convincingly when the writer is damned authentic and has lived the tone she's writing about. That's Selina Rosen to a T. *Queen of Denial* cooks—not just with high energy and in-your-face attitude, but with the metaphorical flavors of grits, red beans and rice, and sweet potato pie.

If there's such a thing as blue-collar sf, this is it. No spiffy interstellar SUVs here—Rosen's characters horse the futuristic equivalent of dented vintage Chevy S-10s around the stars. With plenty of action, violence, foolin' around, and a generous tongue planted just a touch firmly in cheek, *Queen of Denial* takes some old and honored tropes of science fiction, and turns them into the kind of bawdy full-bodied entertainment western literature's furnished since long before Shakespeare.

When MIR morphs into a cut-rate orbital truckstop for space jockeys who can't afford the International Space Station, Selina Rosen's debut novel is the sort of book that'll feature prominently in the spinner rack right between the displays of alien fuzzy dice and zero-gee mudflaps."

—Ed Bryant

More praise for
Queen of Denial

"A rarity of rarities: a book that makes you laugh out loud. Selina Rosen's debut is very much worth noting...sf's answer to Terry Pratchett."—C. J. Cherryh

"Should appeal to anyone who loves a riotous, wickedly funny read."—Jane Fancher

"A rip-snorting space adventure the likes of which we don't see often enough these days!"—Lawrence Watt-Evans

"*Queen of Denial* is a freewheeling, fun and frantic space opera. It takes the usual conventions of pulp action Science Fiction and stands them on their head by featuring a female lead character as tough as any man in the book, and twice as smart. The story moves at a take-no-prisoners pace, keeping you turning the pages fast as possible. And, in the end, arrives at a most satisfactory conclusion. It's a wild ride and quite an accomplishment for a first-time novelist."—Robert Weinberg, author of *The Termination Novel*

"*Queen* is funny and pointed. Ms. Rosen takes a Star-Trek-like plot, introducing the social ills of a world that could be our own, and attacks them with ruthless humor. Drewcila Qwah isn't your everyday heroine, with a foul mouth and almost every other bad habit known to civilization, but she's likeable and honest. The language may not be to everyone's taste, but it's no more than a working spacer's dialect. As Drewcila might say, get the %&#^* out of here if you don't like it. It's not applied gratuitously, and you'll get used to it. The style is as rough and ready as the heroine, but *Queen* is a fast read with a satisfying conclusion."—Jody Lynn Nye

Queen of Denial

by

Selina Rosen

Queen of Denial

An MM Publishing Book
Published by Meisha Merlin Publishing, Inc.
PO Box 7
Decatur, GA   30031

Editing & interior layout by Stephen Pagel
Copyediting & proofreading by Teddi Stransky
Cover art by Don Maitz
Cover design by Neil Seltzer

ISBN: 1-892065-06-1

http://www.angelfire.com/biz/MeishaMerlin

First MM Publishing edition: May 1999

Printed in the United States of America
0 9 8 7 6 5 4 3 2 1

For Lisa, Tad, and Tania.
for being the best sisters in the world.

For Mom and Dad;
I didn't turn out at all like they wanted me to,
and they love me anyway.
What more can I say?

And for Lynn and Meyer,
incase I never sell another book.

An introduction to Selina Rosen

For the last generation or so the readers, writers, and illustrators of science fiction have been getting together for weekend parties at some of the stranger hotels on the planet, and almost always during their off seasons. We call these gatherings "cons," short for conventions. At their best, cons are gatherings of such excitement that you can't walk ten feet down a hall without meeting or making a good friend. You don't sleep because you don't need to—every time you open your room door you feast on the energy of the sun gone nova.

And sometimes a con is three endless, relentless days of the Night of the Living Dead.

The con I'm thinking of was a con of the second kind, a con so dull that I couldn't tell the paying guests from hotel staff, a con so poorly organized that the fun-loving folk who'd conceived and ran it spent most of their time trying desperately to sell the several hundred t-shirts they'd commissioned for the event to the somewhat less than fifty people who'd bothered to show up. Eyes were glazing over by Friday afternoon and the pros—the fun-loving folk like myself who delude ourselves that there's a living to be made in the SF genre—had retreated to the bar, where we can usually be found at any con. From our perches behind the potted plants we rescued the few lively faces from the lobby and swapped horror stories of other weekend disasters—because, frankly, cons of the second kind are at least as common as cons of the first.

So when Selina rolled in, vibrating from the usual vehicular misadventures incurred while getting from western Arkansas to anywhere else in the universe, we called her over and bought her a beer. I knew Selina and she knew me; our paths had been criss-crossing since I'd moved to Oklahoma a few years earlier. We had friends in common but I'm frequently mistaken for the sort of librarian who can cast a pall over a room by raising her eyebrows and Selina—well, Selina created the woman who got your attention on the cover of this book and whose story you should be reading right now instead of this introduction!

I'm getting ahead of myself.

The better-organized cons which Selina and I had attended together had taken note of our different styles and decided in the interest of entertaining the widest audience possible we would always be scheduled at the same time, in different rooms—especially for our readings. A pro can skip out on a panel, a reading, though, is a one-person-show: no author, no reading. I knew Selina had this unpublished novel she was reading from; I'd heard people raving about it; I'd heard them laughing, but I'd never heard word one of it myself.

The Con of the Living Dead would change that: there were only about six scheduled events during the entire three day convention, including Selina's and my readings, and none of them were scheduled against each other. I was finally going to hear the opening chapters of what I knew as *The Princess and the Garbage Scow*.

If we could find a room.

The con had faltered so badly on the money side, that by Saturday afternoon, when the reading was scheduled, the hotel wasn't letting us into their so-called function rooms. We were thinking stairwells when one of the attendees volunteered the use of his room, which the hotel maid hadn't visited. Undaunted, we cleared away the debris, rearranged the furniture, and sat Selina down behind a chip board desk that had never seen better days.

There were aliens in the air ducts; their spores—plus the chlorine wafting in through the pool-side door we opened in an attempt to beat back the spores—gave me an instant migraine headache. Naturally, I'd forgotten my migraine meds. I hunkered down in the darkest corner, eyes closed and clutching a pillow with the hope that I wouldn't do something terribly embarrassing, which sometimes happens with bad migraines.

Then Selina began to read.

Now, one of the truths of the writing business is that most authors can't read their own words for love nor money. Most of the sentences I write are too long to be read in one normal breath and take advantage of the fact that reading is a less linear process than listening (there's also no danger of biting your tongue on a phrase like that last one). But Selina's one of those very rare writers whose prose is a natural extension of her speaking voice.

The opening scene wasn't humorous, not the garbage scow I'd been expecting—then again, Selina had chickened out and was reading from *In Memory Something* (on account of the headache, I hadn't caught the last word of the title). I was hurting and disappointed—not an ideal audience for the scene she was reading: the poignancy of a proud, lonely man determined to undo the past and reclaim the woman he'd loved and lost. I know how novels work; I know how a man's decision, made at the end of Chapter One will inevitably create consequences he can neither foresee nor control. In other words: I knew he was doomed to experience the entire plot and he wouldn't enjoy the experience.

Even without migraines, another author is a scary thing to have in the audience when you're reading, but Selina had caught me. I cared about this man I couldn't quite see yet in my mind's eye. I hoped she wasn't going to treat him too badly.

She turned the page and started reading Chapter Two: change of scene, change of character, enough profanity to earn a medal in the merchant marine, and what to my linear ears sounded like an ice chest filled with beer cans caroming across the bridge of a space ship during liftoff. The skeptical, nit-picky part of me wanted to object: an ice chest in space? beer cans in space? But the story moved too fast; it was indeed *The Princess and the Garbage Scow* and I was caught in a tractor beam of humor.

Natural dialog is a bitch to write; ask any script-writer. And if you're writing a novel, you've got to fill in all the camera stuff, too. Usually, what the reader "hears" is the writer's voice telling a story about the characters. More rarely, the reader "hears" the writer as a character who paraphrases all the dialog and summarizes the camera stuff; done well, we call this "style". Very rarely, the reader is treated to pure character, a total immersion into the mind behind a fictional set of eyeballs. Raymond Chandler did this as well as it's been done, but he was writing in the first person; Selina does it in the third.

And it's funny. Painfully, delightfully, barking seals and whooping cranes funny.

Funny is worse than natural dialog. In "real life" spoken humor relies on timing and nuance while physical humor happens at a speed that cannot be captured with an alphabet. And a lot of what seems funny when written down, dies a lingering death when read aloud. (This I know for a fact.) To write a story that is as funny when read aloud as it is when read silently, and poignant, too, is an act of genius—or dementia, possibly both.

I can't begin to describe the many creative processes that have to be going on to create this sort of synergy. I don't think they can be described. A writer either can do it, or she can't; Selina Rosen can, and she did it with her first novel. If I didn't know her, like her, and respect her, I'd probably have to kill her.

The easy, natural humor of the space merchant-marine; the poignancy of a man searching for something that can never be found; a plot that brings these two elements together in a thoroughly believable, yet unexpected way. In hockey, they call this a hat trick. In science fiction, it's a book that won't ever be lost in my memory.

—Lynn Abbey
February 1999

Chapter 1

Zarco looked out into black, endless space and sighed. "It's like a dream, I don't dare believe and yet I must. Finally, after all this time…I had given up hope. I had begun to believe what everyone had been saying for years—that she was dead, and I would never see her again. Ironic that as I gave up praying for her safe return we should find her, and now all my previously unheard prayers are finally being answered. At last I shall be reunited with my great love. My Taralin will once again embrace me…"

"Sire, please remember. Taralin has been at the mercy of our enemies for the last five years." Fitz's voice lacked the younger man's idealistic enthusiasm. "Who knows what horrors she's been forced to endure. It may be a while before she's her old self."

"She is alive, Fitz. I had given her up for dead, and she's alive. So leave your pessimism behind. Whatever has happened is in the past now. Whatever damage has been done, we will fix. Our love will put things right. I have tried hard not to think of what she may have been going through. But on those endless, tortured nights when I could not sleep I thought of every possibility, every perverted thing they might have done to her, and I don't care, Fitz. If they've used her body, I want her back. If they've broken and twisted her body, I want her back. If they have marred her beauty beyond repair, I still want her back. This is my wife we're talking about, and I shouldn't have to remind you…" Zarco hissed through clenched teeth, "…your Queen."

"My King, I was in no way suggesting that we should discard the Queen." He smiled apologetically and added with a chuckle, "Let's not forget that I have known her since she was an infant. I just don't want to see you…well…expecting too much.

I don't want to see you disappointed. The transmission we received from Facto said that the Lockhedes had run some of their filthy experiments on her..."

"Enough!" Zarco held his hands over his ears. "I will hear no more of your negativity, Fitz! We will go and pick Taralin up, and everything will be fine." He looked back out the porthole. "It has to be."

"Get your feet off the console!" Erik screamed.

She didn't budge, so he shoved her feet. "I said get your feet off the console!"

"It's my fucking ship," the woman said, putting her feet back exactly where they had been and giving the pudgy, balding human a look that said she dared him to do it again.

"It's my operation, Qwah."

"Yeah, this week," she said with a shrug.

"What the hell is that supposed to mean?" Erik asked.

The woman grinned impishly back, "Told ya, Erik. Someday I'm gonna take it away from you."

Erik just laughed, then stopped abruptly. "Well, until you do, get your fucking feet off the console."

"So who shit in your cereal?" She took her feet down, but only so she could walk to the cooler and pull a beer out of it. "Want one?" she asked, holding up the bottle.

Erik's face turned red and she could see the little veins sticking out in his neck.

"I guess that means no." She flopped back into the command chair and opened the bottle of beer on the corner of the console, letting the cap land where it may. Then, just to make Erik's day complete, she plopped her feet up on the console again.

"Do you have any idea how unprofessional your entire attitude is?" Erik hissed, tucking his shirt back over his belly.

Pot calling the kettle black, she thought, but just said, "Junk don' care..."

"Yeah, but passengers do. Did you at least clean out the personal quarters, like I asked you to?"

"Yes siree, Bob! Hosed it out myself." She hooked a thumb in the strap of her gray overalls.

"Damn it, Drew. This woman's real important. Some King's lost wife…"

Drew twirled her index finger around in the air. "Whoop de shit."

Erik blew his oversized belly up, then exhaled slowly, trying very hard to keep his cool. He decided to talk in the only language Drewcila Qwah respected.

"We're talking big bucks here, Drew."

"Well, why didn't you say that in the first place?" Drew smiled. "How much?"

"A lot."

"How much is a lot, Fuck-head?"

"I'm your boss," Erik protested.

"I work for your operation because it's the most profitable one around—today. You are not now, nor have you ever been, nor will you ever be my boss."

"I helped you get your own ship…"

"Because I'm the best Salvager in space, and you damn well know it."

"Why you egotistical little shit-head! I most certainly know nothing of the kind. I have lots of men who bring in…"

"Half of what I do," she grinned unashamed. "Everyone knows I'm the best. Now give me some incentive. How much is a lot?"

"Your part is twenty thousand Inter-Galactic Dollars…"

Drew jumped to her feet, spilling her beer. "What a dick on a baby! Say that again."

"Twenty thousand IGD's."

"She's got plague?" Drew asked suspiciously.

"No."

"We've got to go pick her up out of a radiation field?"

"No, they're going to bring her to the ship. All you have to do is move her through space…"

"I don't fucking get it. That's more than I make on six hauls. Why are they paying so much?"

"I told you. She's a very important lady, and I'm a very shrewd businessman. You should be thanking me about now."

Drew looked at her feet and squinted her eyes. "All I gottah do is haul em?"

"That's right." He looked at her expectantly, waiting in vain for her words of thanks.

"How much you gettin'?" she asked with a raised eye-brow.

Erik grinned from ear to ear. "Enough that it's worth it to put up with your shit."

Drew sat back down and watched as Erik left the bridge. She shook her head. "Anything that looks too good to be true, usually is." She mumbled to herself.

"Twenty thousand iggys!" An excited voice screamed out.

Drew spilled beer all down the front of herself and almost fell out of her chair.

"You fucking asshole! You damn near gave me a cardiac!" She held her chest as if her hand were the only thing keeping her heart from jumping out onto the floor. "And you made me *spill beer*!"

"Did I hear right?" The fur-covered humanoid sat down on the console in front of Drew.

Drew nodded affirmatively. "Damnedest thing I ever heard. Twenty thousand iggys to haul some princess' lily-white ass a few light years. God, how I love the free enterprise system."

She tossed her half empty beer to him and he caught it easily. She dug in the cooler till she found another one, and opened it the way she had the first one. She took a long swallow then looked up at her big friend.

"Erik's feeding us some cock and bull story, though."

"What do you mean?"

"Ah, come on, Van. You really think anyone in their right mind is going to pay that kind of money to transport some royal bitch? There's got to be more to it, that's all. Not that I don't think we're up for the challenge."

She stood up and finished the beer. "Come on, let's go celebrate."

"You really think that's a good idea?"

"Probably not. Which is all the more reason to do it."

Erik moved through the room towards the back where they had planned to meet. He slid into the booth.

"Sorry I'm late. I had to fight a price war with Drewcila. She seems to think that with all the risks she'll be taking it's worth more money..."

"I think that twenty million Inter-Galactic Dollars is more than a fair price..."

"That's exactly what I told Drew. Don't worry, I can handle her. Just do yourself a favor and don't talk about the hazards. Any reminder of the danger she's putting herself and her ship in and she'll be trying to up the ante again. That's just Drew."

"Is it safe? I mean, can she be trusted?" The man asked.

"Drewcila?" Erik laughed. "She's a little unruly and she can be ruthless, but I've never known her to welch on a deal, and I've never known her to leave a job half done. You and your lovely companion will arrive at your destination safely. I can promise you that," Erik said with assurance.

"Now let us dispense with business. Please introduce me to this charming creature."

The man seemed only too happy to change the subject.

"It is my pleasure to introduce our most noble and beloved queen, Taralin Zarco. My Queen, Erik Rider."

Erik stood for the introduction, taking her offered hand and kissing the air just above it, as was proper. As he sat back down, he really looked at the woman for the first time.

She was lovely, with aristocratic features and long thin fingers. Like the man with her, there was no doubting her planet of origin. Their hair was jet black, as were their eyes. The eyes were the real give away. In Barions it was almost impossible to distinguish the pupil from the iris, making their fair skin look even paler. These two were hauntingly beautiful beings, as were most Barions, made more exotic by the fact that one scarcely saw them off their home planet.

Barions didn't trade much with other worlds, though they had the technology for interstellar travel, and spoke intergalactic. They seemed more than happy to stay at home and fight amongst themselves. On Barious, one nation was constantly fighting with another. In fact, the joke around the space ports was that war was the Barions' only real sport. Other than that, no one really knew much about them.

Of course, Erik knew more than most. After all, he'd been working with Drewcila Qwah for years, and Drew was every bit as Barion as the woman he sat across from now.

"It's…it's a pleasure to meet you," Erik stammered when he realized he had been staring far too long. "I was sorry to hear of your abduction," he added quietly, back in control.

"It was…" she shuddered delicately. "Well, at least it is over at last, and I can go home to my people and my husband."

"Please accept my sincere hope that your home coming will be…Son of a bitch!"

"Excuse me?" The man was too surprised to be angry at Erik's outburst.

"A thousand pardons, your Excellency. Please excuse a barbarian who has spent too much time with Salvagers. I stubbed my toe on the leg of the table."

Erik glared across the room at the couple who had just walked in, the tall slender Barion woman dressed down in her very grubbiest coveralls. And the huge, fur-covered male Chitzky, Van Gar, wearing the match for what Drew was wearing—right down to the grease and the "Garbage Scow" insignia over the upper right-hand pocket.

For some reason it always galled Erik to see her with that thing. Probably because he wasn't so sure that they weren't really a couple in the truest sense of the word. Of course, tonight their presence here was burning his britches for another reason.

"If you could excuse me a moment, I think I'll just go to the rest room and check on my toe." He rose, bowed low and made his way through the crowd once more.

"I don't trust him, Facto," Taralin said.

"Don't worry. All he cares about is money, and he's getting enough of that to keep him honest. He gets nothing until we reach Jabar. Then the transfer to his account will be made, and he'll get the second half of his money."

"He's stopped to talk to someone at the bar."

"Can you see who?"

Taralin squinted her eyes and shrugged. "Not through the smoke."

Facto laughed, and patted her shoulder reassuringly. "Don't worry, we will not miss our meeting with Zarco."

"I hope not," she looked troubled. They had gone too far, and been through too much to fail now.

They saw him before he was halfway across the room, and waved broadly at him as if he were supposed to meet them there.

"Erik! Darling! What a pleasure bumping into you here," Drew drawled out. "Join us for drinks, won't you…"

"What are you playing at," Erik whispered angrily. "You've got an important shipment to deliver tomorrow…"

"We gottah eat," Drew said.

"Not here you don't," Erik said hotly.

"Why not?" Drew's curiosity was aroused. "Ya got a girl here daddy?" She yelled. "Mama's been waiten' home all night!"

"Shut up, you gaping renal pore," Erik hissed. "The clients are here, and I would rather they didn't see what morons they have entrusted their lives to. So pick your rude fucking asses up, and haul them outtah here before you get drunk and play a game of 'let's see how far we can pitch the bartender'."

The bartender's eyes got big, and he smiled his warmest smile at the two Salvagers.

"We only did that one time," Drewcila assured him sweetly.

"He was being a jerk," Van Gar added solemnly.

"What can I get you?" the bartender asked, smiling his most helpful smile.

"They're not staying," Erik assured him.

"I'll get you something in a carry out."

The bartender started mixing a drink in a take-out glass.

"On the house," he added.

"Now get up and go," Erik said.

Drewcila smiled and held out her hand. "What's it worth to ya?"

"Fucking bitch," Erik grumbled, digging into his pocket. He took out a handful of oval-shaped coins and handed them to her.

She took them, and stuffed them quickly into her own pocket.

"Now go."

"We have to wait for our drinks," Drew said sweetly.

"Here you are," the bartender put two drinks on the bar in front of the Salvagers.

"Thanks."

"It was a pleasure to serve you. Come back any time."

"Don't get drunk," Erik warned.

"That'll cost ya extra," Drew smiled back.

"You listen to me, Drew. You and this fur-ball had better be ready for take off in the morning, or..."

"Don't get yer panties in a wad, Erik. I'll be ready for take off. Just like I always am."

She patted Erik on the head, then linked her arm through Van Gar's. "Come, Van, I grow weary of this place."

Arm-in-arm, they sauntered out the front door.

Erik gritted his teeth together and headed back for his table. No one was there. Erik sighed. They probably got antsy and left.

"She'll be the death of me yet."

Drewcila and Van Gar walked down the crowded space-port street, oblivious to the colorful night time crowd. They were busy counting the money Erik had just given them. Drew held it in her hand while the Chitzky counted it, neither of them being willing to trust the other with their free drink.

"Wow! Damn!" Van whistled.

"How much?" Drew asked.

"Twenty fucking iggys." Van breathed. Drew stuffed the money in her pocket quickly. But not before a hooker saw it.

"I'd do you for that, tall, dark and furry." The hooker called, following them down the street.

"Not interested," Van said.

The hooker ran around in front of them, so that they had to stop or run over her.

"I'd do you for that, hot babe."

"Bite me."

Drew elbowed around her and they started walking again.

"Would if you wanted me to," the hooker said, continuing in hot pursuit. "Do you both for twenty. That's a real bargain. Come on, what do you say? Two for the price of one. That's my final offer."

Drew stopped and Van Gar followed suit. Together they turned to face the determined whore. They looked at each other, then back at the whore.

"Nah," they said in unison, then turned and started walking again.

"Ah, come on! It's been a lousy night. Give a girl a break," she whined as she continued to follow them.

"We said we're not interested," Van said hotly.

"You don't have to be so mean," the whore shouted back.

Drew turned around. "Tell you what, honey. Go and boil your pussy for ten minutes, and then maybe we'll talk."

Drew gave her a little shove. "Now beat it."

"You'll be sorry!" The whore screamed over her shoulder as she took off running in the other direction.

"Not as sorry as we could have been!" Van shouted after her.

The Salvagers laughed and started on their way again. Their drinks were almost empty, and they were trying to pick a good dive in which to buy a refill, when two big human males crawled out of an alley in front of them.

"Suppose this is the sorry that slut was talking about?" Van whispered to Drew.

She smiled up at him. "Either that, or a welcoming committee for crabs."

"Hey, fur ball, where ya get off puttin' down our whore?" The bigger one gritted out through yellow teeth.

"Sticks and stones may break my bones, but words will only piss me off," Van Gar sneered back.

"So, ya wanna get smart, do ya?" The smaller one cracked his knuckles.

"Why? Are you guys teachers?" Drew asked facetiously.

"Give us the money, and maybe we'll let ya live," the big one snarled.

"Get the fuck outtah my face, and maybe I'll let you live," Van Gar answered with a smile.

At six-six, and carrying two hundred and twenty pounds of muscle-bound flesh, wrapped in a protective coating of fur, there weren't many things in the universe that intimidated the Chitzky.

"Now, now," Drew chided, clicking her tongue. "Can't we find a peaceful solution? After all, the universe would be a much nicer place if people would just talk things out instead of always resorting to violence..."

"You've gottah be kidding, lady," the bigger one said.

"You interrupted me when I was talking!" Drew screamed as she took a step closer to him. "I hate it when people do that!" She kicked him in the balls as hard as she could, and he collapsed, screaming in agony. Then she kicked him in the head for good measure.

Without waiting for the other man's reaction, Van Gar landed a power punch to his face, and he hit the sidewalk next to his friend, out cold.

Meanwhile, Drew was finishing her lesson, punctuating her speech with solid kicks to her victim's ribs.

"What I was going to say before you so rudely interrupted me, was that people should learn to dwell in peace with one another. That we should nurture each other instead of always destroying each other."

Her speech finished, she quit kicking him, and she and Van Gar started back down the street without a backwards glance.

"Well, the whore was right," Drew said.

"Huh?"

"I am sorry. Sorry that I didn't hit that diseased bitch first."

"Amen, Sister." Van Gar laughed.

Drew took his hand. She liked the way it felt—all warm and hairy. He squeezed her hand till it was almost uncomfortable, and she warmed with the familiar feel of it.

"Hey, Chitzky. Why don't you find your own kind!" Someone screamed from the safety of a crowded bar. Van started to drop Drew's hand, but she held his tighter.

"Fuck em," she said.

"Fucking jerk," Van mumbled. "Hell, it might have been Erik. He makes no bones about the way he feels about me."

"Erik's human, Van. You know how they are. They hate everybody."

"It's not just the humans, Drew. Not with the Chitskys. We no longer have a home world, and because of that all races look down on us."

"Aw! Come on, Van. We're supposed ta be havin' a good time. You're not going ta start that poor-down-trodden-Chitzky crap again, are you? So you don't have a planet. Whoopy shit. Some people will find any reason to whine. Now snap out of it. We're celebrating, remember? Fuck Erik. The only reason Erik doesn't like you is because you have hair everywhere, and he doesn't even have it on his head."

Van Gar laughed and followed her into the first of a series of ten bars.

Chapter 2

Drew held her head between her hands and tried to make the screens in front of her come into focus. Through the fog of pain, she was about to decide that there really was such a thing as having too good a time.

Van set a steaming cup of liquid in front of her.

"I told you not to drink that Get Outtah the Truck Bitch. You get sick every time you drink them.

"I am aware of that, Van Gar." Drew spoke carefully, so she wouldn't wake up the sharp pains in her head again. "After all, you only said 'I told you so' seven hundred times last night while I was throwing up my liver and spleen."

"Well, that's seven hundred and one, then." He worked at keeping the smile off his face. "I've just about got the mess cleaned up now."

"I don't know what I'd do without you."

"Drown in vomit?" Van suggested.

"What a pleasant thought," Drew said with a snarl.

She let her head flop on the console in front of her, and then fought the wave of nausea that washed over her.

"Oh! Please! There couldn't possibly be anything left in my stomach. Oh, never again, Van. Tell me. Did I make an ass of myself?"

"No more than usual."

"Did I dance naked anywhere?"

"Just topless. No one seemed to notice."

"That's always comforting. Did we have sex?"

"No," Van said with a laugh. "Not unless you consider holding your head outtah the toilet to be fore-play."

"You will tell me if we ever have sex, won't you? I mean, I'd hate not knowing." She groaned loudly. "Oh, God, Van! I wish I would just die and get it over with."

"No such luck, babe. Drink your medicine, you'll feel better. I'm going to go finish cleaning up the mess."

"Oh, that's right. We couldn't have the ship messy when the royal bitch gets here. Go ahead—abandon me in my hour of need…"

"Your hour of need was about three o'clock this morning. Why have you already decided to hate this woman?" Van Gar pushed the cup closer to Drew, and she picked up her head and made a face at the smell.

"There's just something that galls me about the thought of royalty. The idea that someone is better than me simply by right of their birth. Like being born is something you have any say in. I mean, what happens? Does a sperm scream out, 'No! no. Don't put me in that wretched pussy, I want to go in that Royal cunt!' I don't fucking think so."

Van Gar laughed. "You're a twisted bitch, Drew." Still laughing, he left to go finish cleaning up the ship.

Drew waited till he was out of sight, then she stumbled over to the disposal chute and tossed the Chitsky's hang-over remedy away. Then she went back and sat down.

"I feel better already," she mumbled, looking at the empty cup.

She decided that no matter how hard it might be, she was not going to let Erik know she was hung-over.

"So! You must be Drewcila Qwah," declared a booming male voice.

"Why? Doesn't anyone else want to do it?" Drewcila answered, as she spun around in her chair to face her boarders. "And besides thats *Qwah* as in my *way*!"

"Excuse me?" Facto asked.

"Drew's attempt at humor, I'm afraid," Erik said.

"Stop screaming," Drew said holding her head. "I've got a headache."

"And I'll just bet I know why…" Erik started.

"Are you sick?" Taralin asked with real concern.

"Get Outtah The Truck Bitch," Drew answered

Taralin looked taken aback, and Erik laughed nervously. "It's the name of a drink," he explained.

"Are you trying to say that she's hung-over?" Facto asked in disbelief.

"Hey! Erik! I thought you said this guy was dumb," Drew said.

"I never said that," Erik assured Facto.

"I am Taralin Zarco, and this is my chamberlain Facto." Taralin tried to change the drift of the conversation.

"How come you get two names and he only gets one?" Drew asked suspiciously.

"Drew! For God's sake!"

Erik threw up his hands in defeat.

"I took on the name of my husband when we married…"

"Cause ah him being King and all, I suppose?" Drew was tired of making idle chatter. She turned back to the console and gave them directions over her shoulder.

"You'll find your quarters down the corridor and to your left. You can't miss it. There's a big sign made outtah cardboard that says 'VIP Quarters'. I made the sign myself."

There was no doubt in any of their minds that they were being dismissed. Facto grabbed the two small bags and headed down the hallway, and the Queen followed him.

"Pleasure to meet you," Taralin said, turning at the doorway.

"Uh huh," Drew grunted out.

"What the hell are you playing at, Qwah!" Erik screamed when he was sure they were out of hearing range.

"Hey! I made 'em a sign, didn't I?"

"You're a God damned smart-assed little bitch," he screamed, his face turning red.

"And you're a hairless, pencil-dicked old fuck," Drew said calmly. "But I love you anyway."

Erik took a deep breath and counted to ten. "What's that awful smell?" He asked after a second.

"Did you ever smell a Get Outtah The Truck Bitch?"

"Yeah."

"Well, that's what it smells like when it's been recycled."

Zarco had never been to Vares 7 before, and he decided he hadn't missed much. It was the least inhabited of Vares's eighty moons. Really nothing more than a spaceport, consisting mostly of hotels which had rooms which weren't much better than the accommodations on most ships. There were restaurants which looked like they might get shoveled out once a year, and there were trading posts. The trading posts seemed to have a little bit of everything. People traded what they didn't need for what they did. Or more than likely sold it, so that they would have enough money to get drunk, laid, or both at the most prominent business on Vares 7; one of the fifty clubs which littered the main street.

The only people who ever came here were riff-raff and Salvagers, if there was really any distinction between the two. Zarco didn't think there was.

Vares was a pit, a cesspool of a place on the edge of the cosmos, where the dregs of space congregated to share their diseases. But that was a large part of the reason they had decided to pick Taralin up here. He, Zarco, was dressed in normal spaceport clothes, and they were using the least impressive of his twenty private ships. He had given orders that no one was to know that he had left the palace, much less the planet. But he knew that was no guarantee his enemies wouldn't find out that he was gone. Things had a way of leaking out, even when you took every precaution. A servant told a friend. The friend told his wife. Before you knew it, everyone knew. But no one would even consider that he would be coming to a place like Vares 7. No one would believe he would come to such an awful place.

He still wished their reunion didn't have to be in such a horrible place, but he wasn't willing to take any chance that his enemies might stop his reunion with his wife. He wasn't deluded enough to believe that he no longer had any enemies.

Winning a war didn't decrease your enemies, it increased them. If anything, they became more vengeful. There were always going to be those who would not admit to defeat. Those who had lost loved ones and were hell-bent on "justice". If you lost someone in a war that you won, their death seemed some how justified. But if you lost the war...well, it just seemed like a waste.

Still, as he looked around him, he couldn't help but feel that meeting her in this place seemed a high price to pay for safety.

"Sire, I believe this is our hotel," Fitz informed him.

Zarco looked up at the three-storied building and frowned.

"Are you all right, sire?"

Zarco nodded yes.

"We married on the sands of Dradious, with the crystal clear waters of Uratis behind us. I just wish our reunion could take place someplace..."

He kicked a piece of something that might have once been fruit out of his way.

"Someplace cleaner. Less detestable." He forced a smile. "I'm fine, Fitz. I can't wait to see her again. To embrace her."

Taralin walked onto the bridge. She was fascinated by all the flashing lights, the buttons and screens. She knew nothing about how these things worked, but she imagined that it must take a certain amount of intelligence to operate something like this ship. She hadn't had much chance to travel, and this was the only time that she had felt like she had full run of a ship. Take off had been a little rough, and she had stayed strapped in her EV chair longer than she really needed to. But as soon as she'd gotten her space legs, she had started touring the ship and had finally wound up here.

Drewcila sat at the command console and pretended like she didn't see the other woman.

"How long will it take us?" Taralin asked.

"Sixteen to eighteen hours."

Drew stared at the screen harder.

"This is the biggest ship I've ever been on," Taralin said.

Drew raised her eyebrows. Now that didn't sound right. She'd seen presidential ships, and they were huge, flamboyant things. Surely a king would have as good—if not better. She shrugged—who could figure royalty?

"It's freighter class. I have some pretty big shipments. Junk takes up a shit load ah space. Bulky and heavy. The Garbage Scow is seventy-five percent hold, fifteen percent engine and ten percent living quarters."

"Where do you live, when you're not on the ship?" Taralin asked.

Drewcila looked at her like she was a complete imbecile.

"I'm a Salvager."

It was obvious that Taralin didn't understand the significance.

"Yes, so?"

"What do you live in—a bubble? I'm a Salvager. I live on the ship. I spend all my time in space, running junk from one planet to another. It would be kind of stupid for me to own a house somewhere. Not to mention boring. How the hell do you people exist in one place? It's no wonder you're always fighting amongst yourselves. You're fucking bored outtah yer skull."

"But don't you ever wish you had someplace to call home? Don't you ever long for our home planet?"

Drew thought about it for only a second and then shrugged. "No. The Garbage Scow is my home, and all of the universe is my back yard. I can't imagine living any other way."

Drewcila punched half a dozen buttons on her panel, and watched the screen for the effect. She nodded in a satisfied way. She punched a button all the way to the right of her panel.

"That's got it, Van."

"Good. It's hotter than the hubs of hell down here," a voice spoke back out of the console.

"What was the problem?"

"A fucking rat chewed through a couple of the wires."

"Which ones?"

"The blue one and the green one."

"What's the green one do?" Drew asked shortly.

"How the fuck do I know? The coating was off it. I taped it, I killed the fucking rat, and I'm coming up," Van screamed back.

"Touchy! Touchy!" Drew laughed.

"Was that why take off was so rough?" Taralin asked.

Drew shrugged and smiled.

"Who knows? Guess we'll find out next time we take off."

"I hate fucking rats," Van Gar said.

His voice startled Taralin, and she swung around to face him. She took one look at the alien that had walked onto the bridge, let out a screech and jumped back. Almost at the same time she became aware that he was wearing the same uniform that Drewcila Qwah was. She felt like an idiot.

"I'm sorry," Taralin and Van Gar said in unison.

Van Gar laughed and walked over to her, holding out his hand.

"A pleasure to meet you. My name is Van Gar and I have the misfortune of being Drewcila's first mate."

"Some men will believe any story ya tell em," Drew mumbled.

"Ah," Taralin reluctantly took his hand. "I am Taralin Zarco. It's…ah.. nice to meet you. I'm afraid you startled me a little."

"I would imagine that my appearance would be a little startling to anyone who hadn't had the opportunity to meet a Chitzky before."

"Brown noser," Drew said, punching buttons for no better reason than she was bored. "Don' buy his line ah shit. He's as big an asshole as I am."

"Believe me," Van Gar hissed, "no one can compete with you when it comes to being an asshole."

Van Gar glared at Drew, and she grinned back and stuck out her tongue. Van ignored her.

"So, I would imagine that you're excited about seeing your husband again."

"I don't know if you'd call it excited…"

"Lousy lay, huh?" Drew guessed.

"And so she proves my point," Van Gar said shaking his head.

Drew shrugged, got up and walked to the cooler. She dug through the ice, pulled out a can, threw it to Van, and he caught it instinctively. "You, Queenie?" Drew asked.

Taralin shook her head no.

Drew grabbed one for herself, then launched herself into her seat, opening her beer at the same time without spilling a drop. Drew looked at Van to see if he had witnessed the elegant execution of this act. He held his thumb up and grinned.

"So, is he?" Drew asked after a long pull on the can.

"Drew! You're such a shit head!" Van Gar cursed.

"Is who what?" Taralin asked a bit confused.

"The King. Is the king a lousy lay? You know, is he bad at the bad thing? Does his willy not tickle your twat?"

Taralin looked at Van, who seemed to be much easier to talk to than his employer.

"She wants to know if the King is good in bed," Van interpreted.

Taralin blushed scarlet. Then stammered out. "Ah…that's just the problem. I don't remember."

"Well, I'd say that speaks volumes!" Drew laughed.

"You're…Fuck you, Drew!" Van Gar stomped of the bridge.

"Wonder who tied his shorts in a knot?" Drew asked with a shrug.

"You don't understand," Taralin said. "I don't remember Zarco at all. I didn't even know who I really was 'til two days ago. They told me that the Lockhedes removed part of my brain. That I can't ever remember. Those memories are gone totally. I don't remember being Queen. I don't remember my parents, or my sister. And I don't remember him. Not at all. I don't even remember what I was like before they did this to me. I've been waiting tables on Jors for the last five years. That's all

I remember. Now I'm supposed to go be Queen, and I have no idea how to be a wife much less a queen! I'm afraid Zarco is going to be terribly disappointed."

"Ah, Fuck 'em!"

"Excuse me?"

"I mean...Look, if you meant so much to him he should ah come after you before this. If someone took Van Gar, I'd go after him. And I wouldn't stop till I found him—an killed them in a really horrible sort of blood-gushing way. I mean, he can be a moody pain in the ass sometimes, but he's my moody pain in the ass! And it wouldn't take me no five years to get him back!"

"But they explained that to me. He didn't have a choice. The country was at war, and..."

"Ah, that's a fucking cop-out if ever I've heard one. He probably found someone else to fuck, and then he just wasn' in any hurry. I know men, honey. Take my word for it. They're all the same. I don't care if they're royal or not. No man goes for five years without getting his willy wet."

Taralin was blushing again. "I don't think he's that kind of man. They say he loves me. That he has mourned for me..."

"I guess that's the difference between a King an a normal guy. A normal guy has to make up his own bullshit stories. Listen to me, an you'll be OK. Ride this Royal shit for all it's worth. You've fucking been through hell, an he owes you. I'll tell you what I'd do if I were you. I'd put me an industrial sized ice cooler under the Royal throne, and I'd hire me about half a dozen naked dancing boys with pecs of death and dicks that hang to their knees. And when I got bored with that, I'd get me a bunch ah money outtah the Royal safe and I'd buy me half a dozen of the fanciest freighters you've ever seen. I'd become Queen of the Salvagers, that's what I would do."

She took a long slug of beer and checked the instrument panel.

"But...That would be wrong. Shouldn't I do the best job I can to be a good wife, and to serve my people?"

"Honey, all you know how to serve them is a hot cup of Java. As for wrong. Well, wrong is kind of a relative thing, isn't it? I mean, who's to say it's any more wrong than a man leaving his wife to rot in a hole like Jors for five years while he screws everything that moves."

"He didn't do that!" Taralin said.

"Does he have a dick?" Drew asked.

"Of course he does!"

"Then take my word for it. He's been balling every bimbo who ever wanted a piece of Royal meat."

Taralin didn't want to follow this line of conversation any more. Besides, there was something else she was curious about.

"Are you and Van Gar, well, are you a couple?"

Drew was a little shocked by the question.

"Van and I?" She laughed nervously.

"Well, you did say you'd go after him."

"That's what I git for bein' nice," Drew mumbled. "Van and I have never made the beast with two backs. Not that I remember, anyway. We will have to one day though," she said matter-of-factly.

Taralin was confused by the resolve in the other woman's voice.

"Why do you say that?"

"Because that's what always happens when men and women are friends. They get really close, but they always avoid sex because they know it will ruin their friendship. But all along they both secretly know it will happen. They keep waiting for the right moment. That moment when they think they may be able to pull off having sex and not have it ruin their friendship. In the end, they give up and wind up having sex when they most need the closeness. Then he never forgives her because she must not have thought he was any good in bed, or she wouldn't have been able to stay out of it. And she never forgives him because he didn't fall in love with her."

"And that's what's going to happen to you and Van Gar?"

Drew smiled broadly, and stood up. "No. Because I already know that Van loves me. And I always go back for seconds."

She strolled off the bridge, beer in hand.

Taralin watched her go with a feeling of dread. This reunion was not going to go at all as she had planned.

Zarco leaned back in the cheap hotel chair, and hoped that it would hold him.

"Are you sure you were not followed?" He asked the man who had joined them only moments ago.

"I am," the man assured him.

He looked nervous, and for the first time since Zarco had been told that Taralin had been found alive he felt true dread at what his enemies might have done to his wife.

"You saw Taralin?"

"Yes. She didn't remember me."

"What? That doesn't make any sense, Holm! I mean..."

"The Lockhedes did a very cruel thing to Your Queen and to You, my King," Holm said solemnly.

"Is she mad, Holm?" Zarco asked quietly.

"No, sire. She is as sharp as ever she was."

"Disfigured, then?"

"I have never seen her look more lovely."

"Is she...Is she barren, Holm?"

"Sire, there is nothing physically wrong with Your Queen."

"Then she is mad."

"Sire, please allow me to finish. What I should have said is that the damage is not obvious. The Lockhedes operated on her brain. They removed her memory. She has absolutely no memory of her life before her abduction..."

Zarco sighed with relief.

"I thought it was something serious," he laughed. "The moment she sees me her memory will come back to her..."

"Sire! Please listen. They removed that part of her brain. She can never remember, not ever. It's simply not there anymore."

"But she will remember, Holm," Zarco smiled. "You are younger than I, and have not yet felt the kind of love that lasts more than a night. She will see me, and she will remember."

Zarco looked at Fitz. "She must remember."

Drewcila and Van Gar sat on the bridge.

"So, do you believe that shit about losing half her brain?" Drewcila asked

"It could happen," Van Gar shrugged.

"Maybe she's jus puttin' it on so that she doesn't have to fuck 'im. You know, kindah like 'Not tonight, dear, half my brain is gone.'"

"You are such a sick, skeptical bitch. I can't believe that you, of all people, wouldn't believe her story…"

"Ah, come on, Van. A girl shakes her hips the right way and you believe she's virginal. If I was her, I'd be looking to take this fucker down. And what better way than to say 'I don't remember where the Royal safe is, I don't remember the combination', and then when they believe you, Wham! Bam! Thank you ma'am! You take every fucking dime from the kingdom, and head off for parts unknown with Joe-Joe the horse-hung boy."

"See, that's what I'm talking about. This guy could have had a perfectly good reason for not coming after his wife before now."

"Yeah. Like he's boffin' the serving girl, and the upstairs and down stairs maids." Drew laughed. "Meanwhile, she's waiting tables on Jors for five years with half a brain."

"She didn't say she only has half a brain. She certainly does not seem like a half wit."

"My point exactly. It's all an act."

"Just because you are a vindictive bitch doesn't mean that everyone else is." Van Gar shook his head.

"I am not a vindictive bitch. Well, I may be a bitch, but I am not vindictive. I simply have a very strong sense of justice…"

"You've already tried this guy and found him guilty. I think this guy really does love his wife, and that he just couldn't find her. If he didn't love her, would he be paying twenty thousand iggys to us, and God only knows how much to Erik?"

"You've got a point there," Drew said, thinking for a moment. That was an awful lot of money. "Ah, but how do we know that isn't just a spit in the bucket for him?"

"I swear Drew, you would find bacteria in the milk of humanoid kindness," Van said. "Do you always have to be such a pessimist?"

"What's with all the labels, Van? Are you really mad at me, or are you just trying to increase your negative vocabulary?"

Van Gar laughed. "You're impossible."

"If I was, I wouldn't be here."

The ship rocked violently. Drew looked at Van Gar.

"The green wire goes to the detection system," they said in unison.

They jumped to their feet, spilling beer everywhere and ran for the gun cabinet, where they grabbed the two biggest, ugliest rifles they had and started at a dead run for the cargo bay.

Facto stepped out of his cabin.

"What's going on?" he asked, stepping into their way when he realized they weren't going to stop. "What is it?"

The ship lurched again, and they were all thrown into the wall. "We're being boarded," Van Gar told him, regaining his footing.

"By whom?"

"By fucking Boy Scouts! Who the fuck do you think?" Drew shoved past him.

Taralin stepped out of her cabin, and Drew saw iggys falling into a bottomless pit.

"Get her and go lock yourselves on the bridge. Don't open the door for anyone. The ship is on a set course, and with any luck you'll reach Vares 7 before they can break down the door."

"What is all this?" Taralin demanded.

"Pirates. We're being boarded," Van Gar told her. Then chased after Drew, who had already started back down the hall.

"No! Wait!" Facto started to go after them, and Taralin grabbed his arm.

"There's nothing we can do, Facto. I have faith in her ability to deal with this."

"But, my Lady…"

"Let's do as we were told."

Van Gar and Drew stood on either side of the door to the cargo bay.

"Ready?" she asked.

"Let's party. I'll take point."

Drew punched a button and the doors opened. Van Gar jumped through the door and opened fire. Drew came in after him, and the door clanged shut behind them as someone returned their fire. They ran for cover behind a pile of transformers.

"Fuck." Van Gar took a deep breath. "I count five."

"Seven," Drew corrected.

She jumped out from behind the pile, opened fire, and then jumped back.

"Now there's five of em." She grinned. "Man, I hope you dumb fucks don't bleed all over my scrap!"

"Fuck you!" someone yelled back.

"Hey! You can't talk that way ta me! I'm a lady!"

She looked at Van. "Shall we?"

"You take the left; I'll take the right."

"On three."

"One, two, three."

Drew ran around the left side of the junk, and Van Gar ran out the right. He dodged behind an old truck, and she dove behind a bin of copper wire as a blast went past her. She lay on the floor, still for a moment.

"Fucking up my junk," she mumbled as she started crawling on her knees and elbows. She grinned when she poked her head around the corner of the bin and saw the two guys perched on the top of an old nuclear regulator.

"Kiss me, fuckers!" She fired a hail of bolts on them, and they fell together from their perch. She heard gunfire from the other side of the cargo bay.

Van Gar saw the two men fall and made a dash for the airlock doors. The doors were open, and coming through the tube which the pirates had connected to the hull of the Garbage Scow, Van Gar could see reinforcements from the pirate ship. He couldn't risk firing at the pirates while they were in the tube. If he ruptured the sides of the plastic tube, both cargo bays on both ships would be instantly and explosively depressurized. He stepped to the side of the door as the men inside the tube fired on him, and quickly loaded a nasty looking projectile into his weapon. He counted to three, jumped into the doorway, and fired over the heads of the boarding party, into their ship. Then he ran for the airlock control button.

The men in the tube knew what he was up to, and they ran faster in an attempt to get into the ship before the doors closed.

Van Gar punched the button. It made a grating sound.

"Fuck fuck," he looked around the opening, and someone fired at him out of the tube. "Damn, damn," he slammed his closed fist into the button. It started to close, but much slower than it should have.

"Open it, fur ball."

Van Gar felt something very hard and very cold against the back of his head.

"Buddy, I just launched a nerve gas canister into your ship. If I don't close this door, we're all going to die."

"Fucking liar."

Van Gar heard the man's finger moving towards the trigger. Then there was a gurgling sound, and the gun fell away from his head. He turned and the guy was just staring at him. Then he staggered a little, and fell to the ground, sliding off the bayonet of Drew's rifle as he did so.

Van Gar smiled at Drew. "What took you so long?"

"I broke a nail. Cover me."

Van Gar nodded.

She put her weapon down, pulled a tool from her pocket, and pried the cover off the control panel.

"You better fucking hurry. If they make it to the airlock…"

"You worry so much."

She snipped a couple of wires and twisted them together, apparently oblivious to the shower of sparks which erupted at her finger tips.

Van Gar heard feet hit the airlock floor, and then the doors hit high speed and slammed shut, leaving a hand flopping around on the floor.

Drew made a face. "Ugh! I hate it when that happens."

She played around with the wires, trying to override whatever the pirates had done, so that she could first close the exterior doors just enough to break the pirates' tube seal and suck them all into the vacuum of space, and then close the door completely. She could hear them banging on the airlock door. Either they thought one of their buddies would open the doors, or they were just plain desperate.

Drew was working as fast as she could when Van tapped her shoulder.

"You can slow down. I wasn't lying about the gas canister. They got maybe five minutes before the gas reaches them."

"You send a control beacon at the same time?"

"Well, of course," Van Gar said indignantly. "What do you think I am, a rank amateur?"

He saw the man on top of the stack of rubber tires.

"Fuck! Drew!"

He shoved her to the ground and opened fire on the man as blasts rained down all around them. The man flew back through the air, screaming all the way to the floor.

"You OK, Drew?" Van Gar asked, looking around carefully for any other attacker.

"Yeah," she groaned. She stood up and went back to work on the controls. "Keep an eye out. There should be one more."

"Hey! You little fucker! We know yer in here! Ya might as well come on out an make it easy on yerself," Van screamed.

Behind him he could hear the sound of the exterior doors closing, and Drew picking up her weapon. To the lone pirate, that sound must have been like hearing his own death screams. This guy had nothing to lose.

"I'll check this way," Drew said.

They split up. Ten minutes later, they met at the cargo bay doors.

"I counted seven bodies."

"Me, too," Van said, sounding disappointed. "We must have hit the last one with random fire."

"Too easy?" Drew asked.

"Yeah. I hate it when they finish before I do."

"I hate this." Facto hissed through clenched teeth.

He looked around the bridge and wished that he had any idea what any of the flashing lights or sirens were indicative of. He kept walking around, looking at various screens and trying to get any meaning out of the jumbled letters and symbols that looked back at him. Wishing that any of the data was in a familiar language, instead of code.

"We have no way of knowing what's going on. I should have gone with them. I should have."

"That's not going to change things one way or the other, Facto. Try to relax."

"Relax. This woman is a lunatic!" The words had barely cleared his lips when the doors opened and Drewcila Qwah strode onto the bridge.

"Now, now, Fatso." She knew that wasn't his name, but it wasn't much more stupid sounding. "Is that any way to talk to the people who just saved the Royal piece ah ass?"

She flopped into the control chair and leaned her weapon against the console beside her. Van Gar was not far behind her. He rushed in and sat in the navigator's chair directly across from Drewcila, and their fingers busily flew over their respective keyboards.

"Our coordinates have been re-established, and we are prepared to continue our course," Van Gar reported.

Drewcila just nodded, her fingers caressing the keyboard as if it were a lover she knew well. Finally she smiled.

"The beacon has been activated, and we now have full control of the Purple Cat."

"A purple cat?" Taralin asked.

"The pirate ship," Van Gar answered. Then he turned to Drew. "With the gas on board we don't have to worry about anyone stealing it."

"Stealing it? But it's…Isn't…Doesn't the Space Patrol have to make a report? Isn't that ship evidence?" Facto said.

"Hello! Hello!" Drew screamed. "Are we living in the same universe? According to Article twenty-six of the Salvagers' Code…" she cleared her throat and intoned: "'If you find it, it's yours.' And Article number Six of the Space Patrol Code states:" she cleared her throat again and quoted: "'Any derelict ship containing a Salvager's beacon shall be considered the property of said Salvager under Article Twenty-six of the Salvager's Code.'"

"So what just happened?" Facto demanded. "How were they able to board us in the first place?"

"A rat chewed through a circuit wire and fouled up our detection system. But how they board—now that is really quite ingenious. What they do is match your ship's speed exactly, then they shoot out this tendril and it grabs onto your ship like a huge suction cup, and…"

"I'm sure they can wait for the book, Van Gar," Drewcila said shaking her head. "Look at this shit." She transferred the data on her screen over to his.

He was going to take a glance at the screen and say "so what", no matter what she had transferred, just because she had pissed him off. But when he saw the read-out, he couldn't control his excitement.

"What is this? Most pirate ships are held together with baling wire and used gum," he said in disbelief.

"Yeah, well, not this one," Drew said. "Look at their weapons system. We're damn lucky they didn't fire on us."

"Look at the fucking third level. There's a fucking whirlpool on it…"

"If I might be so bold…" Facto started.

"I wouldn't, if I were you," Drew hissed back. She was checking out her new acquisition, and she didn't want to be bothered. Facto made a rude sound and stomped off the bridge, making as much noise as possible.

Taralin followed quietly behind him.

"I thought they'd never leave."

Drew went to the cooler, finding that it had slid all the way across the control room. She dragged it over to her chair, sat down, and started rifling through the contents. Soon she pulled out two beers and two cigars. Handing one of each to Van Gar, she leaned back in her chair, sniffed her cigar, and smiled.

"It's a whirlpool."

Van wiped an imaginary tear from his eye.

"I'm so proud."

Chapter 3

"No, no, and no!" Drewcila shook her head furiously. "I got paid to bring you here. You're here, and my job is finished. I'm gonna dump my shipment and I'm outtah here."

"I was told by your boss..."

"I ain't got no boss." Drewcila grinned impishly. "No one ain't ever had that kindah money."

"The man you work for, then."

"Don't work for no man." Drewcila grinned back.

"Erik Rider said..."

"Why didn't you just say that bloated pile of shit."

"Qwah!" Facto took in a deep breath and exhaled slowly. "Erik Rider assured me that you and your friend would be giving us escort to the hotel. From there the King's guard will take over."

"Why ain't the guards here to meet her? I'm very busy here."

She watched as the crew of dock workers unloaded her scrap. One of the forklift drivers had just pulled out of the ship with a pallet load of generators. Sprawled across the top was the battered remains of a pirate. The driver was saying unhappy things about Salvagers who didn't dump their trash in space.

"Hey! Hey!" Drew screamed at the man till she got his attention.

"You're going to have to pay a disposal fee on these corpses, Qwah."

"Don't be looken for reasons to dock me on my scrap, bugger head. I know how much I had. And if you try and short me, you and him will be makin' butt-head book ends."

Facto breathed deeply again and tried to put himself into a kind of meditative state, but this wasn't such an easy task around the likes of Drewcila Qwah.

"So, Fuckto. What were ya saying?"

"Erik Rider assured me of an escort. It's part of what I paid for."

"Yeah, well he didn't tell me any such thing. I sure as hell didn't get paid to escort anyone anywhere, an I ain't stretching my neck out for nothin'."

Drew watched as some of the dock workers pulled the bodies off the top of the scrap. They knocked one of the generators off the pallet and it landed with a crash.

"Hey! Hey! I saw that shit! I'm gonna charge you if my scrap is damaged."

She saw that Facto was still standing there.

"You still here?"

"I'm not going without an escort."

"Then call up your lily-livered monarch and have him send you one. I can't leave these morons to unload my scrap. Surely you can see that. I'd lose a small fortune here."

"It's not that easy. We are trying to keep a low profile. The King didn't bring that many guards, and most of those are on the ship."

"Then go to the ship. Hell, I'll escort you there."

"But the King is in town!"

"So? He can come back to the ship. I don't get the big problem here." Drew motioned for Van Gar, and he nodded and started towards her.

"Our king has many enemies. He risked great danger in coming here in person. I shouldn't have to tell you how dangerous a spaceport is. Here there is no real law."

"The Galactic Police…"

"My point exactly. We wish for their reunion to go as smoothly as possible."

He looked to where Taralin stood, looking scared and lost. "She's been through so much already. Please just help us get her to the King safely. I'm not expecting any trouble, but you know what these spaceport towns can be like."

He saw Drew's outstretched hand. He looked at it and then at her face. She was grinning.

"Don't try to appeal to my better nature. I don't have one. Money talks; bullshit walks."

"But I've already paid."

"Erik. You paid Erik. I don't see him puttin' his ass on the line here, do you? You want me," Van Gar reached her then, and she put an arm around his waist, "and Van to escort you, then you need to pay us."

Drew looked up at Van Gar. "How's it going?"

"They say we're short on our load," he said.

"What!"

Drew threw a black look at the dock workers.

"Fucking space leeches! Dogs of the space ways!"

"You're supposed to have fifty converters!" a portly dock worker screamed back.

"Well, excuse me all the hell!" Drew screamed back. "The converters turned out to be shit, and he wanted twice what they were worth."

"Whatever the song and dance, Qwah, your load is still short and that means you lose ten percent."

"Screws! Roaches of the air-ways! Sphincter of the universe!"

Drew turned to Van Gar. "So, how much ahead did we come out?"

"Well, we paid a quarter of what we declared. So, with the ten percent docking, fuel, penalties, etc…" he punched the buttons on his wrist computer, then grinned "…we're 2,000 iggys up."

"Oh, how I do adore the free enterprise system, Van."

She glared at the dock worker taking inventory.

"Double-dealing, penny pinching…"

"You're crooked!" Facto hissed.

"I'm a good business woman."

Drew held out her hand again without looking at him. Facto dug deep into his pocket and dumped what was left of its contents into the Salvager's open hand. Drew looked at it, and seemed less than happy.

"That's all I have left," Facto said.

Drew turned up her nose.

"It ain't much."

"Maybe you can get the rest from your boss," Facto said shortly.

"Erik Rider is a lot of things, but he ain't my boss, Factoad."

Facto didn't want to have this conversation again. "That's all the money I have left. If you don't want it…"

"OK, OK. But you'll have to wait till they finish unloading my scrap…"

"My King and Queen have waited to be reunited for five long years."

Drew smiled. "Then thirty minutes isn't going to make that much difference, is it?"

"You are…" Facto bit his tongue.

"Yes, and so much more." Drew grinned widely. "As soon as I'm unloaded, and I have my money, we'll go. Until then I suggest you go back in the ship and make yourselves comfortable."

"I want more money," Drew said in a whisper.

"Why? We're almost there and nothing has happened," Facto pointed out.

"My point exactly. I'm bored. I hate being bored."

Drew looked at Van Gar, who nodded in agreement.

"While we were escorting the Earl of Pedonia we got bored, and he paid us an extra seventy-five iggys."

"What kind of scam are you trying to run now, Qwah? You never got paid seventy-five IGD's for being bored, and I doubt very seriously you ever escorted any Pedonian Earl. How stupid do you think I am?"

Facto had come to the end of his rope. Drewcila Qwah held not a single redeeming characteristic that he could find.

"I think you'd get really pissed off if I answered that." Drewcila grinned.

Facto doubled his pace and was soon a good five feet in front of the others.

Drew looked at Taralin.

"Now how the hell am I supposed to protect him if he's way up there?"

"You're supposed to protect her. I can take care of myself," Facto assured her.

"In that case you're not as stupid as I thought you were, Fuckto."

"Facto, my name is Facto."

He stopped and turned to face her.

"You are the most irritating…"

"Facto!" Taralin put a hand on his shoulder. "We're almost there now. Just ignore her a few more minutes."

Facto nodded, turned and started to walk again.

"How can he ignore me when it's so obvious that he wants me? He yearns for me. My warm sensuous body pressed close to his—my squirming hips playing against his."

"Enough!" Facto screamed; his face burning bright red.

"Chill, baby."

Drew strode forward, kissed him on the lips, and then walked towards the door of the hotel they had stopped in front of.

"Look! We're here. And tomorrow I'll just be a warm, wet memory."

Facto walked up beside Taralin and they started into the hotel.

"I am not attracted to her," he assured Taralin.

"It's OK, Fuckto."

Drew opened the door and the other three walked in.

"It's not easy to be an object of desire. I live with it…Bar!" As if she were steel, and the bar a magnet, she let herself be pulled in the direction of the hotel bar.

"Come back here!" Facto ordered.

"You said to the hotel. We're in the hotel, and you're out of money. You're on your own."

Facto looked appealingly at the Chitzky, and he shrugged.

"Bar," he answered. As if that explained it all.

He took Taralin's hand and kissed the back of it.

"It was a pleasure to serve you."

"Thank you," Taralin said. "For everything."

"Facto," the Chitzky held out his hand, and Facto took it reluctantly. "Learn to loosen up, dude," he winked at the man and then ran to catch up with Drew in the bar.

Drew sat at the bar.

"Blow Me Hard And Often—with a twist," she ordered.

The bartender nodded and went to work.

Van Gar came in and sat beside her.

"Brown noser," she accused.

"I was just being nice," Van Gar defended. "I know that's hard for you to recognize."

"I'm nice," Drew protested.

Van Gar just laughed.

"I am!"

The bartender put her drink in front of her.

"Thanks," she said. Then turned to Van Gar.

"See?"

Behind them, a man's voice boomed through the crowd.

"Taralin! My love! My life!"

Drew turned to see the long-awaited reunion, and a strange man threw his arms around her, spilling her drink.

"Fucking idiot!" Drew swore, pushing the man harshly away, and wiping the drink off her jump suit. The man looked deep into her eyes. At least he tried to; she didn't cooperate.

"Oh, Taralin! At long last!" He pulled a very surprised Drew into his arms, and kissed her on the lips. Drew pushed him out to arms length and held him there.

"Listen, jerk. I know it's been a long time, so I'm going to let you live." She pointed to where Taralin stood across the room looking hurt. "That's yer old lady over there."

Zarco looked from the woman in front of him to the trio which stood in the door. His face fell.

"You...you really don't remember, then? Not me? Not any of them?"

"No. She don't remember you. But I don't guess that matters too much, since you don't remember her either. I am Drewcila Qwah. I'm the Salvager that Fuckto hired to haul your wife here."

"His name is Facto, and it is you who are my wife. My wife, Taralin Zarco."

"Buddy, I don't know you, and you're starting to piss me off big time. First off, you spilt my drink."

Facto and the others joined their King then.

"I am sorry for the deception, but, well, you were so changed, my Queen. We didn't know how to make you believe us."

"I am your sister, Stasha," the woman who had called herself Taralin announced.

Drew took a step backwards and hit the bar. Suddenly, she didn't feel so good. A wave of nausea washed over her, and sweat gathered on her upper lip, so she took a long sip from her drink. Feeling somewhat calmed, she said carefully, "I am Drewcila Qwah, I am a Salvager. I am not now—nor have I ever been—anyone's Queen."

Van Gar looked at Drew for a long moment, and then at the others.

"Drewcila was in a pirate raid five years ago, and she suffered complete amnesia—or so she was told. She has no idea what her life was like before that. She doesn't even remember the raid."

Drew gave him a betrayed look.

"You might be this person, Drew. Wouldn't you like to know? Once and for all, wouldn't you like to know who you were before?"

It took some doing, but they finally talked Drewcila into going back to the suite with them.

"I'm sure this must all come as a big shock to you," the one called Fitz said.

"Well, this may come as a big shock to all of you, but I ain't goin' no where with you bunch of wackos."

She pulled her hand away from Zarco for the fifteenth time.

"You should listen to them, Drew," Van Gar said.

"Why? This is their fairy tale, not mine. Fucking queen of some country! We all know who I am."

"Taralin Zarco," Zarco answered. "My queen and my love." He took her hand and kissed it.

"Would you stop doing that!"

Drew pulled her hand away. She glared at Van Gar as if he had forced her to commit some terrible and unnatural act just by helping them to convince her to come here at all.

Zarco got up and moved across the room. He could not be so close to her and not touch her, and it was obvious that it was distressing her. Zarco sat across the room and stared at his wife. She looked like Taralin. Except for the hair cut. She had cut her hair in some strange alien fashion—short on the sides and back-long on top. It was attractive, but he missed her long, flowing mane of jet-black hair. Still, the woman he sat across from looked exactly like his wife.

But appearance was where it stopped. Taralin did not walk or move the same way, and she certainly didn't talk the same way. Her voice had taken on a harsh raspiness, and every other word out of her mouth was alien profanity or slang no doubt picked up in her travel from spaceport to spaceport. In spite of all this, it was more than he could handle to have to look at her and not touch her. Because this woman—however strange she may seem—was his wife. The only woman he had ever loved. He only prayed that they were all wrong, and somewhere in her mind was locked away some memory of him and of their love.

"Quit staring at me. Yer giving me the creeps," Drewcila ordered. "Who do I have to kill to get a drink around here?"

"At once, my Queen," Fitz bowed low and ran off to a liquor cabinet. He opened it and peered inside. "I'm afraid it is not well-stocked. Does my queen have a preference?"

"Well, I've always found myself hopelessly attracted to men, though of course there were a couple of times when I was really drunk that…"

"He was talking about the drink." Facto sighed.

"Oh. Anything. Something in a bottle," Drew said.

She watched as Fitz pulled a shot glass out and started to pour a shot from the bottle.

"No, no just bring me the bottle."

He looked unsure but brought it to her all the same.

Drew put the bottle to her lips and downed half of it before coming up for air.

"This has got to be a mistake. I could never be anything like you stuffy bunch of pin heads. Nothing personal." She belched loudly. "I'm sorry you lost yer queen, but I ain't her." She belched again. "Hey! This ain't bad shit!"

"I couldn't agree more," Facto said. "And I'm not talking about the liquor."

"We know that she is Taralin, Facto. DNA doesn't lie. She is our queen." Fitz said.

"Oh, I have no doubt that this is Taralin's body. But I have been with this woman for the better part of a day, and there is no part of Taralin in her. Not one trait of our gentle queen is present in Drewcila Qwah. This woman is a rude, loud, drunkard, and a slut. When they removed part of her brain, they removed Taralin. They killed her."

Facto looked appealingly at his king.

"My King, bury Taralin's memory and find a more suitable mate than this Salvager."

"There can be no one for me but Taralin. What has happened to her is my fault. All our faults, because we cared more for our country than we did our kin."

"Sire, you did the only thing you could do. No one could ask you to act differently. You sacrificed your own happiness for the kingdom. You have punished yourself enough. Don't punish yourself or your country by bringing this mockery of Taralin home. Don't let this woman ruin your people's memory of a kind and noble Queen. What has happened is done, and nothing can undo it. I wish I could tell you truthfully that you could turn this thing back into Taralin, but in all truth I think it would be more suitable to put the crown on a Dridel Beast."

"What are you suggesting, Facto?" Stasha screamed. "That we leave my sister here to play Salvager—to the tender mercies of a Chitzky?"

She looked at Van Gar.

"No offense meant."

"None taken," Van Gar said with a shrug.

"Your sister is dead, Stasha. I can't believe that you wouldn't be sure of that, having spent time in the company of Drewcila Qwah."

"She is my sister, Facto. They may have removed her memory, but her basic traits—the part of her brain that made her what she was—that is still there, still the same."

"How can you say that? This woman waded into her hold with a weapon as big as herself and brutally killed people."

"She protected what was hers. That was very like Taralin." But now Stasha sounded unsure and defensive.

"She killed them, and then she came back to the bridge bragging about what she was going to get off their ship, and she ate a sandwich!"

"I was hungry," Drew said, defensively.

"I don't consider it a bad thing to kill pirates," Stasha said. "They would have killed us if they got a chance."

"She's a crook. You heard her on the docks. She's completely unscrupulous."

"Enough, Facto. I will not hear you talk of my wife— your Queen—in such a manner. You've said your piece, and we have heard it. No more. Taralin will return to her throne beside me where she belongs, and we will make her remember who she is and how to act."

"OK! Hold it right there!" Drew yelled. "If you guys could just stop talking about me like I'm not here, and calling me dead and implying that I'm walking around with half a brain, I've got a couple of things to tell you bunch of coconuts, then I'm going to make like a baby and go."

She waited to make sure she had everyone's attention.

"Now listen, cause I am only going to say this one more time. My name is Drewcila Qwah. I have always been Drewcila Qwah. It's true that I was in an accident and I suffered amnesia, but I have my whole brain, thank you, and I know who I am because they told me. Everyone knew me and everyone still does. I'm a Salvager, my parents were Salvagers, and their parents before them. That is my heritage, and I don't appreciate you saying Salvager like it was a dirty word. It is an honorable and useful occupation, as well as a profitable one. Unlike being some do-nothing Royal fuck. I have worked all my life. No one ain't never give me shit. And if I talk a little too rough for you, or act a little strange in your eyes, or put a little too much store in trash, maybe it's you that's fucked up and not me. I have my memories."

"Which were mostly fed to you by Erik Rider."

Van Gar looked at Zarco.

"She doesn't remember shit past five years ago. There is a scar on the front of her head, just under her hair line which Erik said was caused from impact, but it could have just as easily been caused from an operation." Drew gave him a heated look.

"Drew, if you're this Taralin person, this is your family. Aren't you even curious?"

"If this is my family I prefer the dead one. You know how I feel about these Royal shits. Living off people they look down on. People like you and me who keep the universe going."

Drew downed the rest of the bottle.

"Hell, these people don't even know how to make a decent drink."

"Sire, surely you can see that she can never be one of us again," Facto said in a pleading tone. "Would you really trust her to lead beside you? To give her control of all the kingdom's wealth? All the riches of the palace—all the treasure of your fathers?" Drewcila's eyes grew wide, and she smiled.

"You know," she said thoughtfully, "I have always felt lost in the world of Salvagers. Like an outsider. Like I just really didn't fit in."

Van Gar sighed and ran a hand down his face. He could see a scam coming on.

Chapter 4

"She has been talking to the Chitzky for thirty minutes, Sire. Can't you see that she has only agreed to go home with you so that she can get her hands on your wealth?" Facto pleaded.

"Can't you see that I don't care why she is going with me, only that she is with me?"

Zarco stared at the woman standing with her back to him across the vastness of the spaceport.

"Once we are together, all will be put right. This time apart shall be erased like it never was."

"But, Sire, surely."

"No more! I told you before. Your words border on treason, and they are falling on deaf ears."

"But, my King!"

"Not one more harsh word about the Queen," Zarco ordered.

He took a deep breath.

"Please, my old friend. I need your help more now than ever I did before. All that has kept me going these long harsh years has been the hope of being reunited with Taralin. Now we have found her, and she is whole, but she no more remembers me than a drunk man remembers his balance. I am all too aware that she may never be the woman that she was. That she may never again love me as she once did. But please don't tell me that I am a fool to try. Because if she is gone to me forever, then I'd just as soon they remove my memory so that I don't have to remember what I have lost. I'd rather be dead than never feel her love again."

"An entire fleet of ships. No! Why stop there? Two fleets and our own spaceport!" Drew wiped the drool from the corner of her mouth. "All I have to do is play my cards right, and I can be Queen of the Salvagers. We'll pick these Royal bastards till their bones are clean."

"Drew. That woman is your sister. That man is your husband. They are your past." Van Gar reprimanded her gently.

"Ah, bullshit," Drew said. "I ain't buying that brain-re-moved shit for one minute. I know who I am."

"You know they're telling you the truth."

"They think they're telling me the truth. I know they be-lieve I am their Queen."

"You do, too. I saw the look on your face the moment you realized that they were telling you the truth."

"You read too much into an attack of gas. I didn't come from shit like that. I couldn't. They're just flash and air. I'm real."

She paused, re-gathering her thoughts.

"Now, here's my plan. I'll go with the Royal fucks. You take the Garbage Scow and follow. Don't stay too far back, just out of detection range. Land at the space port at Delta Ray station and wait for me. I figure it will take me about a week to make them decide that they want me as no part of their Royal Court, then they'll give me any amount of money I ask for just to be rid of me."

"Why can't you just admit that you are curious about your past and your people?" Van Gar asked.

"I don't need your asteroid belt analysis, Van. Wait at Delta Ray, and I'll come for you when I've cleaned them out."

"As you wish, your Royal Majesty," Van Gar said, bow-ing low.

"Knock it off, fuck head."

She turned and started to walk away.

"Aren't you even going to say good-bye?" Van Gar asked in a hurt tone.

She turned to face him, and smiled.

"Ain't goin' nowhere, fur ball." She winked at him. "See you in a week."

She turned and walked towards Zarco and the others.

Van Gar watched her go. *Oh Drew, if you stay too long with this King, I'll lose you forever.* He turned away quickly and started for the Garbage Scow. She didn't even realize that this was the first time they had been apart (really apart) in over four years. She didn't even bother to kiss his cheek or hug him. She'd gotten him a navigator and she thought he should be happy with that. Like just anyone could take her place for him. Hell, he couldn't remember the last time he had flown a ship with anyone but Drewcila Qwah. In fact, for the last few years he really hadn't had any continual contact with anyone else.

He looked back just in time to see Drewcila board the Royal ship. While its lines were sleeker, it wasn't half the size of the Garbage Scow, and didn't have near the character. Van Gar dragged himself onto the ship, thinking that he couldn't possibly feel any lower—and then he met the new navigator.

"Hi! My name is Tim," he announced in a voice that would grate on gravel.

Tim was a short, slightly over-weight male in his late twenties. To put the icing on the cake, he was human.

Van Gar made an unpleasant noise in the human's direction, and then he started to make a routine check of the ship.

Tim followed him around like a stray puppy, and occasionally Van Gar told him something he thought Tim should know.

Everything was checking normal, when the computer indicated a blockage in the number two exhaust port. Van Gar started stomping down the hall leading out of the ship.

"Damned Humans, spreading their filthy vermin through space."

Tim followed closely behind him, apparently oblivious to what Van Gar had just said.

"Everywhere they go, disease, war and pestilence follow in their wake. They brought us flies, and roaches, and ants..."

"...and Velcro, and duct tape, and bubble gum," Tim said defending his race.

Van Gar picked up a section of pipe off the ground, walked over to the number two exhaust port and gave it a good hard whack. When the chiming stopped, a half dozen fur-covered creatures fell from the pipe.

"And rats, Tim. Humans and rats."

Van Gar laid into the dazed rats with his feet and the pipe till they were all dead.

"There's only one thing I hate worse then rats, Tim…Tim?"

He found the human laying on the ground, obviously out cold. "Humans, Tim. I hate humans."

Across the spaceport he heard the Royal ship powering up.

"Shit!"

He ran over and shook the human till he opened his eyes.

"Listen to me, monkey boy. Run up and get me the rat extractor, and hurry it up, or Drew will have both of our hides."

Tim jumped to his feet with help from Van Gar, and with a little shove in the right direction he started for the ship.

"Fucking humans!"

He slammed the pipe again and went after the rats with deadly perfect aim.

"Fucking rats!"

He watched as the Royal ship lifted off across the spaceport, sheltering his face with his arm to shield it from the sand and dirt the lift-off kicked up. Damn. She was gone. Maybe he'd see her again, but then again, maybe he never would.

"Good-bye, Drew," he whispered into the dust, choking back his tears. His only friend was gone and he was left in a world of humans and rats.

It was a nice ship, but Drew had seen better. Drewcila indulged them by letting Stasha take her on a tour of the ship and oohing and ahhing at all the right spots. When they finally got to the bridge, Drew parked herself in the captain's seat and started playing with the terminal. The captain nervously hovered around her.

"Uh, my Queen, this is a very sophisticated piece of machinery…"

"Honey, I have forgotten more about flying than you ever knew. Why don't you do some bowing and scraping and shit, and leave me alone?"

The captain looked at Stasha in disbelief. Could this be their gentle queen?

"She's been through a great deal," Stasha said.

"Actually, I didn't think it was all that great. Half my brain sucked out. Left to fend for myself in a cruel and unsympathetic world. Where the fuck are they?"

"My Queen?" The captain asked.

"Uh," Drew smiled nervously, "…coolers, you should really have ice coolers full of beer on the bridge. Nothing gets your beer really cold like real ice. Frozen H2O. How the fuck do you stay in space for any length of time without beer? Really!"

She got up and started pacing back and forth.

"Maybe you'd like to go change into something else," Stasha suggested.

"No. Once today is quite enough."

Stasha just gave her a lost look.

"For God's sake, Stasha. It's a joke, don't you get it?"

Stasha just shrugged. Drewcila took a deep breath.

"OK," she started slowly. "You asked me if I wanted to change into something different, and I said once a day is enough."

Again, Stasha just shrugged.

"OK. Let's try again. This morning, I was a Salvager, right?"

Stasha nodded her head, obviously glad to understand.

"And now I'm the fucking Queen."

Stasha forced a smile and shrugged.

"It's not funny, though."

"Of course it's not funny now. The moment is gone!"

Drew threw up her hands in disgust.

"You're hopeless, Stasha. Are you sure you're my sister?"

Stasha looked hurt.

"Yes, I'm sure. Why do you ask?"

Drew shrugged, and started walking around the bridge looking at the read-out screens.

"Oh, I don't know. I guess I just always figured that if I had a sib out there somewhere they'd be more…well, you know, more hip."

"Hip?"

"Yeah, you know. Cool. With it."

"Cool? With it?"

Drew threw up her hands again and headed for the door.

"That proves it," she mumbled, "there ain't no way that I am this Queen bitch, because there is no way that I could have such an uncool, uptight chick for a sister."

She stopped walking, and Stasha ran into her.

Drew jumped about a foot in the air.

"Don't follow me!"

"You know, Taralin…"

"Don't call me that! Don't you understand at all? Any of you? You may as well be calling me Rover or Fido. I am not Taralin Zarco. Maybe I was once; I don't know for sure anymore. But I'm Drewcila Qwah now, and Qwah I'll stay. Hey! I made a rhyme!"

"We used to be so close!" Stasha started crying. "You know, in many ways you are so different, but in other ways you are just the same." By now she was screaming. "You are still selfish, willful, and full of yourself. They keep saying you're so changed, but they didn't know you the way I did. I look at you and I see my sister; changed and yet the same. You were always strong, and you always spoke your mind. You always had things your way, or not at all. You always treated me like a baby, and I always loved you, even though you were an arrogant, pigheaded…Oh! One of those nasty Salvager words you use all the time!"

She turned on her heal and stomped off in the other direction.

Drew watched her go and smiled. "Then again, maybe she is my sister." Shrugging, she decided to go on a quest for alcohol of any kind. Right now she'd even settle for the rubbing kind if she could get a glass of cold water to wash it down with.

An hour of extensive searching turned up not even a bottle of isopropyl, and so, feeling defeated, she headed back for the bridge. As she passed the Royal quarters, she could hear people talking inside, so she did what any good Salvager would do, and pressed her ear to the door.

"It's too much for her to absorb all at once, can't you see that Zarco?" Drew smiled at the fact that not only could she hear through the door but she could recognize Stasha's voice.

"I see that everyone has some reason why I shouldn't be with my wife," Zarco said. "If I could be with her I know she would soon feel the same way about me as I do about her. I know I could make her remember."

"You'd probably catch something," Facto mumbled.

"Snotty bastard," Drew mumbled. "Little toady dirt-eater." She missed the next remark, then a general shuffling warned her that they were all about to vacate the cabin. She moved quickly on down the hall towards the bridge.

A few seconds later, Zarco and his entourage entered the hall. They quickly caught up to Drew.

"Why are you not resting in your quarters? Are they not suitable?" Zarco asked in a concerned tone.

"With a capital NOT. First off, there is no bar," Drew replied. "Where are you guys going in such a hurry, and why do you always go everywhere together?"

Zarco laughed and smiled at her indulgently.

"There's safety in numbers, dear one."

Drew gave him a hard look.

"I swear, if you pat me on the head I'll slug you. Where the hell are you going in such a hurry?"

"The captain seems to think we're being followed. I'm sure it's nothing for you to worry about."

They passed her quickly, and Drew let them. After all, she knew who it was, and it was about time.

"By the way, 'safety in numbers' is a fallacy," Drew said to their backs.

Zarco stopped briefly and turned to face her.

"What do you mean?"

"Running."

Zarco shrugged, and once again started for the bridge.

"What a strange answer. I wonder what she meant?"

Facto looked over his shoulder at the grinning girl and she winked at him.

"Actually," Facto's fingers worked at his collar, which was suddenly too tight, "it's a rather good answer. A concept of Trigade, a martial arts form practiced by the United Peoples of Trinadad on the planet Caldeed. It states that," he cleared his throat, "There is no safety in numbers if the enemy is equal to you or has an equalizer, i.e. an attacker has a gun, and the group has stones. In a free area, whether we are talking about one man or one ship, you can more easily dodge an attacker. If there is only one, you may run from the greater attacker but if there are more of you...Well, say for instance we are facing an attacker with a gun right now. Your only real chance is to run. But could you really do that and leave all of us behind?"

"I would hope you would run as well," Zarco said.

"But you couldn't be sure, and in that moment of uncertainty..." Facto threw up his hands. "Trigade is not the most chivalrous of martial arts but it does take practice, patience and discipline."

"Are you saying that my Queen may have retained more of her former self than you previously thought?" Zarco asked with a smile.

"Perhaps. After all, Drewcila Qwah doesn't appear to have that kind of discipline."

The King gave him a hopeful look.

"Of course, she also could have picked that particular concept of Trigade up during a conversation in a Salvager bar."

"After you, Sire," Fitz said with a wave of his hand.

After the King had passed through the entrance, Fitz gave Facto a heated look, and Facto shrugged.

Drew watched them walk onto the bridge, then she punched up the buttons on her comlink which should connect her to her ship. She waited for the channel to be opened.

"Of all the stupid, ignorant…you'd think that anyone with half a brain would understand that following at a good distance does not mean up the ship's butt." She looked at her comlink. There was still no flashing light. "What the hell is taking them so long?"

She tried again with the same luck. Which could mean only one thing; Van Gar and the Garbage Scow were not the blip on the radar screen. Drew took off at a dead run. Once on the bridge she knocked the Captain and the others away from the radar screen.

"My Queen, I'm afraid I must protest," the Captain started.

"Blow me, rat boy. I was running ships when you were poppin' zits. Hey! I made another rhyme!" She checked the radar. "Ah, fuck! See that little blip right there?" she pointed.

"That's just a glitch on the radar," the Captain said through clenched teeth.

"Shit for brains! That's the ship. The other is just an image the smaller one is projecting to fuck you up. The smaller one is a cloaked ship, a ship which will no doubt be docking any minute if it hasn't already. The worst part is, it's not my ship."

"If a ship had docked us we would have felt something," Zarco assured her. "I think you are over-reacting."

"You need to get off the planet more, Kingy. There are pirate ships that can dock you and you won't even spill your coffee."

Suddenly the ship rocked violently.

"Then there are ships that dock like that. I hope your crew is armed, and that they know what the hell they're doing."

The warning sirens started screaming, and the doors to the bridge clanged shut. Drew hopped up on the scanner table and tried her comlink again. She ignored Zarco, who seemed to be taking command of the ship. "Come on, fur head…where the hell are you? I'm stuck here with a bunch of pinheads."

"What are you doing?" Stasha asked.

"Well, I had this really great plan on how to get rich, but part of the plan called for Van Gar to grow a brain!" She took the comlink off her arm and stuck it around her ankle, under her pants. "But none of that matters now that we're all going to die here on this big cow of a ship. A very expensive fucking ship. A ship which doesn't even have a detachable bridge."

"We have escape pods." Zarco grabbed Drew by the arm. "I won't lose you now, come on." He started to go and was spun around quickly by her dead weight. "Please, Taralin."

"You hear that?"

They could hear the sound of blaster fire getting ever closer.

"Even if we could beat the odds and get to the escape pods, chances are we'd run out of fuel before anyone could find us. That's the problem with escape pods in deep space. You might as well open the doors and surrender. I doubt very seriously that we are dealing with the kind of riff-raff that I'm used to, and one way or the other they're going to get us." Suddenly a fog started pouring in the air ducts.

"Computer, shut down ventilation to the…"

Before he could complete the order, he fell to the floor.

"What did I tell you?"

Drew fell from the scanner table.

Chapter 5

Her head was pounding, and she rubbed at her temple. One too many Bend Me Over And Fuck Mes. She was really going to have to seriously consider maybe doing something about her drinking.

"I'm going to have to drink more. That's all there is to it. If I drank more, it wouldn't be such a shock to my system," she mumbled out.

"Oh, my Sweetness. Thank all the Gods. I thought perhaps you had perished," someone said.

No doubt the same someone was stroking her hair. Slowly she began to remember what had happened. She instinctively moved her hand towards the inside of her shirt.

"Forget it, Qwah."

She heard a bunch of clanging sounds and looked up in time to see a pile of weapons; all hers, cascade onto the floor.

"You keep weapons in the damnedest places, but a really thorough check turned them all up."

"I feel so cheap and used." Drew got to her feet and suddenly realized she was naked. She looked at the large greasy guy talking to her from behind the laser bars. "Do I know you?"

"No, but everyone's heard ah ya, and from what I been told my bosses made you who you are today."

His attention turned to Zarco. "Just so you won't be too shocked, the explosion which will be rocking our ship presently will be your ship and crew blowing into a billion tiny space particles."

The ship rocked violently, and the greasy guy laughed. "Sorry you had to miss the fire works, folks." He laughed again as he left up the stairs.

Drew looked around quickly. Stasha had been spared, as had Facto and Fitz, though they had probably all been saved for a fate far worse than being blown up on a ship.

"Ever notice that when a bunch of naked people are standing around they never quite know where to look, or where to put their hands? It's hell not having pockets."

She looked out the bars at the pile of weapons and her comlink. No way of getting them, they were just out of reach. She looked up at the ceiling and found the monitors. "Well, at least they're not sloppy."

She had been in better positions in her life. And she had felt better. She held her throbbing head and leaned against the back wall of the cell.

She looked Zarco up and down and smiled. "Now I know for certain that I ain't your wife, because *that* I would not have forgotten," she said, pointing.

"This really sucks. I'm not even one of you Royal fucks, but I'll be tortured just the same, and I don't know shit. I'll die a horrible, cringing death and all because I let my greed get the better of me. Van has always told me that my greed would be my undoing. It fucking pisses me off when he's right."

She started pacing back and forth across the cell, throwing her arms around flamboyantly.

"At least I won't die stupid like that poor shlep that was just down here. He's so stupid he doesn't even realize the trillions and bezillions of iggys he could get ransoming you Royal dicks off to the highest bidder. That's what I'd do if I were him. I'd get rid of whoever hired me and go after the gold myself…"

"Why you mercenary little wretch," Facto swore, "you would sell out your own people!"

"Hey man, what ever greases your weenie. Ethics really don't matter for shit now since my plan to swindle you out of all your trillions and quadrillions will no doubt die with me."

"So what's the plan, Qwah?"

The greasy guy reappeared outside the bars with a little weasel-faced man. Drew smiled and turned to face them.

"Boys, stick with me and we'll all get out of this very, very rich," she rubbed her hands together.

"Now, first…"

"I can't believe you!" Zarco looked as if someone had stolen his last breath. "You aren't Taralin. You are nothing more than Salvager trash."

"Right on both counts," Drew said with a smile.

"I denounce you!" Zarco swore.

"Ooh! Does that hurt! Listen, Kingy, baby. At least I'm saving your Royal asses. That's a lot more than they would do. You don't really think that the Lockhedes intend to let you live? They'll use you to get control of your country, and then once they have it, what the hell do they need you for? You'll just be so much excess baggage. My way, you get to live. You get to keep your country. And a whole lot of hungry smugglers get to get rich. Look at it as a political move to help keep the space lanes clean. You know, Kingy, helping to make space travel safe for decent folks."

"I'd rather be dead." Zarco spat venomously.

"Sire, however mercenary and disloyal you may find the Queen's plan, it will save us and the kingdom from the hands of the Lockhedes," Facto said.

Drew leaned against the wall of the cell, and appeared to be counting. Suddenly the ship rocked violently, followed by a few moments of silence. Then the motors seemed to kick back on with a sickly-sounding grind.

Drew smiled at the others. "Phase one."

Jaco was commander of the Lockhedes on this mission. Till now, he had been quite pleased, as everything had gone according to plan. He had been reluctant to use the smugglers, but they were the only people he could find that knew how to dock a ship without being detected, and their price had been more than reasonable. Besides, this way no one could trace the King's disappearance to the Lockhedes or their government. Not and make it stick, anyway. The wreckage of Zarco's ship would be found, and Zarco and his staff would be considered dead. He could extract the necessary computer codes from Zarco and his staff, and then the take-over would be easy.

"I told you, Jaco. A piece of cake."

Erik Rider sucked on a big cigar, puffing the cabin full of smoke.

The ship lurched violently.

"What the hell is that?" Erik demanded of the ship's Captain over the comlink.

"One ah the motors has gone out," the smuggler answered. "We'll be some slowed, but it shouldn' be no trouble."

"Don't let it be," Erik ordered.

One of the greasy smugglers walked right into Jaco's quarters without knocking.

"What do you think you're doing?" Jaco demanded.

"The prisoners 'ave come to."

"It's about time!" Jaco got to his feet.

"Coming?"

Erik hesitated for a moment. He would really rather not deal with Qwah's wrath, but it was all going to have to come to a head sooner or later. He nodded and got up to follow Jaco.

The prisoners were each pacing their own path through the cell, looking at the ceiling instead of each other.

"So, the mighty King," Jaco laughed. "Brought to his knees for the love of a woman."

"Jaco!" Zarco hissed. "I will not grace you by making a comment."

"Oooh! Snappy come back," Drewcila mumbled.

"Here, put these on." He threw in a pile of white robes.

Drew had just grabbed one, and started to put it on when she saw Erik. "Erik! You fucking piece of shit!" She jerked her arms into the robe, which almost went to her knees. "You...you sold me out!"

"How's it feel?" Zarco mumbled.

Drew ignored him.

"How far into this shit are you, Erik?" Drew demanded.

"I've been in it since the very beginning." Erik looked at his feet. "They brought you to me right after the operation on your brain. You understand, don't you, Drew? It's a big pay-off.

Biggest of my life. The smuggling operation is bringing in a mint, but it's only a matter of time."

"Fucking smuggling." Drew hissed. "Kidnapping is one thing, but smuggling. Van Gar was right about you. God damned, rat-loving, Velcro wearing, roach eating, human."

"Why didn't you just kill us out-right?" Zarco asked.

"You truly are a stupid man, Zarco. The codes to shut off and turn on the computers that run your country are locked in the minds of you and your two top aides, both of whom you conveniently brought off the planet with you. The women are just to help guarantee that you will behave yourself."

"Did you really do that?" Drew asked in disbelief. "Did you really bring every man who knows the codes with you?"

"Of course not! Many competent men at the capital know the access codes."

"Not only are you stupid, but you're a shitty liar," Drew said in disbelief.

"It will be days before they give up all hope on you. In a few hours, we will land on an obscure little moon where one of my men will extract your memories, and thus your code key numbers, and leave you like your lovely wife. Of course, since that part of your brain has already been removed, Miss Qwah, and since you have no information we need, I'm afraid you'll just have to be terminated. Perhaps slowly, while Zarco watches."

Drew yawned, and stretched dramatically.

"Now wait a minute, Jaco, we had a deal…" Erik started.

Drew turned to Stasha. "How sweet. He just sold me out, but he didn't actually want me dead."

"Surely you understand, Erik. I can't let anyone live who knows what we're doing. I can't take the risk. Not when we are so close to reaching our goal."

"But you promised me you wouldn't hurt Drew. She's the best Salvager I've got," Erik pleaded.

"I'm so touched," Drew drawled out.

"Come on, man," Erik said. "Drew has no quarrel with you, give her a couple of iggys and she'll…"

"I'm sorry, Erik." Jaco pulled a laser. "But like I said. I can't let anyone live."

"No!" Drew tried to grab him through the bars, but it was a useless attempt. Erik hit the wall and fell down it, a small hole burned through his forehead. "Mother fucker!" she screamed.

Jaco smiled.

"I can't afford witnesses, but you can think about that for awhile."

"You bastard, you're going to kill us all."

"Down to every scum-sucking smuggler on this ship. When we land, they'll walk into what they think is a de-tox chamber, and they'll all be killed. Then we'll blow up their ship, and there will be no tracing us." He laughed and left the brig.

"You catch that, Jack?" Drew asked when she was sure that Jaco was out of ear shot.

"Loud and clear, Drew. Time for phase two?" A voice asked over the intercom.

"Time for phase two," Drew said calmly.

Jaco sat on the bridge and gazed out at space. He supposed he should feel guilty about the human. After all, without him, their plan couldn't have worked. But orders were orders. The ship rocked violently again. When the engines kicked back in this time, they really sounded sick. "What's wrong now?" Jaco asked impatiently.

But no one seemed to hear. Everyone seemed to be running around in a panic.

"I said, what's wrong?"

"We've lost all of our power. Something has drained it. Our air is going; everything. We'll all be dead in an hour," the Captain screamed in a panic.

Jaco saw something hanging in space in front of them.

"What's that?"

"It appears to be a ship. Wait, we're getting a signal now. It's a salvage ship, and it's been claimed."

"Is it operational?"

"Yes sir," the Captain smiled broadly. "It looks like we've been saved."

"Start docking procedure immediately."

"Yes sir," the Captain said. "Cocky son of a bitch," he mumbled.

"What's that?" Jaco demanded.

"It's an old earth saying. It means good call."

Jaco made a noise and walked out of the cabin. In the hall he got on his comlink.

"Number One and Number Two, go and get the prisoners and go to the airlock. All other units, arm yourselves and go to the airlock. Kill anyone who gets in your way."

Jaco then made his way towards the airlock.

The cell was opened, and two uniformed Lockhedes ran in the cell. One grabbed Zarco, and the other grabbed Drew.

"The rest of you, come on," number one screamed. "We're all going for a little ride."

They led them down to the airlock, where Jaco and the rest of the Lockhedes waited. They were pushed roughly to the front. The smugglers arrived just as they were opening the airlock doors and found themselves facing a line of heavily armed guards.

"What the Hell?" Jack screamed.

"You'll be staying here," Jaco pronounced.

"Like hell you say. Our ship's lost all power. Soon there won't be any air," the Captain told him.

"Who knows? Maybe you can fix it," Jaco said with a smile.

"There's not a chance of that," Jack yelled.

"There's more of a chance of that than you'll have if you choose to fight us."

He pushed the prisoners out the now open airlock into the ramping tube.

"Move it," he ordered.

As they neared the derelict ship, the door opened as if by its own code. Jaco laughed.

"The idiots! I figured they'd forget to stop the door open sequence." They rushed into the ship. When the last of the Lockhedes were on board, the doors closed.

Jaco laughed again. "It's a little late now." He coughed. "Too late for them." He coughed again.

Drew smiled.

"What have you done?"

The other men started coughing.

"What have you done!"

Jaco grabbed for Drew, but she moved easily out of his way, and he fell to the floor.

"People who deal in betrayal, shouldn't be too surprised when they get conned."

Drew kicked the dying man in the ribs.

Jaco looked up at Zarco with eyes that were growing dim.

"I've still won, Zarco. I've won because this woman will never be your queen. I have made her into..."

He spasmed and died as his men began to fall around him.

"Yes, yes? Go on," Drew said, "into...into what? I hate it when people don't finish their sentences. Well come on, boys and girls. We're burnin' photons."

Drew took off at a dead run for the bridge, and the others followed. She threw the dead pirate captain out of his chair, and turned the filtration system on high. Then she started powering the ship up. A voice came at them through the ship's comlink.

"Hey, Qwah! I thought you said that ship didn't run."

"Hey, what can I say? I lied." Drew laughed and flopped herself down in the Captain's chair.

"Come on, Qwah, you owe us. If it wasn't for us, you'd all be dead."

"And if it wasn't for me, you'd all be dead. I think that makes us about even."

"Damn it, Qwah. A deal's a deal. You do us outtah our part, and..."

"What, Jack?" Drew laughed. "This is a pirate ship. Do I have to get vulgar, or do you understand how much instant fire power I command? Not to mention my sterling reputation for dog fights. No. I'd say that in a fire fight you have a more than ninety five percent chance of getting fried. But if you're feeling froggy, go ahead and jump. I feel like a good fight. Besides, my hyper-power just reached the ready mark."

The ship took off with such speed that it sent everyone standing crashing to the floor.

"Ladies and gentlemen, take-off will be a bit rough, so be sure and buckle up. Oops! I'm afraid that I did that all out of order."

The ship stabilized, and Zarco and the others got up.

"Why did you do that?" Facto demanded, pulling the robe back down to cover up his privates.

"I said oops," she said. "Besides, you had it coming after the way you all treated me when you thought I was selling you out. I may be mercenary, I never claimed that I wasn't. But I'm a Salvager, and we have codes we live by, too."

Zarco fell on his knees beside her, picked up her hand and kissed it. "Oh, my sweet love, can you ever forgive me?"

"Oh, you're not going to start all that kissy-faced crap again, are you?"

"Forgive me also, Majesty. And thank you for sparing my miserable life." Fitz said, bowing deeply.

Stasha smiled. "I knew you could never really betray us."

Drew smiled and looked expectantly at Facto, coughing a little.

Facto shuffled his feet. "I'm sorry," he said flatly.

"But…How? I don't understand." Zarco looked at Drew. "This ship appeared as soon as their ship was done for."

Drew looked at him as if he were an idiot. "There was never anything wrong with their ship. The Lockhedes were in a big-ass hurry, so we needed to slow the ship down so that we wouldn't pass this ship."

She looked at Facto and Stasha. "Aren't you glad I gassed the ship now? We all knew their plans. I knew they wouldn't allow the smugglers on board, and knowing about the gas, the smugglers wouldn't want on board."

"Speaking of the gas, can I take this thing off?" Facto asked.

Drew bent over a screen and punched some buttons. "The air seems to be clear now," she watched Facto remove the clear hose from his nose, and then pull the filtration bag off his back.

"No, read that wrong."

Facto tried to cram the apparatus back on, and Drew laughed loudly. "Just kidding." She took hers off, and threw it on the floor.

"How did you know they would have filtration packs on board?" Fitz asked. "They aren't exactly standard equipment."

"They are on smuggler ships. Besides, they came and got us off your ship after they had gassed us, didn't they?"

She got on the ship's comlink and punched in a code.

"Hello Garbage Scow, do you read? This is Purple Cat."

"Great Gods, is that you, Drew? When we went past what was left of the Royal ship I thought you'd gone to that big junk yard in the sky. What the hell are you doing on the Purple Cat?"

"Now, that's a long story."

Chapter 6

The ship was running itself at this point, so Drew and the three men were moving the bodies into the airlock. Stasha couldn't make herself do it, and had in fact been crying for the better part of an hour. They were about to close the airlock door when suddenly Drew got a wild gleam in her eye.

"Damn! I'm really losing it." She ran in and started going through pockets, occasionally finding some money or an expensive trinket. "Would you look at this," she screamed in excitement, "these pants are real leather. I'm telling you these pirates, they know how to dress. I think they're my size, too."

To their horror, she stripped the pirate's pants off and held them up to her.

"Cool!" She pulled them on. "Now, if I can just find a decent shirt."

She started rummaging through the bodies again.

Stasha dried her eyes and decided that she was being silly. She decided to go help the others with their efforts. As she rounded the corner she saw the three men. Behind them she could see the airlock full of bodies. Taralin stood in the middle of the pile. She grabbed the hand of one of the corpses, and held it up out of the pile.

"Hey, sis. What do you think? Is this shirt me, or what?"

Stasha fainted dead away; Zarco caught her.

"Are you happy now?" Zarco asked harshly.

"Is that a rhetorical question, or do you really want me to answer it?" She took the black and red striped shirt off the corpse and smelled the armpit. She made a face, then took off her robe and threw it on the floor. She put on the pirate's shirt, smiled, and looked back to where Zarco held Stasha, who was starting to come around.

"Geez, all I wanted was an honest opinion."

She waded out of the bodies, carrying three knives and a bag filled with loot. At the airlock, she closed the door and pushed the button to open the exterior airlock.

"What are you doing?" Fitz asked in horror.

"Well, why do you think we carried them here, Fitz? For ornamental purposes? I'm giving them burial in space. A moment of silence please, followed by a loud bellowing fart should be appropriate." She was silent, then farted loudly, and started back towards the bridge. "I'm hungry. Wonder if these bastards left anything worth eating." She turned and looked out the portal just in time to see the bodies sucked into space.

"There, we're all cleaned up now. Would someone please close that exterior door?" She turned and walked towards the bridge again, but stopped when she realized no one was following her. They were all looking at her in shock.

"Ah, come on people, they were dead anyway. Most spaceports will hold you at dock for days if you have a body on board. Then the whole crew and the ship have to go through de-tox; which costs the ship's Captain a fortune. So, if your mother dies out here, you bury her in space. That's just the way we do things."

"Well, let me tell you how we do things," Zarco said hotly. "Our religion preaches reverence for the dead. Even if they are our enemies. There is a service and then the bodies are cremated and their ashes spread to the wind."

Drew shrugged and started walking again. "So what's the big difference? Bodies torched and tossed to the wind, or bodies cast into space to implode. That's the problem with religion, there's always all this nit picking."

Drew was sitting at the controls of the ship when the others returned. She pointed at the view screen where a green planet hung in space.

"So, there you go, people. I've punched up co-ordinates, and in eight minutes we will start re-entry procedures. I suggest that you strap in." She got on the comlink.

"Purple Cat to Garbage Scow, do you read?"

"You might have told me you were dumping bodies, Drew," an angry voice spit back.

Drew laughed. "Don't blow a gasket, Van. It will all burn off on re-entry. Come in closer. I'm not expecting hostiles, but considering my cargo, who knows?"

"I read, and am changing grid in accordance."

"Oh, baby, I love it when you talk that comlink lingo. Hey, Van…"

"Yes?"

"I miss you."

"I miss you, too."

"Over."

"Over and out."

"Why is that thing following us?" Jealousy dripped freely from Zarco's lips.

"Because I have no reason to trust you people. For all I know, you need a good Salvager for your war efforts. Lots of governments have tried to buy me before. You might have heard of my memory loss and cooked up this whole thing. How do I even know you are who you say you are?"

"But the Lockhedes!"

"You might have fooled them, too."

"What about your friend, Erik? You heard what he said!" Fitz said.

"Hell, Erik was running smugglers. Which means he'd sell his sister into prostitution to turn a buck. No, I hate to tell you all this, but you still haven't convinced me that this whole thing isn't just some cock and bull story."

"But the war is over. We have never had any need for Salvagers and we sure don't need any now that we're at peace," Zarco said.

"Maybe you'd better tell the Lockhedes the war is over, because I'm not sure they know it. Besides, usually after the war is when you need a good Salvager most. The country is usually going through a post-war depression, and they could really use all the metal and parts that got left on the battle field."

"I have crews…"

"That can't get half as much use out of scrap as one good Salvager. And I'm the best." She smiled, and her ego all but glowed right through her teeth. "Everyone knows that."

"My country is quite solvent. We don't need to trade in trash," Zarco started.

"Salvage." Drew corrected.

"You are ridiculous!" Facto hissed.

"Yeah, well, you're a shit-head."

"I still want to know why he's following us," Zarco said.

"Protection. Plain and simple." She didn't elaborate.

"Commencing re-entry in 5, 4, 3, 2…"

The ship started to rock as they hit the planet's atmosphere.

"This looks like it could get rough…"

A siren started wailing.

"What's wrong?" Stasha screamed in obvious panic. She hadn't lived her sister's life of the last five years, and she'd had just about all the excitement she could handle for one day.

"Shit!" Drew started punching buttons. "Fuck!"

"What's wrong?" Zarco demanded.

"Purple Cat calling Garbage Scow. Fuck it! Van, do you hear me?"

"Loud and clear."

"What's wrong?" Zarco screamed.

"We're all going to die horribly if you Royal fucks don't shut up!" Drew screamed back. "That's what's wrong."

"Van, the descent engines won't kick in. I've got no forward thrusters."

"Go to manual."

"Oh, gee, fuzz head. I never would have thought of that. I have taken it off computer. The computer isn't the problem. So, unless by 'manual' you mean that I should go turn the propeller by hand, we'd better come up with something else, because the gravitational pull is only going to increase."

"Can you reach escape velocity?"

Drew checked her readings.

"I don't have enough fuel to break the planet's pull now. Why didn't you think of that earlier?"

She looked out the front screen at the planet rushing towards her, and had to swallow the lump in her throat. "God, this isn't my fucking day!" Think, she had to think, there was always a way out. Damn pirate ship, if only she was on her good ole salvage barge…Salvage barge.

"That's it! Van, snag us with the tow-line and tow us in."

"That might rip your ship apart."

"I'd rather die up here than down there. Come on, Van."

"Get ready."

Van Gar looked at the human. "Hang on to your hat, monkey boy, we're going to lasso us a ship."

He turned the Garbage Scow's descent engines off for awhile, and allowed it to get dangerously close to the other ship, then he released the tow-line, slammed the descent engines back on, and turned on the electro magnet at the end of the tow-line.

"Prepare for hook-up."

When the tether caught hold of the other ship, it jerked both ships roughly.

"You're on tether."

"Really, Van? I thought my head just wanted to go visit Mr. Back Wall," she spit back. "Are you going to be able to guide us in?"

"Not really."

The ships shook violently.

"You have to realize, Drew, that most of the time we're towing in something that doesn't have anything living in it. Besides, when we have towed something, it has always been behind us."

"What are you saying, Van?"

"Well, let's just say that I'm in a wagon, and you're pulling me, and there's a hole in the road, so you have to stop."

"Yeah, so?"

"Well, let's say that you don't see the hole, and I have to make the wagon stop by dragging my hands on the ground."

Drew thought for a minute. "When I finally see the hole and stop, you still won't be able to."

"It's taking everything the reverse thrusters have now to keep us from plowing into the planet. I have no control over where the Scow is going, it's just following your lead."

"So, I'll lead, then," she answered thoughtfully.

"Drew, what are you going to do?"

"Put on protective headgear and start looking for a hole."

"Good luck."

"We're going to need it."

Drew had her hands on the ship's control, manually guiding both ships. Her eyes hurriedly went over charts and graphs.

"Van, we're going in."

She could practically hear the whine of the Garbage Scow's engines as it strained to keep both ships from crashing into the planet's surface. They were getting close now.

"Van, release the tether. Now!"

"Roger." He pulled up on the release, and the smaller ship dove like a rock. He ran well over the top of it and landed roughly in a pile of sand. He shut the ship down and then he quickly threw off his helmet and started out of the ship.

"Come on, monkey boy." There was no answer. The human sat limp in his chair. "Ah, damn. I wish I'd been nicer to him, now."

Van Gar exited the ship, stepped into the soft sand and sank up to the top of his boots. He looked down at the Purple Cat, which lay at the bottom of the dune he had landed on top of. A good quarter of its nose was covered. It lay there in the bottom of the hole like an egg in a bird's nest, and seemed to be intact. Of course, the Garbage Scow appeared to be intact, and the navigator was still dead. The sand slowed his pace, and it seemed like it took hours for him to reach the ship, when in fact it took only a few minutes. He beat on the hatch.

"Drew, Drew, can you hear me? Drew!" He had just turned to go back to the Scow and get the torch when the hatch opened, and Drew stepped out of the ship.

"So, I fell in the hole. What happened to your wagon?"

Facto appeared to have broken an arm, and they were all pretty shaky, but aside from that, they had all survived their crash. They started the climb up the dune towards the Garbage Scow.

"So, do you know where we are?" Van asked Drew.

"Some big desert on the planet Gar. I was just looking for a soft place to land, I wasn't taking in place names."

"There is only one desert on the planet, and that is the Galdart," Fitz sounded less that happy.

"So, we are in the Galdart desert." Drew shrugged. She looked at Facto. "What's the big deal?"

"This desert is two thousand miles across, the temperatures can reach one hundred thirty degrees in the day and thirty-two at night. There is no water, and the only organic life form is the Hurtella," Fitz informed them.

"So, we put out a distress signal, and someone will come pick us up in less that an hour."

"The Galdart desert is in the middle of the country of the Lockhede," Facto said harshly. "Of all the places to land us, you would land us here."

"Would you rather I have smashed you into a mountain closer to home?" Drew said hotly. "Besides, it's not even hot here."

"That's because night is falling, even as we speak."

"Oh."

She looked at Van Gar, whose jump suit was hanging open till it was almost indecent. She also noticed that his cuffs flapped in the breeze. "Van, fasten up your suit, you're going to get sand all in your hair."

"I can't, I ripped the Velcro off of them," he said, adamantly.

"Why?" Drew asked, shaking her head.

"Rats," Van answered, and stomped into the ship.

Drew looked around at the others. "Did I miss something?"

Drew went and got a beer out of the fridge and opened it.

"Could we send a message to your people?" she asked Zarco.

"I'm afraid any transmission would be picked up by the Lockhedes, and they would get here first. And they are our people, yours and mine." Drew made a gurgling sound, which could have meant anything, and began punching up screen after screen of what looked to him like nothing but garbled letters and numbers. But it was obvious that she was reading it.

"Couldn't we take this ship and go to our country?" Zarco asked

"The Scow won't be going anywhere for a long time." It was obvious by the tone of Van Gar's voice that he blamed Zarco personally for what had happened to his ship. "Bringing in both ships like that burned out all four thrusters. We're lucky we're not all dead."

"Speaking of dead," Drew shook her head towards the navigator.

Without a word, Van Gar went over, picked him up and carried him out.

"Where the fuck is everyone?" Drew asked Zarco.

"Fitz and Facto went to find medical equipment with which to fix Facto's arm, and I believe your sister went to her quarters. I'm afraid it's all been a bit much for her, and the sight of one more corpse was more than she could handle." He looked around. "So, at long last, we are alone."

She turned to face him, then looked around quickly to see if it was true. Her distaste showed on her face.

"You really don't remember me, Taral...Drewcila, but I remember you. You are so different, and yet in so many ways, you are so much the same. If I scrape away all the hardness, I can still see you. I have to wonder if we are not all just victims of our circumstances. I see in you all the same traits you once had, but they have twisted to fit your new life. Your keen mind has saved us more than once. In a way, I love you more than I ever have."

He moved close to her, and took her in his arms. She started to push away, then decided to see just what he was up to.

"Please, just this. I ask no more of you now. Please, it has been so long. I know you don't know me, but believe that I know you, that I love you. If I could do it again, it would all be so different. Oh, how I have ached to hold you, to caress you."

Curiosity over came her better judgment…the way it usually did…and she wrapped her arms around his neck. When his lips met hers, she responded. She felt him warm against her, and she was not repulsed. He wasn't a bad little kisser, either. But she certainly didn't feel any deep stirring within herself.

Someone coughed, and then coughed louder. She pushed easily away from Zarco. "What do you want, Van Gar?"

"Sorry to bother you, but I thought you would be interested to know that I have disposed of the corpse now," Van Gar said through clenched teeth.

"Thank you, Van Gar," Drew said.

"I'll just go check on the others," Zarco swept off the bridge, giving Van Gar a heated look as he passed him.

Van Gar walked purposefully over to check a read-out which he then didn't even bother to look at.

"Don't think I'm trying to tell you what to do…" Van Gar started.

"I don't know why not, since that sentence is always followed by you doing just exactly that," Drew said.

"I was just going to say that if that was part of your plan to make him hate you, I'm pretty sure that it's not going to work."

"He kissed me," Drew said plainly.

"And a mighty battle you did put up," Van Gar hissed.

"How I choose to conduct business is up to me, Van Gar." She crossed her arms in front of her chest. "I think I know what I'm doing. I have a plan."

"I didn't know your plan included sleeping with Zarco!"

"Maybe I've changed my plans."

"What changed your mind, Drew? His tongue down your throat?"

"Maybe," Drew turned back to the screen, already tired of this argument, and not quite sure what they were arguing about. She frowned.

"That couldn't be right." She punched some buttons. "Damn!" She started walking off the bridge, and Van Gar followed.

"What is it?"

"According to the read-outs, the ship has sunk three feet since we hit."

They opened the hatch, and walked out.

"At least three feet," Van said.

"Van, look!" Van turned, and looked down the dune at where the Purple Cat had lain. It could no longer be seen.

"That doesn't make any sense. The Garbage Scow is twice as heavy."

"And spread out over ten times as much surface area. Still, at the rate it's sinking, it will be covered by morning."

Drew looked at Van Gar. "Life sucks! My beautiful Garbage Scow, doomed to sink into the sands of this stupid planet. I've only been here a few hours Van, and I already hate this place. It was a stupid plan. I wanted to be Queen of the Salvagers, now we're gonna wind up Hurtella food. Whatever the hell a Hurtella is."

"It's not your fault, Drew."

"Damn right it's not! If you had kept up with me the way you were supposed to none of this would have happened!"

He ignored her outburst, put his arm around her shoulders and pressed her hard against him. "You can fool everyone else, and tell them whatever you like, but I know you didn't decide to do this because of the money. You did it to find out who you are, and no one could blame you for that."

"What utter crap," Drew said in a not-very-convincing tone. "I wasn't lying. He really did kiss me first."

There was a long silence, and then Drew looked up at Van Gar and smiled sadistically.

"Of course, that's not to say I didn't enjoy it."

Van Gar laughed and pushed her down in the sand.

"There's a chance that we may be able to take all the thrusters apart and make one of them work."

"We can't take off with one thruster," Drew said standing up and trying to wipe the sand off of her jump suit.

"No, but we can keep the ship from getting buried in the sand long enough to figure out how to get out of here."

It didn't take them long to rebuild a thruster. Of course, clearing the sand out of the exhaust was another story. They took turns shoveling.

"This damn shit runs in the hole faster than we can shovel it out." Van Gar stopped for a minute leaning on his shovel. He tried to wipe the sand off of his stomach.

Drew smiled. "Why did you rip the Velcro off your jump suit?"

"Rats," he answered, and started digging again.

"I still don't get it." Drew laughed. "Maybe I should go in and get those Royal fucks to help us?"

"While you're at it, why don't you just get some fairies to wave their magic wand and just put the Scow back in orbit?"

"Want me to take over for awhile?" Drew asked.

"Nah. Why don't you do me a favor? I keep hearing something over on the other side of the ship. Maybe it's one of those creatures old what's his face was talking about."

"A Hurtella?"

"How come you can remember that, but you can't remember to clean the garbage chute?"

She ignored the question. "Fitz didn't say that they were hostile."

"Well, he didn't say they weren't. Just take the blaster and go check for me."

Drew got up and carefully dusted herself off. She picked up the blaster, and threw it over her shoulder. "Sissy little mama's boy," she yelled back.

Van Gar kept on shoveling. "Pain in the ass," he grumbled. "Stupid Royal fucks."

"Hey, Van!"

Van raised up so fast he hit his head on the bottom of the ship. He backed up against the wall of his pit and stared at the human in amazement.

"Tim?" Van asked, holding his shovel in front of him as if it would ward off evil spirits.

"Yeah," he coughed and spat out some sand.

"I must have fainted. Guess I don't handle stress well. How'd I wind up in the sand?"

Van hated to tell him he had thrown him away for dead. "Uh…Last I knew, you were sacked out on the bridge, guess you sleep-walked, dude."

The human shook his head as if the answer made perfect sense. "I woke up and the only thing sticking out was my nose. I had to dig myself out. It was a very frightening experience."

"I'm sure it was."

He was interrupted by the sound of blaster fire. He quickly climbed out of the hole and ran towards the noise, shovel in hand. About half-way round the ship he almost ran into Drew. She laughed at the sight of him.

"Better bring a shovel—make that ten shovels." She held up an armored creature about twelve inches long from tip to tail. "If you don't, the terrible Hurtella will get you for sure."

"Very funny, Drew. While you're fucking around, our hole, which we have been digging for about forty-five minutes, is filling with sand." He held a hand to his heart. "One of these days you're going to give me a heart attack."

Drew smiled, threw the creature down, and followed him. "Do you care about me, Van?"

"Where the hell did that come from?" he asked doubling his pace.

"I've had a shit of a couple of days here Van. I'm feeling a little weird, indulge me."

"That's a stupid question, Drew," he said flatly.

"You know what I mean, Van."

"Would it matter if I did?" he asked, continuing his pace.

She ran to catch up with him and caught at his hand. "Now you're asking stupid questions."

"What's going to happen to us, Drew?"

"We'll be fine."

"I meant us?"

"I don't know, Van. It seems like yesterday our lives were all orderly."

Van shot her a look.

"Well, you know, like a dirty room, but you know were everything is—that kind of orderly."

"But don't you see, Drew? You didn't know where everything was. Now you do, and things are going to change. We don't know exactly how right now, but it's gottah change."

She tripped over the human on her way into the pit. "What the fuck?"

"Damn it, Tim." Van leaned down and slapped the human's face.

"Come on, Tim, snap out of it."

"I thought he was dead," Drew said.

"No. It seems that this really great navigator you got me goes to sleep if he gets scared."

"Oh, you're fucking kidding me!" Drew laughed.

"No, he walked up behind me right after you left, and like to scared the shit out of me. I told him he sleep-walked."

The human started to stir.

"The port's still clear. Let's go start the thruster before we have to dig it out again."

"Ten more minutes, mom," Tim mumbled as they pulled him to his feet.

"Come on, monkey boy," Van Gar pushed him forward. "Time to go home."

Chapter 7

Someone screamed. Drew sat straight up in bed. From her cabin she could hear the conversation taking place in the hall outside her door. "What's with her?" Tim asked.

"She's never seen such an ugly human before," Van Gar answered lightly.

Drew lay back down. Obviously, seeing a dead guy walking around the ship had startled Stasha.

"I'm surprised they didn't both faint," Drew muttered and buried her head deeper in her pillow. She heard the gentle humming of their one remaining thruster—all was well. She started to go back to sleep, then jerked to a sitting position again.

Well! Things were far from being well! Stuck in the middle of a desert belonging to the very people who had chewed up part of her brain and thrown it away. Yes, she had finally admitted to herself that she was one of them. It was confusing as hell to know who she was and have all these people tell her that she was someone else.

But all that was unimportant; at least for the moment. Their fuel would only last just so long, and then the ship would be buried in the sand. They were stuck in the middle of a desert, which from all the readouts was every bit as harsh as Fitz had indicated. She didn't have time to sleep. She got up and looked at the clock.

"Eight hours. Hell, my body will start to deteriorate with so much sleep."

She walked to the bathroom. A quick look in the mirror, and she decided she looked every bit as bad as she felt.

"Ick, it's the incredible Hurtella-faced woman, and her side-kick, hair of death."

She stuck out her tongue.

"Yuck, there's stuff growing there that remembers when the humans first gouged big holes in the galaxy."

She picked up the electric mouth scraper and spent five minutes cleaning the gross stuff out of her mouth. She stripped and got into the shower. She looked at the sand which gathered by the drain.

"I hate sand."

"So do I." Without further ado, Van Gar got in the shower with her.

"What the fuck are you doing?" She laughed.

"Would you believe conserving water? After all, there is a desert out there, and this is the only water."

"Yeah, and you know just like I do that it has been recycled seventy times, and can keep being recycled till the ship runs out of power. Which will take days."

"I saw you kiss him last night."

"I told you, Van. He kissed me."

"The point is that even if we live, I'm going to lose you to him."

"I'm never staying here with that tight-assed pansy. And since when do you own me?"

"There's a good chance you will stay here."

He held a finger over her lips as she started to speak.

"Let me finish, Drew."

He ran his hand over her wet head.

"We have played a game with each other for years, and now may be the only time we'll have to see how the end of the game will turn out. I won't pretend to know how you feel about me, but I know you are as curious as I am. We have never been as close to death as we are now. Things don't look good, and do you really want to die never knowing?"

"That's one hell of a line, Van," she said with a smile.

"Did it work?" Van Gar asked.

"Rather well, actually."

She wrapped her arms around his neck.

"Then I'll have to use it again sometime."

Their wet bodies met, and they kissed.

The water kept recycling.

Stasha had watched Van Gar enter Drew's cabin, and she waited to see how long it would take one or the other to emerge. Van Gar was the first to leave. His hair—all of it that could be seen—was wet, and he was whistling a happy alien tune. When Drew emerged a few minutes later, her hair was wet, and she looked around as if checking to see if she had been caught. She smiled broadly when she saw Stasha standing partially concealed behind a metal brace in the wall.

"So, how long were you standing there?" Drew asked.

"How could you?" Stasha asked. "You wouldn't sleep with your own husband."

"I didn't sleep with Van Gar," Drew said with a wicked grin.

"Poor Zarco. All these years he's saved himself for you, and you're nothing but a common whore."

"I don't think there's anything common about me," Drew said in mock anger. She laughed and shrugged. "Did you know that Chitzky males have multiple orgasms, just like you and I?"

"Of course I didn't," Stasha said indignantly.

"Neither did I."

Drew grinned wildly, started whistling the same tune Van Gar had been whistling, and sauntered off in the direction of the cargo bay.

Drew and Van had spent the last thirty minutes walking around and around the vehicle in their cargo bay. It was a huge covered thing with tracks, that they used to pick up salvage in areas so dangerous it just wasn't safe to carry anything of value, even scrap, without armored transport.

"I don't know, Drew."

"Well, I do. You're amazingly good at the sex thing."

"I ah…I was talking about the transport, Drew."

His face was bright red.

She gave him an expectant look, her brow arched questioningly.

"What?"

"What?" she asked hotly. "What! I should have known better. Males of all species are just alike. I said you were good in bed. The least you can do is lie to me and tell me I was good, too."

"OK," he said simply.

He started looking the transport over again.

"Well?"

"Right now?"

"Yes, right now!" she screamed.

"You are so good in bed, Drew. How can I put in mere words how fine you really are," he droned in a monotone.

"Fine!" She walked out from underneath the transport to stand in front of him. She poked him in the chest. "Say what you like, you egotistical fur ball…"

"I never said I was good at the sex thing. You did."

"Fuck you, Van Gar, I know you liked it!"

"I never said I didn't like it, Drew. I was just a little disappointed, that's all," he shrugged.

"Disappointed!" She doubled up her fist and hit him square in the chest.

He stumbled back a couple of feet.

"Fuck you! Do you hear me, Van Gar De La Trag Iz Trok!" She turned on her heel and started out of the cargo bay. "Fuck you!"

Van Gar watched her leave. "She used my whole name. Damn! She really was mad!" He went back to jotting down all the measurements on the transport.

"So, she's really a lousy lay, huh?" The human jumped out of the cab to stand on the track.

"Why you slimy little, rat-loving human!"

"Hey, I can't help it if you guys forgot that you sent me inside to take down the interior dimensions."

"That was supposed to be a private conversation between Drew and I. It's none of your business."

"I bet his Highship would be interested in it."

"I could rip your spleen out of your ear," Van Gar growled. "Besides, I never said she was a lousy lay. I said I was disappointed. As for telling the Royal fuck—have at it."

"If you were disappointed, she must have been a lousy lay. I mean, one plus one is two, and all that. It all adds up to the same thing."

"Stupid human," Van Gar mumbled and went back to his work. "I never said I was disappointed in the sex."

"In what, then?" The human watched as the Chitzky purposefully ignored him. "You don't like me, do you?"

Van Gar laughed. "And I thought you were too stupid to wipe your own ass."

"Why don't you like me?" Tim whined.

"Where do you want me to start?" Van Gar looked up at the human. "You're ugly, you are without a doubt the most cowardly being I have ever met, you whine more than my grandmother…"

"Yeah, but besides that," Tim said defensively.

"Besides that, you are stupid, and you don't know how to do anything."

"I'm a damn good navigator," Tim screamed back.

"Then navigate us the fuck out of this desert," Van Gar screamed.

"Get me something that runs, and I will." Tim jumped down off the four foot track, stumbled and almost fell. He looked up at Van Gar and thrust the note pad he held at him. "Here's the fucking inside measurements."

He turned to walk out of the cargo bay. He was almost to the door when he turned around. "You know, I may not be too fucking smart, but it doesn't take a genius to figure out what you're disappointed about. Maybe she didn't say she loved you because you didn't tell her that you loved her."

Van Gar gave him a shocked look.

"Maybe I went about it the wrong way, but I was just trying to get you to talk to me. We're probably all going to die out here, and I'm the only one here that's alone. I don't know anyone here, and you know what really sucks? There's no one at home that will miss me if I don't come back."

"That's because you're an obnoxious little twit," Van Gar said.

"Up yours, man!" Tim stormed out of the cargo bay.

"Some people just can't accept creative criticism." Van Gar sighed. He really shouldn't have been so hard on the human, but all he ever did was whine, and Van Gar had troubles of his own. The last thing he could be worried with was the unhappy home life of the galaxy's ugliest human. He had all the measurements, and now he had to go talk to Drew, which considering how they had just parted was not something he was looking forward to.

Drew punched the transport dimensions into the computer and a picture came up on the screen. She punched in the weight of the machine and added the analysis the computer had already done on the sand.

"Fuck." Drew rubbed her hand over her face.

"Maybe we could make it lighter," Van Gar suggested.

"I didn't count us or our supplies yet. It will be heavier than that. Weight isn't our real problem anyway. It's the tracks. According to this, they will just dig us into the sand. Then there are about a billion other problems. For instance, during the day we're going to bake in this tin can."

"How many days can the ship keep running?"

"Three. Four if we're lucky."

She wouldn't look at him. He couldn't stand it. He put his hands on her shoulders. "You weren't a disappointment, Drew," he whispered.

He kissed the top of her head. "But...well, with everything that's going on... You weren't a disappointment."

Drew nodded. She didn't know exactly what she wanted from Van Gar. One thing was for damn sure she didn't like to be mediocre at anything. Being considered by Van Gar to be only a little more than a disappointment in bed was not exactly doing anything for her wounded ego. But right now there was more at stake then her self esteem.

"It looks kind of grim, don't it?" she said.

"Yeah." Van Gar looked at the screen. "Wait. Get up. Damn, we're starting to think like all these normal geeks."

Drew got up and he sat down at the console.

"We're *Salvagers*," Van said proudly. He drew a sled on the front of the transport and added five inches to the tracks. He cut holes in the side of the vehicle and then added reflective shields. This time, the data was much different. "We can get metal off any part of the ship to make the sled, and add to the tracks. We can use the shielding off the outside of the ship as a sun screen. If we use the solar generator we'll have rechargeable power. It's never been much use to us before since we were running in the dark or in the shadows. However in the middle of the desert…it ought to make more than enough power to run the vehicle. Of course, it will mean taking some pieces off the ship, but, under the circumstances."

"Van, right now the Scow is going to sink in the sand as soon as we run out of power to run the thrusters. I've never been one to let sentimentality get in the way of saving my own ass."

As soon as the sun went down, they went to work. The first thing they did was pull enough shielding off the outside of the ship's belly to cover the top of the transport. Then they started to cut the first of the two by three foot windows in the sides of the transport.

Van cut it and then Drew kicked it so that it fell out and landed on the floor with a resounding crash, the human fainted and fell head-first off the tracks, and Zarco walked in. He walked around the machine just checking it out, unnoticed by the two working on the inside.

"Should we see if he's OK?" Van Gar asked.

"Nah, it's no great loss if he's dead, and a concussion might actually improve his brain power," Drew laughed.

Zarco heard the gentle hum of the laser torch as it was turned back on, and watched as the bright light penetrated the vehicle's body.

"I don't see why we can't use what we're cutting out here to add to the tracks," Van Gar said over the popping of metal.

"Sounds good to me."

Then they started talking about what they were going to do with this part and that part. As interested as Zarco was, and as much as he wanted to know what they were doing, he just couldn't follow their lingo. What wasn't part names that he neither knew nor recognized was jumbled Salvager slang which was spoken so fast that he couldn't grasp its meaning. About the time he was going to make his presence known, a huge piece of metal fell from the vehicle to land at his feet with a resounding crash. He looked up, and saw his wife and the creature looking down at him. Taralin smiled at him, and he melted. She was never more lovely that she was now, wearing the clothes she had stolen from the dead pirates, and glistening with sweat.

"Hey, King baby, you better keep an eye out," she warned and winked at him. "As long as you're down there, would you check to see if that human is alive? If he is, roll him off his nose."

"Yes, of course, my love," he went to check. Finding the human alive, he then rolled him onto his back. "He's got a small bump on his head, but other than that, he seems to be unscathed."

"Well, you can't win 'em all," Van Gar said, smiling at Drew, who nodded her head in agreement.

"I actually came down to see if there was some way that we might be of assistance." He looked up at Drew. "I gather that you are building a transport to carry us across the desert. Since crossing the desert alive is in all of our interests, it only follows that we should all work towards this common goal."

"I think Drew and I…" Van Gar started.

"…think that's a damn good idea." Drew finished.

"Then I'll just go and gather the others." Zarco bowed deeply and departed.

"All they're going to do is get in the way," Van Gar grumbled.

"They're not stupid, Van. There are about a billion little tasks that we need done, and there's no reason they can't do them. It will save us that much time."

Van Gar nodded in a defeated sort of way, and went back to cutting out the next hole.

"I bet *he* doesn't think I'm boring in bed," Drew said taking some small pleasure from watching the snarl that leapt to Van Gar's face.

Chapter 8

Even with everyone helping, the ship had run out of power
and was starting to sink into the sand two hours before they rolled
the transport off the ship and into the desert night.

They had cut the transport so that it was completely open
on the sides except for support for the roof. The shields from the
ship formed a canopy extending three feet out all the way around
the transport.

Drew sat at the controls and looked back at the sinking
ship. Five years ago she had lost all memory of her life before
that moment. Now, as she saw the Garbage Scow sinking silently into the sands of the Galdart desert, she felt in a way that
the last five years of her life were being erased as well. Her life at
this moment seemed to have no point past getting herself and the
others out of the desert alive. For a woman who always had a
plan it was a very humbling feeling.

She was married to a man she didn't know, traveling on a
planet she didn't remember, and watching the only home she knew
sink into the sand. In a few seconds, the Scow would be out of
her line of sight, and in a few more hours it would disappear completely in this ocean of sand. All it would be was a memory. And
memories could fade or be removed, and then the last five years
would be gone, too, and she would have no past, no point of
reference with which to judge her life. She'd been there before, it
hadn't been pleasant. Memories were supposed to be all that you
had to judge your life by. But big chunks of her life were missing; erased and forgotten.

Was her life better or worse? Who could really tell? She'd
been happy in her role as Drewcila Qwah. Happy with the life of
a Salvager. Happy with her reputation. But was that her? Or the

life that Erik had chosen for her by telling someone with no memory "this is who you are."

She went over a dune and she could no longer see her ship.

"I am Drewcila Qwah," she whispered. "If I am queen of anything, I am Queen of the Salvagers."

"What'd you say, Drew?" Van Gar asked.

She looked at him. She had almost forgotten that he was sitting there. She looked at the Chitzky, his chest exposed because of the missing Velcro, and smiled.

"Everyone is someone. Aren't they, Van Gar?"

"Are you doing your deep, philosophical thing, Drew? Because if you are, it's just scary, and all that shit is lost on me as soon as you get past the 'life is like an empty beer can' phase. That I can relate to. All that other crap just goes over my head."

Drew laughed.

Something large and dark ran across their path at that moment, and she had to swerve to miss it.

"What the hell was that?"

"What?" Van Gar shrugged. "I didn't see nothin'."

"Something ran in front of us, about the size of a dog."

"It must have been a shadow."

"Of what, dunder head?"

"The only life form in the Galdart is the Hurtella," Fitz reminded them.

"Must of been a Hurtella, then," Van Gar said with a shrug. "It probably looked bigger because it got caught in the headlights. Can't you go any faster?"

"We're using a solar powered motor, remember?" Drew asked. She grinned when he hit himself in the head.

"Then how are we running at all?" Facto asked.

"Batteries. If we keep our speed down, they should hold till the sun comes up. Once the sun's up, we can fly." Van Gar answered at length in an attempt to make up for his earlier statement.

"What happens if we run out of power before the sun comes up?" Stasha wanted to know.

"We won't," Drew assured her.

"But what if we do?" Stasha persisted.

"We sink like a fucking rock into the burning sand of the Galdart," Drew answered, not without irritation.

"Oh." Stasha pulled a face.

"You had to ask," Zarco said with a laugh. "How many days will it take us to get out of the desert?"

"Three, if we're lucky."

Drew looked back at him.

"I have a more important question. Once we get out of the desert, how much Lockhede territory do we have to cross through before we make it to Gildart?"

Zarco moved to where he could see the map on the console. He frowned. "A hundred miles."

"Lovely."

They lapsed into silence.

Drew drove through the night, then Van took over for her, and she tried to sleep. She wasn't having much luck. Even with the reflective shields, all the ventilation, and the breeze that their now very fast pace was making, it was still close to a hundred degrees in the transport. First, she undid the Velcro on her coveralls, then she pulled the tops down. By high noon, she had removed them completely, and lay on top of them in her underwear. She had expected to hear some sort of protest, but a quick glance around showed that her companions weren't wearing much more, and in the case of her fur-covered friend, Van Gar, considerably less. He had to be absolutely miserable.

She still wasn't comfortable, but exhaustion took over and she fell into a restless sleep, filled with dreams she would try to interpret later without much success.

Van Gar looked back at where Drew tossed and turned, and wondered what she was dreaming. It seemed to Van Gar that he had no past either. Nothing that had happened to him before he'd met Drew seemed to bear any significance in his life. A blur of mediocrity. Going no where. Until that fateful day almost five years ago when he had met Drewcila Qwah in a crowded Salvagers' bar.

Van Gar had never liked Erik Rider, so he hadn't immediately understood why he had felt such a loss when Drew told him about Erik's death. Now he realized why—Erik was so much a part of what both he and Drew had become. Because in a way, Erik was as much responsible for making him all that he was as he was for making Drewcila.

"Games within games," Van said with a sigh.

"Excuse me?" Zarco was sitting in the seat beside him now.

Van Gar started to ignore him, but then thought better of it. This was, after all Drew's husband. The man she had lived with before she had stepped into Van's life, and the man she would, more than likely, be living with when she stepped out of his life.

"I was just thinking about how everyone seems to be playing with my and Drew's lives."

"What do you mean?" Zarco asked defensively.

"In a game, when you make a move, you don't always know the outcome of that move. It seems like the best move at the time, but you won't know till later whether it was or not. If you were playing the game without an opponent, you could easily correct any mistake. But most games don't work that way. So, you make your move, and they make their move, and in making their move, they change completely the way you were going to play out your hand."

He looked at Zarco to see if he was listening. He was, so Van went on. "You have everything you want, except that your country is at war. Your enemy steals your wife, and you do nothing." Zarco started to protest and Van held up his hand. Zarco remained silent and Van went on. "That's your first move. A move that could be rectified except that your opponent removes you wife's memory so that you can never regain what you have lost. Erik likes money, so he creates Drewcila Qwah to hide your wife. Then moves her into my life. Drew is ambitious, and becomes the best Salvager in the galaxy. She and I go on without any knowledge that we are only pieces in a game. We still don't know how the game is going to end. It's become more and more complicated. The more players you add, the more pieces you move into play, the more complex the game. The only thing I'm sure of right now is that however things come out, Drew and I are going to lose. Considering that we never even knew that we were playing the fucking game, I think that's pretty crappy."

Zarco just looked at the alien for awhile, taking in all he had said. "You're in love with my wife."

The alien totally ignored his statement.

"You think I should have gone after her?"

"I would have. Failing that, I think you should have left her where you found her. As soon as you found out that she had a new life, you should have let her live it, instead of pulling her right back into your game."

"I'm not playing any twisted game, and I resent you insinuating that I am. Taralin is my wife. Taralin is Queen of Gildart. Would you have me leave her in a world of Salvagers?"

"You already made your move, and now you're trying to take it back. You let them destroy Taralin, and now you're going to destroy Drewcila Qwah."

"What right do you have to tell me how to treat my wife?"

"What right do you have to put Drew in danger? As long as she is Drewcila Qwah, she belongs more to me that she ever will to you. And I've got news for you; Drewcila Qwah will never belong to any male. Own a couple, maybe, belong to one? Never."

"Are you blaming me for our current position? Because I hardly think that you can blame it on me. The Lockhedes, maybe, but I…"

"Drew never would have been a target if it wasn't for you. Drew and I would likely be half way across the galaxy. And having just unloaded a cargo of junk, we'd be spending our earnings in some tacky over-crowded bar and beating up some humans."

"And that's the life you'd have her lead?"

"It beats all hell out of burning alive in the fucking Galdart desert!"

"Holy fuck!" Zarco screamed.

Van Gar was so taken aback by the King's use of Salvager slang that he damn near hit the looming shape in the middle of their path. He slammed on the brakes and slammed the transport into reverse.

Drew awoke with a start. "What the...Oh, shit!" She scrambled to her hands and knees and headed for her laser canon. "Move, move," she yelled at Zarco.

He moved, and she sat down in the seat quickly.

"I thought those damn things only came in small," she screamed at Fitz.

"The Galdartian Hurtella has been known to reach lengths of fifteen feet and may weigh as much as three thousand pounds."

"Why didn't you say that before?" Van Gar screamed.

"I saw no need to startle anyone."

"So considerate!"

Drew sat ready to fire.

"It seems to have stopped chasing us," Van Gar announced. "They're a helluva lot faster that they look."

"Go around it," Drew suggested.

As soon as they started to move, it started to chase them again.

"Shoot it," Van Gar screamed, throwing the vehicle into reverse again.

"I don't know if anything will pierce that shell."

"Then shoot it in the head."

It stopped chasing them again.

"What does something that size find to eat in the middle of the desert?" Stasha asked curiously.

"Idiots that try to cross all this sand," Drew screamed.

"Try to go around it again, Van. This time, make a bigger circle."

It didn't work. The thing moved three times as fast this time, and was almost upon them before Drew could fire. The blast barely missed his head, sending a shower of sparks into the beast's face, which made it stop and think for a moment. Then, much to their dismay, it charged them.

"Fuck!" Drew fired again. The shot, fired in haste, hit nothing but shell, and only served to add speed to the animal's charge. It slammed into the transport, and they lurched sideways. It backed up and then started to charge them again.

"Damn it, Drew, shoot the fucking thing!" Van screamed.

Drew fired. This time she hit the creature in the head, and the animal stopped in mid-charge, a steady stream of blood pouring from the wound.

Then before they had time to rejoice in its death it charged them again. It struck them in the side, and this time there was the unhealthy sound of metal crunching, and someone screamed.

Drew fired again as the transport lurched to a stop.

The bolt hit the beast in the head, and it stopped just as its beak-like mouth looked like it was going to tear a chunk out of the side of the transport.

Drew fired again just for good measure.

Van and Drew looked at each other.

"Fuck," they said.

"What a dick on a baby," Drew swore.

"I think Tim is hurt," Stasha said, kneeling beside him.

"No such luck, he just passes out when he gets excited," Drew said.

"You're kidding, right?" Facto asked.

"I wish she was." Van sighed and followed Drewcila out of the transport and into the sizzling heat of the sun to look at the damage. The right track was damaged and was not going to move without repair. Drew rubbed her hand over her eyes.

"How bad is it?" Zarco asked.

"Well, I hate to dash anyone's hopes, but…we're all going to die."

The canopy gave them some shade to work in, but without the effects of movement, it wasn't much better than being in the sun. Despite the desire to work without any clothes on at all, Drew and Van had put their coveralls on to work in, hoping that they would both protect them from the vicious rays of the sun and hold in some of the sweat which evaporated from their skin as soon as it was created in the intense desert heat.

To make matters worse, the transport was sinking the whole time they worked on it.

It took them a little under an hour to repair the damage done to the track, but the ordeal had taken its toll on them all, and everyone was very quiet as they started out once more.

This time, Drew sat beside Van Gar, canon at the ready. She scanned the horizon with a pair of binoculars every few minutes, looking for any sign of a Hurtella. The idea was to avoid them if at all possible.

It was dark before Van Gar and Drew decided to change places.

"Why don't you get some rest, Drewcila," Zarco said. "You look exhausted. I could drive this thing for awhile."

"Can you fire a laser cannon?"

"Yes."

"Then why don't you take point and let Van get some rest?"

Van Gar started to protest.

"Don't give me any flack, fur ball."

He nodded, and moved to the back of the transport, leaving the other seat for Zarco.

Drew started the transport moving while Zarco got into position. The gun felt good in his hands. While part of his preparation for the throne had included extensive military training, he hadn't had a gun in his hands for years. The entire war had been fought, and while he had called all the shots, he hadn't fired a single one.

At times when the daily casualty reports came in, and lives were counted in numbers, and victories were won on the bodies of the dead, he had felt so removed from it all that in a way it had been, as the Chitzky suggested, a game. He had fought the war with his generals on paper, and with computers and calculators. It was only when he had the time to look at the news, or thought of his missing wife, that he saw the numbers as people.

He had allowed Taralin to become one of those numbers, but no longer. He'd fight for her now. He would sit here with this gun, and watch out for things that wished to hurt her, and he would kill them. He wasn't going to play games. Not anymore.

"You keep scrunching your face up like that and it might become permanent," Drew said lightly.

"I was just thinking."

"'Bout what?"

"Well, mostly about you. About what I should have done. What might have made things different."

"It's about five years late for that shit now, isn't it?"

"What do I have to do to win you back?"

Drew looked only at the desert in front of her. It was a while before she answered. "I'm not a fucking trophy, Zarco. I'm not the same person you knew. In a lot of ways I don't even know who I am. And every second that I am around you, I become less and less sure that I ever knew.

"How can I really be anyone if I don't have a past? After all, a person is only the impressions their memories have left them with. Am I Taralin Zarco, or am I Drewcila Qwah? Maybe I'm a combination of both, or perhaps none of the above? Maybe I will never be whole until I somehow link the past you remember with the person I have become.

"The problem is that I was perfectly happy 'til you came along and told me that I'm not who I thought I was. For now, the only way I can stay sane is to be the only person I know how to be, Drewcila Qwah, and it would help a hell of a lot if you could accept that, and quit trying to make me over in your fucking image."

Zarco nodded and looked out at the desert through the infrared binoculars. "I keep telling myself I won't be selfish, and then I keep falling right back into the same patterns. You'll have to remember that I was taught to be selfish. I'm King, and therefore I have always had everything I wanted. I'm used to people bending to my will."

"And I am a very shrewd business woman. I am also used to people bending to my will, but only after a lot of hard work. I plan to see what's in this for me, and after all I've been through, I expect something for my efforts. If there isn't enough, then I'm outtah here."

"Then we'll have to make sure that you get just what your heart desires." Zarco smiled broadly at her, and she had to admit that she was at least a little attracted to him. She was also not awfully opposed to the idea of having everything her heart desired.

A day and a half later they crawled up out of the desert. All badly sunburned and dehydrated, they worked half-heartedly at removing the shields from the top of the transport and cutting the extensions off the tracks. Now that they were on solid ground, these things not only looked ridiculous, but made travel almost impossible. Especially the sled in the front. Essential in the sands of the desert, it had brought them to an abrupt halt the minute they had hit solid ground. As they worked, they drank freely of their water supply.

"If you hadn't been so stingy with the water rations, we might not all be suffering from dehydration right now," Facto said accusingly to Drew.

"Oh, the joys of hindsight," Drew cooed. "How did we know we wouldn't be stuck in the desert for a week? If that Hurtella had done much more damage, we could have been."

"According to the charts, we'll hit a road five miles that way," Tim announced, pointing West.

"That's the desert, monkey boy," Van said slapping his hand to his head in disbelief.

Tim smiled nervously. "I, ah, meant that way," he pointed East.

"Some navigator," Van Gar mumbled. "Navigate us right back into the desert."

"Anyone can make a mistake," Tim defended.

"Yeah, that was your mother's excuse," Van chided.

Fitz looked at the charts. "We should be able to make it all the way to the border on this road without hitting any major towns. The only problem will be the Wall."

"The Wall?" Van Gar asked as he made the last cut and the sled fell free.

"The Lockhedes' ancestors built a great Wall out of stone all around their country to keep their enemies out. The Wall is ten feet high and twenty feet wide. The gates are well guarded, and no one can get through unless they have the proper paperwork," Fitz reported.

"And what's the good news, Fitz?" Drew asked.

"We're only a six hour drive from home."

Chapter 9

The further they got out of the desert, the prettier the countryside was, and the more vehicles they encountered. The strange
vehicle drew stares, but no one had tried to detain them. Yet. The
longer that lasted, the more nervous Drew became.

"How close are we to the border?"

"Two miles closer than the last time you asked," Tim
answered.

"I don't pay you to be funny, asshole. Just answer my
question."

"Five miles."

Without anyone saying anything, Van Gar pulled off the
road to hide in the brush. He shut all the lights off.

"OK, everyone just stay here and be quiet," Drew ordered. She grabbed the laser canon and jumped out of the
transport.

Van Gar grabbed his favorite rifle blaster and followed.

"Wait a minute!" Zarco ordered.

"Shut the fuck up!" Drew hissed.

"What are you doing?" Zarco asked in a whisper.

"Just stay here and shut up, or bigger than shit you'll get
us all killed. Just trust me."

She and Van Gar strode off into the night, walking towards the road. When they reached it, they hid themselves behind a pile of brush.

"So, do you think he does?" Van Gar asked.

"Think he does what?"

"Trust you?"

"If he does, he's a bigger fool then I think he is," she smiled
at him. "I think I see lights."

They watched the road.

"What do you think?" Drew asked.

"Too small. There are six of us."

"Seven."

"I was hoping we could leave the monkey boy here."

"Here comes another one...too small. Maybe we'll have to leave the monkey boy. Here comes another one. Come on, let's move."

They ran into the road with their guns at the ready, and the car screeched to a stop.

"Get out of the car! Slowly!"

"Why?" the driver screamed back.

Drew looked at Van Gar, who shrugged.

"Because we have really big guns and if you don't, we're going to blast your ass away," Drew answered.

"Oh." The driver got out of the car. "In that case." To their dismay and surprise, he opened fire on them.

"Fuck me!" Drew fired without thinking, and the driver landed some ten feet behind the car. "I'll move the car, and you get the body. Quick, before another car comes!"

Drew moved the car up behind the transport while Van Gar hid the body. He met them all at the car.

"What now? We still don't have any papers," Facto said. "Lockhede is not going to let anyone enter Gildart without the right paperwork."

"Oh they want paper work, I'm so scared," Drewcila said facetiously. "Lockhede isn't guarding the gate, a bunch of guards are. Chances are that only one of them asks to see paperwork. He's the only one we have to get past. The only one we have to convince," Drew said with a smile.

"And just how are you going to convince him without paperwork?"

Drew pulled a big wad of currency out of her pocket. "Inter-Galactic Dollars—IGDs. You can't trace them, and there isn't a bank in the galaxy that won't take them as easily as gold."

"You think you can pay the guard off, and he'll let us pass just like that?" Facto shook his head in disbelief. "Not everyone puts as much importance in money as you do, Qwah."

"That's Queen to you, dick head. Listen. You rich fucks don't get it because you ain't ever been hungry. That guard up there probably has a wife and kids, an aged mother, and a worthless brother he's trying to support. If I wave a year's pay under his nose, he has two choices. He can shaft himself and his family, or he can let a car full of people go through without their paperwork."

"He'd be a traitor to his country!"

"Why? Because he let us into Gildart? You aren't even at war anymore. Why should he care?"

Facto started to say more.

"Its real simple, Fucktoad. If money doesn't work, we kill him and hope we can get out of there before the other guards start firing on us," Drew said emphasizing her words by checking her weapon over carefully.

"So if you can't buy it, kill it. Is that your answer to everything?" Facto asked. "Pay it off or kill it..."

"Enough Facto!" Zarco ordered. "You are wasting our time. We don't really have any other choice."

They held their breath as Drew braked the car to a stop at the guard gate.

"Nice limo," the guard said.

"How would you like to have one just like it?" Drew asked with a smile.

"That would be great. Could I see your paperwork, please?"

Drew held out a bunch of iggys. The guard's eyes got huge.

"Ah, is that what I think it is, ma'am?"

Drew smiled sweetly back. "If you think it's a bribe, then the answer would be yes."

"How much is there?"

"Two hundred."

He took the wad of bills, looked around quickly, and stuck it in his pocket. "Well, boys, this one's paperwork seems to be in order. Go on with you, now, and have a good trip."

They didn't breathe till the guard post was out of sight.

"I can't believe a man would sell his country out for two hundred IGDs!" Facto said in disbelief.

Stasha laughed for the first time in days. "You know," she said to Drew, "I really think he would have preferred to have us all shot through the head than admit that you were right."

"Nonsense!" Facto shot back. "I simply can't believe that the Lockhedes have so little pride in country."

They were stopped at the Gildart border. "I'll need to see your paperwork," the guard on duty said.

"Why, you insolent pig!" Facto sputtered. "Do you not know who he is?"

"Please," Drew held up her hand. "Allow me, Factub." She held out another two hundred IGDs.

"Their paperwork seems to be in order!" The guard grabbed the money. "You may pass, and have a safe trip."

They all laughed as they drove away. All except Facto.

"I can't believe it. We have no protection at our borders. Anyone with a few hundred IGDs can just walk right into our country. Drug dealers, smugglers, spies, revolutionaries, and murderers. We need to fire that man. We need to crack down on all our guards. Make higher standards, make the test harder, make..."

"How much do you pay your gate guards?" Van Gar asked.

"A decent wage," Facto said.

"Compared to what—starvation?" Drew laughed.

"What's your point?" Facto asked Van Gar.

"My point is that it's hard to have any loyalty to a system of government that only throws you enough crumbs to exist. If you want decent gate guards, I suggest you make the wages high enough that an ambitious man would want to do it. Make them high enough that he feels he owes you loyalty."

"Nonsense!" Facto huffed, and was silent the rest of the trip.

The city lights were the first thing they saw. Stasha started to cry. "If I never leave home again, it will be too soon."

Drew watched as the Barions became down right giddy with excitement. The sad thing was that she looked at the lights of the city ahead and felt no more feeling of home-coming than the Chitzky or the human. It was just a place, like so many places she had been to. One more place that she didn't know.

"I can't wait till Mother and Father see you," Stasha said, patting her sister on the shoulder.

Panic weld up inside Drew. She had parents, too. She was just getting used to the idea that she was related to Stasha. In fact while she wouldn't admit it if asked, she was starting to like Stasha. She had expected Stasha to get hysterical several times during the past few days. She had expected her to slow them down and whine, but Stasha had toughed it out. For the most part without bitching. Drew saw a lot of her own characteristics in her sibling. In spite of herself, she felt close to Stasha, as if there really were a bond between them.

"I think we can safely call the palace and tell them we're coming in now," Zarco said.

He found the communicator in the back of the limo. After several tries, he managed to get through.

As they neared the palace, they encountered people rioting in the streets. The military met them, and pushed the crowds back so that they could get through.

"What's all this shit?" Drew hissed. "I expected we'd be greeted with a parade."

"I told you not to leave Seamus in charge of the kingdom while you were away," Fitz sighed. "He's a good man, but he never could communicate with the people, and he complicates everything. He wants letters in triplicate before he'll buy pencils."

"I'm sorry about all this," Zarco said. "It's not much of a welcome. But if it's any conciliation, they couldn't know that it's you in this vehicle. The people love you, Taralin. They worship you. If they knew you were home, that knowledge would quiet even the most violent riot."

"Such a happy people," Van Gar said as some vegetable splattered on the front windshield. "I can tell by their enthusiasm that you really are the Queen here. I admit, Drew, that I had my doubts, but they're acting just like you do on free drinks night at the bar."

"And I was afraid they would all be as stuffy as Fuckto."

"I haven't seen such a riot since the police force went on strike," Fitz said. "Lord knows what Seamus has done in your absence."

"Whatever the problem is, you know the people will calm down and their rioting will turn to rejoicing as soon as they hear I have brought their Queen back to them."

Drew looked at Van. "I don't remember it that way, do you?"

"No. I seem to remember us saving his royal ass about a half a dozen times." Van said.

Drew nodded. "As long as my short term memory's not going as well."

They pulled the car into the spot indicated. "But what if I don't want to park there?" Drew mumbled. As the gates shut them off from the mob in the street, they got out of the limo carefully. The soldiers fell at Drew's feet, and prostrated themselves.

"My Queen, I am your humble servant!" they said in unison.

Drew gave Van Gar a smug look.

"There's no place like home, Van. There's no place like home."

Chapter 10

Drew didn't know how long she had slept. It might have been hours, or it might have been days. She yawned and stretched, loving the feel of the blue silk that enveloped her. She was warm. Not too hot, and not too cold, but just right. Where she lay was soft yet firm—and clean. As was she. None of this was very familiar, but she supposed you could get used to anything, if you had to. She stretched to her full length, and still felt very small laying in the middle of this ocean of a bed.

"Would Her Majesty like anything this morning?" asked a strange young woman.

Drew held her hand to her chest.

"Yes! How bout some fucking privacy! And don't ever do that again!" Drew screamed. "Damn, I'm sleepin' here in the buff because, stupid me, I thought I could have privacy in my own fucking room. If I wanted something, I'd go to the door and yell out, real loud like. 'Hey you peons, get me whatever the fuck it was.'"

The young woman looked more than a little shocked, then she bowed low.

"A million pardons, my Queen," she started to back out of the room.

"Hold on a second," Drew took a deep breath. God, she hated being nice before her coffee. "I'm sorry, I'm just not used to having strangers in my bedroom."

She looked around the elaborately decorated room, and grimaced. It was nice, but it really wasn't to her taste.

"God, who picked out this awful wallpaper?"

"You did, my Queen."

"Me? Purple flowers and pink bunnies? Oh, I don't think so!"

"The King has left your room just as it was the day you were abducted," The young woman assured her.

"My name is Drewcila. Who are you?"

"Drewcila, my Queen?"

"Yeah. Taralin is a suck name. Don't you think it's a suck name?"

"It's your Royal birth name, my Queen. The name…"

"Yeah, yeah. But don't you think it's a suck name?"

"My Lady, Queen, I have no concept of what 'suck' means."

It was Drew's turn to look shocked.

"You don't?"

"Well, I don't understand it the way you're using it."

"What's your name? That's twice I asked," Drew said impatiently.

"Margot."

"Are you married, Margot?"

"No."

"Do you have a boyfriend, then?"

"No."

"And do you know why that is, Margot?"

The girl shook her head no.

"Because you don't know what 'suck' is—that's why."

"Yes, my Queen."

Drew laughed heartily.

"My name is Drewcila, but everyone calls me Drew. Can you say that?"

"Drew."

"Very good. Now. Can that Queen shit, and quit bowing. It's going right to my head. So, why are you here?"

"I'm your dresser."

"Funny, you don't have any drawers!"

Drew laughed at her own joke—lame as it was. Margot just frowned. "Everyone's a critic. So, Margot, where are my clothes?"

Margot held up a yellow satin gown with white fur trim.

"You're fucking kidding me, right?"

"Your mother picked it out for you. Your parents are here, and they are very anxious to see you."

Drew got up, pulling the sheet with her, and started pacing the floor.

"Parents," Drew sighed. The last thing she wanted to do was meet anyone else who insisted that she knew them. "Tell them I'm..."

It was Drew's curse that if she gave being sick as an excuse, she immediately started to run a fever. So she quickly dumped that excuse for the one she usually used instead. "Tell them I'm having sex."

"What?" Margot gasped.

Drew looked at the startled look on Margot's face. "Well, I suppose that old stand-by's outtah the question."

"Don't you want to see your parents, my Queen?"

The Queen gave her a hard look, and it took her several seconds to realize why.

"My...Drew."

Drew's features softened.

"No, I don't want to see them."

She flopped down on the bed, her face set in a pout.

"No, I don't. They're going to look at me expectantly. And when I don't jump up and down for joy, they're going to get this crushed look on their faces. Then they'll say with a big tear in their eyes. 'Don't you remember me? You used to spit your milk all over me.' Or, 'When you were little you were so cute, you used to chew on the pet zombit. Don't you remember?' It's more that I can take."

Margot had been completely filled in on the Queen's condition, and for that reason she hadn't told the Queen that they had been childhood friends who had grown up together and had no secrets from each other. But it had been hard not to. It hurt that there was no recognition in her friend's eyes, so she understood exactly what Drew was saying.

"You've got to see them sometime, Tara...Drew," Margot said softly.

"But does it have to be today? Can't it wait?" Drew felt suddenly lost and abandoned. In a strange place, surrounded by strange things, and strange people. She was surprised by who she asked for first.

"Where's my sister? Where's Stasha?"

"I would imagine that she's with your parents in the morning room."

"Morning room!" Drew scoffed. "Do we also have a noon, afternoon, and evening room? What about a just-thinking-about-morning room, or a not-quite-evening room?"

She ran her hands through her hair, and looked like she wanted to scream.

Margot giggled.

"Now you're laughing?"

"Not-quite-evening room!" Margot giggled again.

Drew shook her head. "Where's my crew?"

"They were given suitable quarters."

"Just great!" Drew had been so absorbed in taking care of her own needs to worry about where anyone else was going. When they didn't try to shove her in a room with Zarco, that had been good enough for her. She could imagine how these people's minds worked, and while she was sleeping in silk, Van and the human were probably sleeping in a drafty box somewhere.

"I want Van Gar put into one of the nicest rooms in the palace. He's not my step-an-fetch-em-boy, he's my Bud, my only friend. The only one I can trust now that I have had my life tossed into the hands of strangers. Van Gar is the only one who knows me, at least he's the only one who knows the same me I know."

She looked at the dress on the floor. "There is no way I am wearing that thing.

"You have a whole closet full of clothes. Stasha had all your clothes cleaned in anticipation of your return." Margot walked to the wall on the right and pushed a concealed button. There was an electrical hum, and twenty feet of silk-covered wall disappeared to expose twenty feet of closet filled with clothes.

Drew rubbed her hands together and trotted—naked—over to the closet, and started going through the outfits. "Cool hologram!"

She pulled out a purple gown, made a face and tossed it into the middle of the room. Thirty minutes later, there was a mountain of clothes in the middle of the floor, the closet was empty, and Drew was wearing a pair of black leather boots Margot had told her were for riding. Drew spun around.

"So, what do you think. Is it me?"

Margot giggled. "Can you not find a single thing to your liking?"

"I can't believe I would ever have worn such crap."

She looked at the bed sheet. "Oh well," she sighed, walked over and grabbed the blue length, then wrapped it around herself in toga fashion. She gazed into the twelve-foot mirror which graced the south wall.

"Divine! Simply divine! Whoever is your tailor?"

"You're not going to breakfast like that!"

"And why not? This is probably the most expensive piece of clothing I have ever worn. Well, that I remember, anyway." She twirled around vigorously, exposing rather more flesh than she believed would be considered proper.

"Well, maybe I should wear underwear. I wouldn't want to appear crude and uncultured."

Margot produced a pair of panties, and Drew slipped them on.

"Well, here I go. Off to meet Mummy and Daddy and all that good rot. Just show me to the just-after-morning-but-not-quite-noon room."

Margot chuckled. "Yes, of course. Would you like me to have these things disposed of?" She indicated the pile of clothes in the middle of the room.

"Disposed of? Are you nuts? Do you have any idea what the re-sale value on that shit is? Just leave it. It looks more homey now anyway."

Margot nodded and opened the door.

"This way, my Qu...Drew." She indicated the direction with the wave of her arm.

Drew looked at the expanse of hallway and the Royal Blue carpet that covered the floor. The whole castle seemed to be an odd mixture of the latest technologies and treasures of antiquity, one giant anachronism. Two huge guards fell in behind them. Drew looked them up and down quickly and winked at the cuter one.

"My, I certainly married well, didn't I?" Her question didn't want an answer, and Margot didn't give one.

"In here," Margot waved towards a door, then pushed the button that opened it.

Drew just stood there.

"You're very nervous, aren't you?"

Drew shrugged.

"They're very nice people, your parents. Your father can be a bit rigid, but he is really a push-over, and your mother...Well, she..." Margot couldn't lie to Taralin. "Your mother can be a bit over-bearing, but she usually means well."

"Great, I have nothing in common with either one of them." Reluctantly, she followed Margot into the room.

Zarco got up from the chair he was sitting in, walked over and kissed her cheek, as if he had some right to.

She made a face and quickly wiped the kiss off.

He stiffened, and backed quickly away. "My dear, your parents, Lord and Lady Straightlaced."

The man was very tall and stern looking, as if he lived in constant fear of smiling and thereby breaking his stone face. The woman was short and plump and grinned broadly enough for both of them, but the grin seemed somehow forced and false. Her "sweetness", if it existed at all, was only skin deep, and probably wasted on people she cared nothing about. The one they called her mother ran to her and hugged her, and almost but not quite kissed her cheek.

"Oh, my darling, I thought we would never see you again."

"Lillith, you heard what the doctor said, she doesn't remember. Don't overwhelm her," the father person said.

Drew's stomach was starting to churn, and she felt as if she were going to hurl. She found herself searching for Stasha.

Stasha met her gaze and nodded. She moved quickly and took her mother's arm and led her towards her seat and away from Drew. The only chair empty was the one next to the husband person.

Drew sat down hard, and she must have looked as green as she felt.

"Are you all right, dear?" Zarco asked.

"All right! All right? Do you realize that I went through a whole closet! A fucking roomful of clothes, and there was not a damn thing there I would be caught dead wearing? I'm wearing the fucking sheets off my bed. I have a fucking dresser; like I need any help wearing my sheets! There are bunnies on my walls. Bunnies! Last time I saw one of those, I was eating it, and spitting the gristly bits at the humans sitting at the bar. Kidnapped by fucking Lockhedes, forced to crash land in the desert. I lost my fucking ship. Hell, I lost two ships, both swallowed up by the Galdart sands. Attacked by giant Hurtellas, then we get to plow our way through a riot. Did you people really have to rescue me?"

Drew jumped up and started to run out the door, but it was closed, and she hit the wall in several places trying to find the button. There was a hand on her shoulder.

"You feel better now, Drew?" Stasha asked.

Drew turned to look at her. She was smiling. Drew shrugged.

"Not really. I could do with a drink about now."

"Let's go get something to eat."

Stasha looked around the room.

"Come on, let's go, I'm famished." Zarco said.

Stasha reached for Drew's hand and Drew let her take it and lead her out.

"I'm sorry about the clothes. It was stupid of me not to realize that in five years your tastes might have changed."

Lillith must have overheard. "The dress I picked was suitable. Whatever you've been doing, Taralin, you must realize that as Queen, you have certain duties and responsibilities. You can't walk about the palace in riding boots and your bed sheets!"

"Mother!" Stasha started to protest.

"If I'm the fucking Queen, I can run about buck naked if I want." Drew spit back venomously.

"Well, at least that hasn't changed. You still have a mouth on you."

"If I didn't, I'd look funny eating. 'I'm sorry my Queen but you've got a lovely piece of lettuce in your ear...Oh a thousand pardons I forgot you don't have a proper mouth.' I need a drink." Drew mumbled and made her very best stupid face.

"Oh, very funny, Taralin," Lillith said hotly. "You always have to hurt my feelings."

"I don't even know you." Drew spat back. "And here I thought all this brain sucking was a bad thing. I need a fucking drink."

"Tar, what's fucking?" Lillith asked the father person.
Stasha chuckled.

"It's, ah," the father person smiled and looked embarrassed. "It's a slang term meaning...I'll tell you later, dear."

Drew excused herself after breakfast, and Margot followed her.

"I thought you said she was a little over-bearing. At no time did you say that the woman is a flaming bitch," Drew said accusingly.

Margot smiled and shrugged. "I don't know what that is. Lillith has always been nice to me, but...Well, you and she never did get along. You got along a little better after you married Zarco."

"Yeah, I imagine that pleased the status-climbing old whore. She probably really loved me only after I had been abducted."

She shook her head. "Erik told me that my parents were Salvagers like me, and that they were slaughtered by space pirates. I had this vision of my parents being bigger than life; bold and brave. Then when they told me I wasn't really Drewcila Qwah, I pictured my father as being the sit-on-his-lap type, and my mother as the home-baked-cookies type. Instead, we're talking the Ice Man and Super Bitch. Do you know where my crew is now?"

"In the guards' quarters. This way."

Margot led her down yet another hall. At the door, the guards bowed, then started to follow them.

"What do you think you're doing?" Drew asked, stopping and turning to face them.

"Our orders are to go with you where ever you go," they said in unison.

"Paranoia in stereo," Drew mumbled. "Tell you what. Let me see that laser rifle."

They both tried to hand her their weapons.

"Just one." She smiled and took one of the rifles.

"OK. This is my rifle now, and I'll guard myself."

"But, my Queen, our orders..."

"I un-order you," she said with a smile.

They must have accepted that, because they stayed at their post.

"Do you know how to use that thing?" Margot asked in shock.

"Use it, hell! I cut my teeth on one of these suckers."

Margot led her to the guards quarters. They were warm, and not uncomfortable looking, but nothing close to the splendor of the palace. Van Gar was laying asleep on a lower bunk. Drew crawled into bed with him. Much to Margot's horror.

"Van," she said softly.

No response.

"Van," she said a little louder, shaking him a little.

He still didn't stir.

"Van, damn it, wake up!" she yelled, shaking him as hard as she could.

He startled awake, and sat bolt upright, hitting his head on the top bunk.

"Fuck!" He rubbed his head. "Damn it, Drew!"

"Where's the dweeb?"

Van Gar shrugged.

"Do I look like a monkey keeper?"

"Do you want me to answer that?"

"If you say yes, I'm going to rip your head off and shit in the hole."

"My, aren't we in a lovely mood?"

"Well, I just love it when you scream me awake, and it just really makes my day if I can follow it up by giving myself a concussion."

Drew rolled over onto his leg.

"Why don't you just use the weapon and get it over with?" he grumbled, rubbing at his knee.

"Ah, quit being such a pussy!"

He saw Margot cringing against the far wall. Obviously, she had never seen anything that looked like Van Gar.

Drew followed Van Gar's gaze. "Margot, I want you to meet my pilot, Van Gar. Van Gar, this is Margot—she's my dresser."

"Your dresser!" Van raised an eyebrow. "And did she dress you in this lovely little frock?"

"This 'lovely frock' happens to be the sheets off my bed, smegma breath."

"Sheets!" Van ran his hand over the fabric, apparently oblivious to the fact that it also happened to be her tit.

"This is real silk, Drew! The real shit. Do you have any idea what the re-sale value would be on this shit?"

"The shit that I'm wearing on my disappointing body?"

"I said I was sorry." Van Gar sighed.

"Apparently I'm the one who's sorry. Anyway, I'm wearing about seven hundred iggys in thread."

"Wow!" Van looked mightily impressed.

"You should see the shit I threw on the floor. There was enough fine cloth there to keep us in beer for ten years."

"Then why are you wearing the sheets?"

"This was funeral shit, Van. Long flowing gowns and drek like that. Nothing I'd be caught alive in."

"You mean dead in," Van corrected.

"No. I mean alive. When I'm dead, you can put me in anything. As long as I'm breathing air, I ain't wearin' none ah that shit."

"Queens don't wear sheets, not even silk ones," Van said.

"Yeah. Well, I ain't cut out ta be no Queen, either. Zarco, he thinks he can kiss me any time he likes, and my parents! You wouldn't fucking believe them. My dad is like some stone soldier, and my mother!" She sat up and threw up her hands.

"What's she like?"

"Imagine Erik in a dress, only a tad bit ruder."

Van Gar made a face.

"Yeah, not a pretty picture. My room you would not even believe. The wall paper has flowers and bunnies on it. And get this; I supposedly picked this shit out myself! It's just too scary."

"Bunnies? You mean those horrid creatures from Earth that almost ate Deltoid 4?"

"One and the same."

"Hell, the last time I saw one of those, we were eating it and spitting the gristly bits at the humans in the bar."

"Exactly! Now you can see why it's so important that we get all we can and get out of this place."

She remembered Margot standing there.

"Margot, could you give us a moment?" The dresser bowed and left the room.

"I gottah get outtah here, or I'm gonna go nuts. I want you to go to the spaceport. Not right away, but in a couple of days. Find out what ships the kingdom owns. I figure they owe us at least two, but we'll shoot for three and a bunch of loot."

"What are you going to do?" Van Gar asked suspiciously.

"When I get done with them at the palace, they're going to be praying to get rid of me. Zarco is going to want a divorce, and I want to know what to ask for in the healthy settlement I plan to collect."

Van Gar smiled and nodded.

"So, basically, you want me to go shopping."

"Hey! This is one of the hardest jobs I've ever done, and it's going to have to have a big pay off to make it worth all the trouble."

"I still don't buy that you're just in this for the money."

"Well, buy this then, baby. My curiosity has been satisfied. I know just enough about Taralin to know that I don't want to know any more." She walked over and opened one of the lockers.

"By the way, you're moving up to the palace. You can bring your monkey if you want."

"Ha, ha."

Drew opened another locker.

"You can rest up in luxury for a few days, and then you can head out to the spaceport in the biggest baddest limo we can find. We might as well live this shit while we can."

"What's all the noise and rioting? You know anything about that?"

Drew shrugged.

"The natives are restless. Who knows. It's a bunch of government shit. As far as I'm concerned, it's just one more reason we need to get the hell out of here. My guess would be that the country is suffering from a post-war depression. And if I'm right, we need to get out while the gettin's good."

"Can you do that, Drew?" Van asked. "Can you cash in while your people are cashing out?"

"These aren't my people. They're just some chumps ripe for the picking. Right now we don't have a whole lot of options. We are shipless. And a shipless Salvager ain't worth a hell of a lot in real space. I don't think we can count on Erik to set us back up. What with him bein' dead, an all. The way I see it, Zarco and his precious people let this happen to me. So, if what I have become eats his lunch…well isn't that just kind of poetic justice?"

Drew met Margot outside the dorm, wearing one of the black and red guard uniforms.

"You can't wear that!"

"Ah, so now the little dresser girl thinks she can tell me what to wear. Not fucking likely. I like it, it fits me, and it goes with the gun," she said, pointing to the laser side arm which hung in a holster strapped to her hip and leg.

"But that's a guard's uniform!"

"And I love it. See, the tight black pants with the red piping up the sides. And I love the way this shirt buttons here and then here to give it that double-breasted effect. It's black on the outside and red on the inside. So that if you leave it open like this, you can see the red, and it just looks so…"

"Scant. You can see most of your cleavage."

"Can you really?"

"Yes."

"Then this is just one of the greatest shirts I have ever worn."

They had reached the palace, and the door guards.

"Well, hello, boys."

They both gave her a shocked look.

"Listen, I left your rifle in the guard house. When you go get it, would you be so kind as to retrieve my bed sheets?"

"Your every wish is my command, my Queen."

"And look here." She unbuttoned one of the guard's shirts so that it hung open, exposing his hair-covered chest. Then she walked over and undid the other fellow's shirt. She stood back and admired her handiwork.

"Oh yes, that's much better. Now listen. As of now, all guards working at the palace must wear their shirts undone in this manner."

"What, my Queen?" the hairy one asked, thinking that he must have misunderstood.

"You heard me, man. By Royal Decree. Now, go on. Carry out my orders. I want to see the chest of every man in this palace by sundown tonight."

At that, she strode into the palace.

"You!" Margot giggled. "You can't do that!"

"Why not? I'm the Queen, aren't I? You screws all keep telling me I am, and then when I do my first official act, you balk. I guess there's just no pleasing some people. By the way, do you know what the people are rioting about?"

"Just about everything as far as I can tell. Not enough work, mostly." She shrugged. "It's not my problem, so I don't bother with it."

"That's typical," Drew said mostly to herself. "Let me tell you something, Margot. If that mob decides it's mad enough, and it starts to crawl over the wall, it will get to be all of our problems in a hurry."

"That won't happen now that the King is back. He'll straighten everything out."

"Yeah, right!" Drew scoffed. "He's probably not willing to get any more involved than you are. His answer will probably be to call out the guard and chase them back. A temporary fix at best—at worst a war between classes. This country's only hope of survival is that the Lockhedes are in the same shape that you are. Of course, chances are that things are even worse there, or they would have won the war. Does Gildart have any more enemies on the planet?"

"Gildart and Lockhede are the only civilized countries on the planet."

"And therefore the only ones capable of making war. That makes a hell of a lot of sense."

She'd seen it before. Planets that had been unaware of technology and space travel until someone "discovered" their planet. Then the rich nations suddenly became technologically superior, and the poor ones became primitives almost over night. It even explained why the castle was such a mangled mass of carved stone and transistors.

She stopped in her stride and stared thoughtfully at the wall. She seemed to Margot to be thinking, and drawing up conclusions. She took her finger and drew things in the air, and then erased them with her fist and started over again.

Margot watched with great interest as her sovereign seemed to be indulging in a bout of insanity.

"And so." Drew nodded her head and made long sweeping figures in the air. "And then...so, if..."

She grumbled and made still more figures in the air. She seemed to study her conclusion and then slapped her hands together, rubbing them as if to warm them.

"There is a fortune out there. It's saved other countries from post-war depressions before. It just might work, and as an added benefit make me the most powerful salvager in the galaxy," Drew mumbled.

"What might work? Where did you learn so much about politics?"

"I don't know a damn thing about politics, but I trade in other people's problems. My job is to extract money from what is no longer profitable. Come on, let's go find Zarco."

"Well, you're going the wrong way. He's talking with his advisors. This way."

In a few minutes they had reached the door to what Margot told her was the council room. It was guarded by four of the biggest guys she had ever seen. Without question, they moved aside to let her pass through the door. In fact, they bowed as she stepped into the council room.

The room was buzzing with conversation. A man at the door announced:

"All rise for her Royal Majesty, Queen Taralin Zarco."

All rose, including Zarco, who had been sitting in a throne in the front of the room. But though the over one hundred men and women in the council room fell silent, out in the street, the people were still screaming. The noise filtered through two doors which opened onto a balcony a story above the street.

Zarco took one look at what Drew was wearing and grimaced, then he smiled.

"I see you have found something to your liking."

"Very," she ran across the room and leapt into the throne beside him.

Zarco laughed and shook his head.

"So, my love, what can we do for you?"

"You do for me? Nothing. But me? Well, I have the answer to all your economic problems."

"Well, then do tell, dear," he said indulgently.

"Salvage. Salvage is the answer. We're in a post-war depression."

"Please don't do this," Zarco pleaded in a whisper.

"Post-war depression?" One of the councilors said.

"For over five years this country's entire economy has hinged on your war efforts. The building of war machines, a military work force, etc., etc. Now that's all gone. Those people out there aren't your enemy, and they're not the problem. A depressed economy is your problem. Your economy was probably in trouble when the war started, but the war fixed it temporarily. A false fix, really. You should have used the boost to take real steps towards fixing the economy. Instead, you obviously decided that what was working didn't need fixing, and now you've got rioting in the streets. But I have the answer.

"Salvage. Salvaging is the fastest growing industry in the galaxy. Recycling and re-sale has made many men rich and pulled many countries—indeed whole worlds out of economic disaster. The same machines that were used to build war machines, and now sit idle, can be retooled to disassemble those now-broken and useless machines. The scrap can then be sold at a huge profit to the state. In the right market, you can actually make two to three times what it cost you to build it in the first place…"

"My Queen," the young advisor stood up. "With all due respect, are you suggesting that Gildart become the trash mongers of the galaxy?"

The entire council room exploded into laughter. Including Zarco. Drew gave him a hard look and got to her feet. "Silence!" she ordered, and all fell silent. She looked around and grinned. "Too cool." She continued. "With all due respect, morons like you, sir, are the reason that your country is in the shape it's in. There is a big difference between salvage and trash."

She looked at Zarco. "Remember when my ship was sinking in the desert? We took parts from it to build a machine that could carry us out of the desert. We are alive now because of an act of salvaging."

"And I can not minimize the importance of that act, but it's inconceivable that all the country's woes could be cured by taking parts off of things and selling them. As a nation, we have a certain standard which doesn't include rummaging through our garbage cans," retorted Zarco.

"Do you have any better ideas?" Drew spat angrily at the King.

For a second, she thought that the advisors had drawn all of the air out of the room with their collective gasp.

"I estimate that it's going to take that mob two, maybe three days at the most, and then they're going to come crawling over the wall after you."

"My dear, this room is filled with the finest minds in our country, and together we will find the solutions to the country's problems. And it won't be in the garbage pail of the galaxy."

"Zarco, in this room you have assembled all the greatest tight asses and fools in the country. I'd bet my sweet little ass that none of these men have worked a day in their lives. How can you sit in a room full of politicians and bureaucrats and think that they can help you understand the needs of the working class? You can't take a room full of bloated, over-paid, desk jockeys and pray that they will understand the plight of the unemployed."

Zarco saw the reporters in the back of the room filming and laughing, elbowing each other for the best view of their Queen.

"We can talk about this later, Taralin," he whispered.

"Oh, don't pull that go away little wife and do needle point shit on me. When is the later that we can talk about it? When the people are stomping on our disemboweled innards? Did you bring me back here so I could be your wife again? Or did you bring me back here because of some archaic ritual in which the Queen must die with the King?"

The press was having a field day.

Zarco took a deep breath. "That is quite enough."

"Enough what? Enough sense for the day? Should I leave now so that you can dish out some more shit?" She stepped down off the dais.

"Tell you what. Next time I come in, I'll wear hip boots and bring a shovel." She walked several feet forward, looked at the assembled group, flung her arms wide and screamed. "A real big shovel!"

Zarco's head spun. His beloved wife was making a spectacle of herself in front of the entire advisory council. The press had the story of the year. Much better than the Queen's homecoming! The Council was all abuzz with whispering, and the noise from the street had reached a deafening pitch. He couldn't hear himself think. He got up and strode to the doors, flung them open and strode out onto the balcony before the guards could get there.

"People! My people! We can't fix anything if you do not allow us to work!"

Something flew up out of the screaming mob, and hit him in the head. He put a hand to the bleeding wound in disbelief.

As one guard knocked him to the ground, another opened fire on the crowd.

Drew didn't think. She moved across the expanse in a few great strides. "Cease fire, you idiots!" To add emphasis to her words, she hit them. She looked down at the swelling mob. She couldn't tell how many, if any, had been hit, but it was obvious that it had been all the crowd needed to push them into violent action.

"Moron!" She hit the guard again, then looked down at Zarco.

"What now, bright spot?"

"I'm bleeding!"

"Don't be such a pussy. We're all going to be bleeding in a few minutes if you don't do something."

Already they had dragged him inside, and the King's doctor was taking care of him.

"What would you have me do, dear? Bleed on them?" Zarco screamed.

Drew looked startled and then laughed. "You know, honey, yer kind ah cute when you're mad."

The crowd was getting madder. She stood at an angle to the door so that she could see out, but couldn't be hit by thrown debris. She looked back at the room full of advisors.

"So, here's yer big chance, boys. It's show time. Come on, advise something."

They just stared, and whispered, and dithered.

"That's what I thought," Drew mumbled. She looked back at the crowd and suddenly a smile crossed her face.

"Margot!"

The servant ran forward and bowed.

"We don't have time for that shit. Gather up some of these dopes, go to my room and get all of my clothes."

"But my Queen! "

A bottle came flying in the open door.

"Just do it, Margot."

Margot nodded, called for volunteers and then marched them off in the direction of the Queen's bed chambers.

"Give me that!" She took the riot helmet from the guard who had fired on the crowd. "It's too late to worry about brain damage for you. You'd better give me that, too."

She took his gun.

Then she saw Facto where he stood over the King, looking worried. She took the gun to him and held it out.

"Here."

"Why are you giving that to me?"

Drew shrugged. "Because you're the only one here that I know has a brain, and because I trust you not to shoot me in the back."

Facto raised his eyebrow, and Drew shrugged again. "If my plan doesn't work, I want you to shoot up in the air till I can get my lily-white ass back in here."

Just then Margot returned with the first armload of clothes.

"Wish me luck!" She put the helmet on her head and took the armload of clothes.

"Be careful!" Margot begged.

Zarco finally realized that she planned to walk out on the balcony.

"Taralin! I order you…"

He was cut off by her laughter as she and Facto, who stayed just outside the door, strode onto the balcony.

"My people," she yelled.

The mob yelled louder.

She took her gun and fired it above her head.

The mob, having been fired on once, scurried for cover. Then realizing that they were not being fired at, they got quiet.

"My people! We must all bear these ill times. So that I, too, may know what you are going through, I will attempt to live like you 'til this time has passed. As a show of my good will, I give you…my wardrobe."

So saying, she threw the armload of clothes down to the mob below. The women, who made up at least half of the crowd, ran for the garments, all else forgotten.

Drew looked back at Margot. "Keep that shit coming!"

She threw armload after armload to the crowd until Margot informed her there was not so much as a sock left to be found of her old wardrobe. "My people!" she screamed, but the court herald was suddenly at her side.

"Oyeh! Oyeh! All attend, her Majesty the Queen," he boomed.

The crowd was silent.

She looked at him and smiled. "That's quite a set of lungs you've got there."

He smiled broadly back at her and bowed. "It is always a pleasure to serve You, Your Majesty."

Drew nodded her head, and as he stepped back to stand at her left shoulder, she once again addressed the crowd.

"My people. In my long absence from you I have seen many things, and endured indignities you can not even think of.

Believe me when I say that I know and understand the hardships you are now going through. I'm going to talk to this bloated lot of bureaucrats, and see if we can't do something about the mess we're all in. But anything we decide is going to take time before it works.

"We're not in as bad a scrape as you may think. Yes, things are bad, but they can only get worse if you stand out there in the street and yell instead of doing something constructive to help fix the country. Your words are wasted when you all stand here and scream about the problems we face. We know all the problems. What we need are solutions. Why don't you all go home and write a letter to us, telling us what you think is wrong and how you think we might fix it. I promise to read those letters personally, and bring your ideas to the Council. My husband, your King, is anxious to hear your ideas."

"My Queen," one man screamed from the crowd, "is the King injured?"

"He's got a tiny bump on his head. More importantly, were any of you hurt?"

"Gratefully, no."

"Good. Well, that's all I have to say."

She held her hands above her head.

"Go now, and sin no more!" She bowed low and then hurried back inside.

The crowd was cheering. Chants of "Long Live the Queen" echoed through the open doors until the guards closed them and the sound was muffled.

Drew smiled broadly and raised both her hands triumphantly over her head. "I am indeed the Queen of Bullshit! I've never conned a mob before." She lowered her arms and looked skyward. "It's a heady feeling...I think I like it." She looked thoughtful for a minute. "Yes, I like it!"

Zarco was on his feet now, and he used his height to look down on her. It didn't really give him the power he had hoped for. He needed to say something. She had just made an ass of him in front of the whole advisory council. He gave her a hard look.

She smiled broadly at him and shrugged. "It's a gift."

His heart melted.

"Well done, my love." He started to clap. He looked at the others expectantly and soon every person in the place was clapping. "Well done," he bent down and kissed her on the top of her head.

"Quit doing that!" she hissed.

"So, can we do the Salvaging thing?" she asked him.

Zarco smiled for the cameras, knowing that no one else in the room had heard her, and said out of the corner of his mouth.

"Not while I am King."

"Then I'm taking my ball," she holstered her gun, "and I'm going home."

With an elaborate wave to the crowd, she swept out of the room followed by Margot. It had been a full day, she thought she'd go down to the courtyard or perhaps she'd go and lounge in the spa. Or maybe..."Hey, Margot, where the hell is the bar in this dump?"

A lavish dinner was spread. A feast to celebrate the return of the Queen to her palace and her King. Her parents and her sister were there. They had even invited her alien friend so that she would feel more comfortable. They had been waiting several minutes.

Van Gar tapped with his knife on the table impatiently.

"So...where is she?" Lillith asked, lifting her nose a little as she glared across the table at the Chitzky.

"Erik in a dress," Van Gar mumbled to no one in particular. He felt about as welcome as a fart in church.

Zarco's face was a mask of calm. "Stasha, would you please see if you can find your sister the Queen so that we can eat this fine feast that the Royal chefs have worked all day to prepare for her?"

Stasha nodded. "At once, my King." As she was standing up, Drew swept into the room, a liquor bottle in her hand. Margot stumbled in the door behind her, obviously just as polluted as her mistress, but not carrying it as well.

"Van!"

Ignoring everyone else, Drew stumbled over to the table and plopped the bottle down in front of Van Gar.

"Wait till you taste this shit! Best shit I ever drunk, an there's a whole shit pot load of it. A whole cellar full."

Van Gar seemed to be having a hard time keeping from laughing. "What's so damn funny, ass hole?" she asked, slapping him upside the head in a playful manner which almost landed him on the floor. "Is my fly undone?" She looked down quickly to check it. "Not that I have to worry about anything flopping out, but you never know what might try to get in the door if you leave it open."

At the head of the table, Zarco clenched his fists. That she had showed up drunk was bad enough, but it was obvious that she would rather talk to her hair-covered friend than any of the rest of them. She'd rather talk to Van Gar than him.

"Please have a seat, Taralin, so that dinner may be served. We have been waiting for you." His patience was stretched as tight as his smile as he gestured to indicate her chair at the other end of the table.

"Wow!" She picked up the bottle in front of Van Gar and poured his glass full before she headed for the chair Zarco had indicated. She stopped half-way there and held up the bottle. "Where are my manners? Would anyone else like a drink?"

"We have servants for that, Taralin," Zarco hissed, his impatience pushing out his teeth like the air out of a tire.

She looked at the girl standing holding a tray, obviously wanting very badly to set it down.

"And you think they can do it better than I can. Let me show you something." She set down her bottle with care, and held her arms out to the serving girl. "Give me that tray!"

The girl laid it in her hands.

Drew took a half-step and set it down on the table.

"There! Now that wasn't so hard."

She heard Margot giggle as she picked up her bottle and proceeded to her seat.

"So, Margot, pull up a chair. There's plenty for everyone."
Margot gave her an appalled look.

"She's one of the servants, Taralin," Lillith rebuffed her.

"Well, then I guess she doesn't ever eat or nothin'. I have all these new things to learn. It really is mind-boggling."

She flopped into her chair and slammed her bottle down on the table.

"I've been wondering. Now that I'm Queen, do I have to shit anymore? Because I haven't yet today, and I was anxious to know whether that was just a Queen thing, or if I needed to take a laxative."

"Can't you do something with her?" Lillith pleaded with Zarco.

Zarco shrugged and was silent. He looked at Fitz, who sat on his right-hand side, as if pleading with him to do or say something to make the Queen instantly act more like the woman they had all known.

"My Queen," Fitz started, "with all due respect..."

"Why does everyone start their sentences that way around here?" Drew asked.

"My Queen, your behavior is inappropriate for this sort of affair," Fitz finished in spite of the interruption.

"Say what?"

"You're making an ass of yourself, Drew," Van Gar informed her. He took a slow sip of the wine and smiled. "It is rather good," he said, making his most pompous face. "I'm starved, do you think you could shut up long enough for us to eat?"

Zarco looked at the herald and nodded.

The herald cleared his throat and announced. "The first course is boiled salvoids with buttered carrots."

The course was carried first to the King. Zarco nodded approvingly, and then they carried the dish over for the Queen to view.

Drew looked at the thing that must have once been some sort of bird and made a face.

"Is it dead?"

"Yes, my Queen."

"Then why don't you cut off its head?"

By this point she was turning green. A combination of too much wine on an empty stomach, and the sight of the boiled bird thing with its head still attached was making her feel ill.

"Now I know why I have always preferred eating out of ration packets. You don't have to look at your food."

"Are the salvoids not acceptable, my Queen?"

For answer, Drew threw up on the floor and on the head waiter's shoes.

The waiter's features did not change.

"A simple 'no thank you' would have been sufficient, my Queen." He turned on his heal and headed for the kitchen.

"I'm…" Drew threw up her hands, and got shakily to her feet. "I hope my hurlin' all over the waiter's shoes won't ruin your dinner. I ain't feelin' too hot. Think I'll just go find a toilet and crawl in now."

She got up and stumbled to the door, Margot stumbling after her attentively.

The maids had already cleaned up the mess.

"Please serve the meal, Baxto," Zarco said.

"Oh! What has happened to my poor daughter!" Lillith cried. "What have those Lockhede animals done to my little girl?"

"They took out part of her brain." Stasha got to her feet. "For five years she's been living by the skin of her teeth. She's not used to all of this." She swung her arm in an elaborate arc over the table. "You all just keep pushing her, trying to turn her back into Taralin. Well, that isn't going to happen. The best we can hope for is that she'll learn to like us again. Yes, you heard me right. She like us, because we're the ones in the wrong. There isn't anything wrong with her that needs changing. We just need to get used to her the way she is. In some ways, she needs some refining, yes. But five years ago Taralin wouldn't have been able to save us from the desert, or bring in a damaged ship, or have freed us from the Lockhedes. Five years ago she wouldn't have been able to turn away that mob in the street. So, whatever bad things may come with the skills she has developed over the last five years, you can't let them blind you to the fact that Drew is twice the leader that Taralin was."

"How can you say that? She just vomited at the dinner table," Lillith said. "Call me old fashioned, but I think that goes beyond bad manners."

"She just wants you to hate her because she doesn't want to stay here. She figures the only way you'll let her go is if she makes it impossible for you to tolerate her."

Van Gar's head spun around to look at Stasha.

"Yes, I followed her and Margot when she went to talk to you this afternoon, and I overheard what she said to you," she explained.

Van Gar smiled at her, and she knew exactly what he was thinking. Why didn't she tell everything? That, she imagined, was just what the Chitzky wanted her to do. Make them kick Drew out now so that he and she could go off together. But that wasn't at all what Stasha wanted. She wanted her sister to stay here and be happy with her husband, the King. Zarco deserved to be happy after all he had been through, and Drew deserved more than life as a Salvager.

"She really said that?" Zarco asked.

"Yes, and the only way we're going to make her feel differently is to accept her as she is. For instance, the only name she knows herself by is Drewcila. Now I understand that in public we'll have to call her by her name or her title, but in private I see no reason why we can't do her the courtesy of addressing her with a name she's familiar with."

"How can you expect me to call my own daughter by anything other than the name your father and I gave her at her birth, some thirty years ago?"

"Thirty!" Van Gar started laughing out loud. "Thirty! Oh, she's really going to shit!"

Chapter 11

Three days later, Zarco was no closer to a solution to the problems with his wife than he was to finding a cure for the woes of his country. He tried to cater to his wife's whims, but since the only goal she seemed to have in mind (besides driving them all insane) included turning Gildart into the Salvaging hub of the galaxy, she wasn't so easily accommodated. As for dealing with her as his wife, he didn't have the foggiest idea how to approach her.

Five years ago the fact that she had her own room had been a joke. Until four days ago, the bed had never been slept in as far as he could remember. But she didn't remember him, and he was no closer to having his wife back than he had been before he had left the planet to retrieve her. He was trying to be patient. Stasha kept insisting that all Taralin needed was time. But he had waited for what seemed like a lifetime, and pacing back and forth in his room every night was not helping him solve any of his problems, personal or political.

A few minutes ago he had been so sure that he was going to have her. They had been strolling around the grounds, he explaining what everything was, and she cracking jokes in her usual devil-may-care fashion. Then, without warning, her hand had reached out and grabbed his. Then she was in his arms, and they were kissing and caressing. He started leading her back to the palace and their room, and she was following without a struggle. Then she asked if her alien friend might have his own car. Zarco said no, and before he knew what was happening, they were having a row loud enough to wake everyone in the palace. Drew had stomped off to her room, and he had stomped off to his, and that had been the end of that. Now he looked up at the twin moons from his balcony and wished he had just said yes.

Drew stomped into her room. She took her holster off and slung it at her bed, gun and all.

"Well, that's real safe, Drew," Van Gar said.

She swung around to face him, not at all surprised to see him. "You'll never believe what that pompous Royal fuck wanted."

"I can guess."

"Yeah, well he wanted me to do it, and he wouldn't give me a car. He expected me to have sex with him and not get anything out of it."

"Wow! What a strange guy," Van Gar said facetiously.

"I would have done it for a car, but there's no way I'm doing it for free."

"You'd sleep...For a car, Drew? You'd really fuck him for a car?"

"I don't know what you're bitching about! The car was for you."

Drew flopped down on the bed beside her gun.

"What a day!"

She reached back and picked up a book off the middle of her bed, and opened it.

"Did you ever find the human?" She asked.

"No," Van gar looked at the book in Drew's hand, and made a face, "when did you start reading the classics?"

"It takes my mind off of all the shit. But I'm not sure that these books which have been translated and rewritten twenty times follow the original text."

"What's it about?" He sat down on the bed beside her.

"It's about a piece of farming equipment that's possessed by the spirit of an undead creature. The possessed tractor has these huge rows of blades and it runs around tearing the groins off of people, twelve at a time."

"That sounds like a happy little story."

Van Gar lay down beside her and propped himself up on an elbow so that he looked down at her.

"I know something else that would take your mind off the day's events, and help you to relax."

The look in his eyes left no room for misinterpretation.

"I wouldn't want to disappoint you."

"Drew, at any moment that mob may reform outside the palace walls and we could all die. Do you really want to die…"

"You've used that line already," she interrupted with a smile.

"I'll get you a car."

She jumped up and took his hand.

"You're on, you sweet talker, you."

"Where are you taking me?" He allowed himself to be pulled along.

"Why, into the wall, of course, you silly boy!"

He gave her a skeptical look.

"It's a hologram. According to Margot, she and I are the only ones that know where the controls to shut it off are. So, no one will be able to see us. And if someone comes in, I can sling on my robe and walk out, and no one will even know you were here."

"You've planned this all out."

"I wasn't the one that was disappointed."

She dragged him through the hologram into the closet. The copy of Rob Deed's novel, Succumbind, lay forgotten in the middle of the bed.

An hour later, the door opened and two men rushed in.

"So, where is she? Where is the Queen?"

One of them walked to the bed and picked up the book. Then he slung it down in disgust.

"We don't have time to look for her, come on. We've got what we really need."

They ran out and the door closed behind them.

Drew had almost finished putting on her robe when they ran out. She looked at Van Gar and shrugged.

"I guess it couldn't have been very important." She started taking the robe off.

"Who were they?"

Drew shrugged, and slung off the robe. "I don't know, but they certainly have no regard for art."

"Drew, Drew!" Stasha screamed. "Oh, no!" She looked at the two guards with her. "They must have gotten her, too. Go and tell the others…"

"My lady, perhaps one of us should stay with you…"

"That won't be necessary. Go! Go!"

As soon as she was sure they were gone, she flopped down on the bed and started to cry. Suddenly she felt a comforting hand patting her shoulder. She assumed it was her mother or father, and she cried all the louder, knowing that she had support.

"Geez, Stasha, what's wrong?" Drew asked in the most comforting tone she could muster.

Stasha spun around.

"Drew!" She hugged her sister tightly.

"Stasha this is to kinky, even for me."

"I thought they took you, too."

"What the hell are you talking about, Stasha?"

"Some of the guards," she wiped her nose on the back of her hand in a very un-lady-like fashion. "They were apparently part of some internal rebellion. They are holding Zarco, and they say that unless their demands are met, they'll kill him."

"I guess that's who those two clowns were who ran in here last night. I was in the closet so they didn't see me."

"Why were you in the closet?" Stasha asked. She saw the evil grin on her sister's face. "On second thought, don't tell me." She started to cry. "Oh Drew, they're going to kill Zarco. You have to do something."

"Ah, they ain't gonna kill him. Rough him up a little maybe. But if they kill him, they'll lose their bargaining power, and they're not so stupid as to think that we could let them live. I doubt they are desperate enough to want to die for their cause."

Stasha dried her eyes.

"Where were you?"

"I told you, I was in the closet."

"Why?"

"You said you didn't want to know," Drew said with a smile.

"He's here, isn't he?"

"Who?" Drew asked with well-fiend innocence.

"Well, unless you're a bigger whore than I think you are, Van Gar."

Drew smiled eagerly and clapped her hands together. "If it is Van Gar, does that mean I'm just a tiny whore?"

Stasha shook her head as Van Gar walked out of the closet wearing the Gildart guard uniform that he, like Drew, had taken to as everyday attire.

"Oh, Drew! What about Zarco?"

"No, I'm not sleeping with him."

"That's rather the point, Drew. You're not even giving him a chance."

"Hey!" Drew said in self-defense. "He wouldn't even give me a car!"

"What?"

"Don't ask." Van Gar warned dryly.

"We'd better go tell them that you're still here. Come on." Stasha got up and started pulling her sister along after her.

"Oh, it's so good to be Queen," Drew droned in a dull monotone voice as she allowed herself to be pulled along.

"I can't believe it," Fitz said, shaking his head in disbelief. "Members of the palace guard abducting the King—traitors among our own ranks."

"Remember what the Queen and her friend said about low pay? Perhaps they were right," Facto said.

"The King and the Queen stolen right from under our noses! Abducted while they slept!"

"Well, like it or not, Fitz, you know who that leaves in charge."

The door opened and Stasha swept into the room, pulling Drew behind her.

"The Queen!" Facto screeched in horror.

Drew smiled broadly, rubbing her hands together. "Well, boys, there's gonna be some changes roun' here."

Fitz fainted dead away.

Drew sat in the King's throne, wearing her uniform and her side arm. She had a beer in one hand a cigar, in the other.

"Whenever you're ready, my Queen," the camera man said.

Drew took in a deep breath. This was it, the biggest scam of her life. This was the deal she was going to be talking about when she got old. This was the story all salvagers would know by heart. This was the moment of truth. She was about to become a legend. "Roll em!"

She watched the light they had told her would indicate when the cameras were running. When it lit, she began.

"My friends, I'm afraid the news I must relay to you is not happy. In the night, some misguided souls broke into the palace, killed several guards, and abducted the King. I was only spared capture by the diligent efforts of the palace guards. The abductors now ask for a huge amount of money to release the King. As you know, it is not the policy of this reign to negotiate with terrorists. My five year absence is the proof of just how rigid we are on this matter.

"Until the King is released, I will be in charge, and I hope that I can serve you well. The cards and letters have been flooding in, and I am reading as many as possible. Hopefully, the terrorists will realize that their only chance for survival is to deliver the King safely to us. But, in the meantime, I will fill my empty time by working night and day to cure the ills of our ailing country. Thank you." She worked up a tear.

The cameras went off, and she stepped down. She looked at Facto. "Call a meeting of the advisory Council at once."

"Are you sure, my Queen?"

Drew glared at him.

"At once my Queen." He bowed and went off to do her bidding.

The advisory council and the newsmen waited patiently for the arrival of the Queen. When she appeared, Fitz, Facto, Van Gar, Stasha, and five well-armed guards accompanied her.

"All hail Taralin Zarco, Queen of all Gildart," the herald announced.

She smiled at him as she walked by. "Nice touch." She walked over, flopped down in her chair, and the others assembled themselves around her.

"Sorry to keep you waiting. Now, let's see, what did I have in mind? Oh, yes. You're all fired."

The noise from the group was deafening.

"Silence!" The herald ordered.

"You are all fired. Your salaries are to be stopped at once. Why am I being such a hard-ass? Well, maybe it's because I woke up on the wrong side of the bed. Or maybe it's because my cereal lost its crunch in milk. Or maybe it's because I have a whole lot of trouble believing that a bunch of fat-assed bureaucrats, whose idea of struggling is when their holo-deck won't work, have any grasp of what real people go through at all. Maybe it's because I believe that being unemployed in the middle of a post-war depression will give you a better grasp of what is really needed to turn this country around, and make you more able to advise me in the future. But for now, consider yourselves on the unemployment line with everyone else."

She paused for effect, then went on.

"Now, a message to the people. A hundred positions are now open. The jobs will pay minimum wage, and will be temporary. The job is to read the tons of mail we are receiving from the public, and keep a tally of the gripes and recommendations so that I may tackle the most egregious problems first. Apply at the palace gates. Oh, and before I forget. Former members of the advisory council are eligible to apply. That will be all for now."

As the room started to empty, Drew turned to Fitz.

"Get me all the files pertaining to the war. Specifically, any files which deal with the statistics on the loss of equipment in the field, and where that equipment was last known to be. Also, I want to know the location of every re-cycling plant in the country, and how much of what it puts out is used here."

"I can answer that now," Facto hissed. "Gildart does not use its trash. We throw it away."

"Then you're all idiots!" Drew screamed in his face. "Don't talk to me in that tone of voice, Fuckto, or I'll have you beheaded, or something like that. While Zarco's away, I have the power." She laughed wickedly. "Now," she cleared her throat authoritatively, "I want to know how much trash we make a year in tons. I want to know how many spaceports we have, what we import, what we export, and how many ships there are in the Royal Navy."

"So, that's it, then," Facto frowned. "In the King's absence, you're going to implement your maniacal plan to make Gildart the center of the Salvaging universe."

"Ooh you're pushing the beheading thing, Fatso." Drew smiled. "I didn't get to be the best Salvager in the galaxy by not jumping on opportunity. Trust me. Yes, of course I am doing this for purely selfish reasons, but the country will benefit from it. In fact, it will thrive."

Facto nodded. This at least was something he could believe. Drew would do what was best for the country, as long as it profited her.

"What about the King?" Fitz asked.

"What about him?" Drew asked.

"Shouldn't we try to find him?"

"Do you know where he is?"

"No," Fitz answered.

"Well, neither do I," she shrugged. "OK, we've wasted enough time on that shit. On to more pressing matters. I need an inter-stellar comlink, and I need it yesterday."

"There is one in the King's office," Facto announced.

"Good, then I'll get right to work. Oh, and while I'm thinking of it, bring me a guard's contract. I want to see what we're doing wrong and correct it at once."

"As you wish, Your Majesty."

"And bring me a case of my favorite beer...Oh, and get me ten of the finest naked dancing boys on the planet."

"Will there be anything else, my Queen?" Facto asked through clenched teeth.

She looked thoughtful for a full minute. "Nooo, that ought to just about do it for now." Then she let out a peal of near-maniacal laughter, rubbed her hands together and looked at Van Gar. "Now I, Drewcila Qwah, shall become Queen of the Salvagers. All trash shall come through me, and all men will bow their knee and cry when I pass, 'Praise Drew, from whence all garbage flows.'"

Facto wondered how far from the truth her statement was.

Chapter 12

Despite the guards' protests, Drew had gone to the garden alone. She sat silently in the dark, contemplating the day's events. Everything she had ever dreamed of was right there within her grasp. All she had to do was play her cards right, and she would have the fleet and the salvaging port she'd always dreamed of. But certain things were not as easily manipulated as an empire. Everyone made such a big deal out of absolute power. Drew didn't know what they were bitching about. The so called burden of power was probably the easiest thing she'd ever had to deal with. Yeah, like, it's so awful always having people waiting on you hand and foot, and having everything your way.

But power couldn't fix everything. She was confused about being this other person that she couldn't remember. Surrounded by people who should fit into her life, but just didn't somehow. Zarco was her husband, but all she felt when they told her he had been abducted was the joy of being able to carry out her plans without him getting in the way. Yet in the garden with him, she had felt something. If he hadn't told her she couldn't have that car, she would, more than likely, have spent the night with him instead of Van Gar. Not because she had any real feelings for him, but because he had feelings for her. When she was with Zarco like that, and no one else was around, she could feel the love he had for her, hear it in his voice. He wanted more than her body, he wanted her love. In the life she could remember she had never had anything close to that. She had always imagined it would be different with Van Gar. But while the sex was incredible, it was obvious that he saw her in no different light that any other sex partner had; a convenient, and in Van Gar's case, only mildly amusing, fuck. She didn't know why that bothered her so much, but it did. No one else had ever complained, and here he was, her best friend, and he had the utter gall to tell her that she was a lousy lay. Even more amazing than that was the fact that even after he had blasted her sexuality, she had slept with him again, and she had enjoyed it. She decided that if Zarco ever was returned, and if she was still here when he was, she was going to have sex with him and tell Van Gar that Zarco was much better in bed. That would get the old furball's goat.

She felt something cold against her neck.

"Don't make a sound."

"I was beginning to think you'd never get here. A person could get piles sitting on one of these concrete benches, you know."

"Don't pretend that you planned for this meeting. I know you ordered the guards not to follow you."

It was about that time that he felt something cold and hard in the middle of his back. He allowed the gun to be taken from his hand by the Queen, and moved to face her as the beast ordered.

"Good job, Van."

She looked the man up and down and recognized him as one of the door guards.

"Marcus, isn't it?"

"Yes, my Queen."

Drew smiled at the contradiction of action and words. Kidnapping the King, but still addressing her in the proper manner.

"Marcus, I am not a fool. I knew there was a traitor among the guards. Why would I tell them anything but what I wanted you to hear? I figured if you knew I was walking in the garden alone you'd either surface to abduct me or talk to me. So, which is it?"

"Why did you say what you said about the abduction? Why did you lie?"

"How much faith can a people have in their kingdom if the King's own guards have turned against him?"

"We wish the King no ill will. We only want the changes we have outlined, not cash as you said."

"Zarco's well, then?"

"He sends this message." Marcus handed her a folded piece of paper. She didn't open it.

"He will remain well as long as I do," Marcus threatened.

"I meant what I said about not dealing with terrorists."

"I am not a terrorist, my Queen. I simply want the government to do something about what's happening out there. I want the same things that you do. Just implement the programs, we'll release the King, and no one need know."

"The things you ask for are simplistic, idealistic and utterly ridiculous. If I do what you want it will kill what's left of Gildart, your enemies will easily overrun your borders and we shall all go down together. Where will the money come from to implement your programs?"

"By taxing the rich."

"You would have to tax them till they became the poor to do the things you would have us do."

"Then what do you suggest?"

"I suggest that you keep the King out of my hair for two months and put your trust in me. In my five years away I have learned many things. I can make this country prosper again, if you just give me the chance."

He looked thoughtful.

"There's nothing to think about, Marcus. We play the game my way or we don't play at all. I kill you, your people kill Zarco. Then I do what ever the hell I please. Any way you look at it, I win. The only thing you have to think about is whether you want to win, too."

"I could let Zarco go now," he said in a threatening tone.

"And I finger you as his abductor, you and all your accomplices are tried and convicted, and it takes me a little longer to get what I want." She seemed to calculate all that, then smiled broadly. "I still win, and you still lose. There's only one way that we both win."

Marcus nodded in defeat. "What do I tell your husband, the King?"

Drew smiled. "Tell him that I said that I now understand why he couldn't come after me, and that I am a very hard woman to deal with."

"What about me?" He asked, suddenly realizing that he had not only been seen, but recognized.

"The next time you spend this much time away from your post, you will be fired."

He nodded and ran away.

"So, what now, Drew?"

"There is a giant gap in the salvaging industry now that Erik is dead. You and I are going to fill that gap. Come on, let's start calling."

Facto walked past Zarco's office. He had risen early and hadn't been able to go back to sleep. He had already passed the open door before he realized that the light was on. He walked back to stand in the doorway.

Drew sat at the comlink console. Her hair was a mess, her shirt was undone till it was indecent, and discarded caffeine cups littered the desk. Van Gar lay on the couch asleep, a rifle in his hand. Margot sat asleep in a chair. It was obvious that Drew had been working through the night.

"Yeah, Lue, that's right. Queen of ah fuckin' country...You heard right, I'm taking over Erik's operation. Van Gar and I...What's in it for you? Well, let me tell you, Lue. This country of mine doesn't know the meaning of salvage. There are mountains of textiles here. Cloth, organic fiber cloth, Lue. Not the cheap shit, either. And do you know what they do with it when they're tired of it, Lue? Hold onto your hat. They throw it away."

She pulled the receiver away from her hear, and even Facto could hear the man on the other end screaming.

"That's right, Lue. Tons of it thrown away in the land fills to rot...Yes, there's a huge work force, they just need to be trained and put to work…That's exactly what I was thinking, Lue. Your people would be perfect for the job…Your share? Oh, thirty percent of the profits sounds right to me…Forty is as high as I'm going…Lue, you're taking my heart right out of my chest, my country needs this money!…You're killing me!…OK, OK, Lue. Fifty…Give me a week to get things set up." She hung up the phone and laughed.

"Sucker!"

She immediately started punching buttons again.

"Hello, Cramont?…Yeah, this is me, you old slime…No, I ain't dead. Listen, have I got a deal for you!…"

Facto walked away, shaking his head. Whatever she was up to, things weren't going to get back to normal until Zarco was returned. He could only hope that would be soon.

A week later, the council room was full again, but this time it was a decidedly different advisory council. This group sported weapons of all kinds. Wore clothing that was scruffy, indecent or both. And reeked of alcohol and smoke.

The reporters waited in eager anticipation for their Queen. Covering the news had become decidedly more entertaining since the Queen's return.

The herald ran into the room as if the very devil was at his heels, and started almost before he stopped moving.

"Her Royal…the Queen!"

The reason for his haste was evident when the Queen came bounding through the door, with her entourage practically running to keep up. She walked over to her throne and sat down so hard that she spilled the beer she held in her hand. In her other hand she held a smoldering cigar.

"Sorry I'm late, but I was busy passing a kidney stone."

She looked over her shoulder at Facto.

"How was that?" she whispered, taking a drag off her cigar. No response.

Drew shrugged, coughed, and pulled a sheet of paper from her pocket.

"My people, my friends, my business associates. Please bear with me while I...ah!"

She wadded the paper up, threw it behind her and removed the cigar from her mouth.

"Screw it!"

The crowd roared with laughter. Drew smiled broadly and took a drink of her beer.

"Sheesh I only have two hands, how do they expect me to hold a fucking paper. I've been working in trash for five years, and I know when something stinks. Face it, our country's in the toilet, and at this point we can either walk away and let the shit keep floating, or we can flush and start over again."

The hot ashes off her cigar fell on the red velvet arm of the throne, and she quickly poured beer on it to stop the spreading fire.

"I'm going to ask all of you to think for a moment of the country as a business. A business that is experiencing a sudden, giant loss in profits. Crash! The bottom falls out of your market, and you're stuck with a warehouse full of product that you can't sell. What happens? Any good business person knows that you have to lay off your employees and re-tool! We haven't.

"Factories all over the country have been trading in the business of war. They re-tooled their assembly lines to make the battle machines and tools of war, but now the battle is over. I'm sure another will arise soon. But for the time being, I'm sorry, but there is no war. So, why aren't they going back to what they were making before? Because no one has any money to buy the things they would produce, because they've all been laid off. It's a vicious cycle, and the only way you can stop such a cycle is to bring something completely different into the picture.

"That is where my friends come in. Each one of them is an expert in his own field of salvaging. So, you may be asking- just what is Salvaging? Well, let me tell you. Go to your garbage cans. Are there plastic bottles in them? On the galactic market, plastic bottles are worth money. What about cloth? Did you throw out an old shirt? What about paper? All these things and more are worth money. Not enough to cure the country's woes if considered singly, but multiply your trash by every trash can in the country. Then think of all the machines of war that lie broken and scattered across the land. Think of the cars and planes and space ships littering the country's landscape. Now nothing more that an eyesore, these useless things can make us enough money, and bring us enough jobs to put us back on our feet.

"OK. I know the next question. What happens when all the scrap of war is gone? What then? How do we keep our country from falling right back into the same trap? Simple. By making Gildart the Salvaging capital of this galaxy. By turning our three little spaceports into major Salvaging ports. By training our people in the fine art of Salvaging.

"So, what is Salvaging? Simply put, we will take other people's garbage and turn it into cash. I don't think anyone can find fault with that. Except maybe the people who have everything they want right now. People who still have a job, who don't have bills, and in fact aren't being touched by this economic crunch that is affecting all of you.

"You saw the old advisors reactions to my proposal. All they cared about was how it would look. Look to whom? The Lockhedes? The rest of space? So what! Who is so important to impress that we put our own needs behind the need to look esthetically pleasing? I say being prosperous is impressive. Let them be impressed by how rich our populace is, and let them be impressed by the size of our spaceports.

"And now I'm going to ask the press to leave so that we can get on with this meeting. Thank you."

"My Queen," a reporter in the back protested, "we have always been allowed to sit in on every advisory council for the duration of the meeting!"

"I have said everything that is of interest to the people. All they need to know for now. What will happen from here on is all just complicated bull shit that will be a real snore. We'll be talking at length about such interesting things as weights and measurements, and how many more toilets we'll

need at each spaceport to handle the new traffic. Mostly, I
don't want you here because we plan to do some serious work
here, and I don't want to have to worry about everything we
say. I want the members of this council to give their opinions
on what they know, not on what the home audience may think.
I don't want you to take pictures of someone asleep or someone doodling. I have more important things to do than worry
about giving you my good side, and the people at home have
better things to do than watch my friend Beamer snore. Now,
I thank you for your coverage. Get out."

Despite their protests the Queen's guard hustled out
the press.

When they were all gone, Drew looked at her motley crew
of advisors and smiled.

"So, now to get down to business. Who's going to get us
the scales?"

"Tory found six huge scales on Jastin. He can get 'em for
a song," a big man announced.

"All in favor of buying the scales from Tory?"

"Yo!" They all yelled.

"OK, cool. Now, how many bathrooms to a station?"

"I'd say a total of six at appropriate distances around a
port with twenty-four stools and ten showers in each," Van
Gar suggested.

Drew shook her head thoughtfully.

"I don't know, that's a hell of a lot of plumbing," she said.

"There ain't nothin' I hate more'n ta land at a port and
have ta go back ta m'ship ever time I gottah take a crap," a petite
green-haired girl in the front row said.

"Point taken, Terry," Drew said. "OK, all in favor of the
twenty-four john theory?"

"Yo!" They screamed.

"Well, then I guess that concludes the business for today.
All in favor of getting shit-faced drunk..."

"YO!"

The servants brought in the bar and the liquor.

Zarco looked through the bars of his cell at the man watching the TV. Marcus had only agreed to remove his hood when Zarco had told him that he recognized his voice, anyway.

"Marcus, why do you continue to hold me? Can't you see it's not doing you any good? Taralin doesn't know how to rule the country!"

"No, but Drewcila Qwah does." Marcus pushed the view screen over so that Zarco could see it.

"...just three weeks, Queen Taralin Zarco has brought about amazing changes in the economic climate of the country. Unemployment, which only three weeks ago was at an all-time high of fifty-six percent is already down to thirty-seven and dropping daily as the Queen's program goes into full swing."

They cut to a picture of a land fill and a piece of equipment digging up the piles so that a whole herd of men and women could start to pick the valuables from the trash. A news man stuck a microphone in one man's face.

"How do you feel about digging through trash for a living?" the reporter asked.

The man smiled and shrugged. "I don't look at it as digging through garbage. I look at it as cleaning up Gildart. Making the planet cleaner for my kids. I used to look at taking out the garbage as a distasteful task. Now, instead of making trash, we make money."

The reporter moved the microphone back to himself. "There you have it, Tost. Not only have the Queen's programs given jobs to thousands of people, but she has inadvertently solved the nation's landfill problems. Back to you, Tost."

Tost was grinning when the camera flipped back to him. "We go now to Jen Gaston at the old Hammer Munitions Plant where things are...well, a little different. Jen?" They switched to a young woman walking though a silent factory.

"Thanks, Tost. Well, things are quiet now, but as you can see, Hammer Munitions has new equipment. This equipment will all be used for the country's new industry—Salvaging.

This machine lifts large things, tanks, cars, etc., so that they can more easily be disassembled by these." She held up a pneumatic wrench. "This plant will launch into full production tomorrow morning. So, where is everyone? Well, follow me." She went down a long hall. When she opened the door, you could hear voices. Inside was a room full of people.

"These people are finishing up two weeks of intensive training in preparation for their new lives as Salvagers. All the indications are that the Queen will be making good on her promises. By the end of this year, unemployment might very well be at zero. Back to you, Tost."

Again, Tost was smiling that pasted-on, camera-ready smile. "Thank you, Jen. On a not so up note, there are once again protesters outside the walls of the Royal palace."

They cut to a man standing in the middle of the mob. He had cornered a protester, and obviously intended to interview him whether he liked it or not. "This is Rod Tently, on the street outside the Royal palace. So, sir, what is the problem? I mean, unemployment is on the decline. What else do you want?"

"There is more wrong with this country than just unemployment, man. We think the Queen just doesn't care about anything but making money. She told us to write letters, but so far only the unemployment problem is being addressed. What about medical care and the plight of the farmers? What about crime? She's put a bandage on a scratch, and is ignoring the fact that the patient is still dying."

"But surely there hasn't been enough time to address all the problems we face."

"I don't think our Queen will address any problems unless we make her."

"So, there you have it, Tost. Some people would be suspicious if your gave them a gold brick."

Tost was still smiling, and it was more than Zarco could stand. He turned away from the set.

"Can't you see, Marcus? Her plan is not working. She doesn't understand the needs of the people."

"She understands better than you do. The news man's right. They're not giving her enough time. One thing at a time. The economy was the biggest problem, and she's tackled that one. Rather well, I might add. I've been out there. Gildart used to be such a dirty place. You never saw it, because inside the palace walls things are so clean. But out in the streets there was trash everywhere. No one wanted to claim the trash, so we walked around, over, or through it. Now it's gone. The streets of the Capital are cleaner every day. She's one of us, and she's going to do what's right for us, the working class. She's not going to care what the Lords and Ladies of the court think are worthy causes. She doesn't even care about being popular."

"I could work with her. Let her help me with decisions."

"You'd slow her down, if not stop her altogether. No, you'll just stay right here till the Queen has a chance to fix hundreds of years of Royal stupidity."

Drew watched the screen and tried to block the noise in the street out of her mind. "Fucking peasants," she said lightly to Van Gar. "Why, I gave them gruel just the other day, and would you listen to them? Go down and tax them at once, Fuckto. A 'standing in the fucking road, bugging the shit out of the Queen' tax."

Facto just sat there, his eyes dull, and shook his head.

"I don't think our Queen will address any problems unless we make her," the man on the screen said.

"Oh, damn!" Drew drawled out, "he's figured me out."

"Perhaps you had better start to address the other problems of state," Fitz suggested. "Such as the return of the King."

"Now, Fitz, let's see. Medical, farmers and crime...nooo. No one said a damn thing about the missing King."

"None the less, don't you think it's about time that you at least tried to negotiate for Zarco's return?" Facto hissed. "It's been three weeks since we have heard anything. Aren't you even worried?"

"Give me a little while. Maybe I'll have time to worry about it five years from now."

"You are being so harsh," Facto said. "So unforgiving. You weren't here, and you don't know what Zarco went through every day because of your abduction. If you would just meet with these people, at least make sure they are feeding your husband, and that he's well."

"You know, Facto. I have to ask myself if either of you were so insistent when I was out in space someplace having my brains liposuctioned?" There was silence, and Facto even looked down at his feet to avoid her gaze. "That's what I thought. Now, I happen to know that Zarco is in good hands. As far as I'm concerned, he's reaping what he has sown. He wouldn't come after me, and I'm not going after him. Your efforts would be more effective if used to help me run the country the way you're supposed to, instead of begging me to give in to the demands of these terrorists. Why don't you tell me what you told him? How it's my duty not to go after him."

"Those were different circumstances..." Fitz started.

"Yes, they were. The enemy during a war captured me, and everyone knew they intended to hurt me. Zarco, on the other hand, is being held by some disgruntled palace guards who I believe have no intention of damaging their King." She was mad, so mad that she couldn't see straight, and she really didn't know why. Then it hit her, and she yelled out. "I'm expendable, but he's not! When it was me, no one gave a flying fuck. Well, now it's his turn, and I don't give a diddly damn, either!"

"He cares about you," Fitz assured her.

"But not enough to go against what you two advised, and you two advised him to let me rot."

"You're being unfair."

Drew shot Facto a heated stare. "Unfair! Unfucking fair! Let me try to spell this out so that even you morons might understand. Zarco let the Lockhedes suck my brains out because he didn't care enough to come after me. Because of this, twenty-six years of my life are lost to me. Totally lost—not even a blur. Among the memories lost is my love for Zarco. So now I don't care enough to go after him. In my book, things are just starting to get even. If you can't advise me without giving me shit about Zarco, then you can get on the bread line with the rest of those advising fucks. Now, go to bed or something, I'm tired of dealing with you."

She glared at them and they bowed low and left.

Drew ran a hand through her hair. "That's something I'm never going to get used to, " she mumbled.

"What's that?" Van Gar asked quietly.

"People bowing when you've just told them to go fuck themselves." She turned her chair so that she could look out at the screaming crowd in the street. It was now ten at night and they didn't look or sound as if they were going to stop anytime soon. "Arg, Van, the crown weighs heavy on my brow." Drew only half laughed. This Queen thing was starting to be a real drag.

"Maybe it's time you stopped trying to build your own little Salvaging empire and started trying to be Queen." It was obvious by Stasha's tone that she was in no way happy with Drew. "Face it, Drew. You found a quick fix for the unemployment problem, and I'm not saying that was any small task. But you don't really have any more idea what the 'people' have to deal with than Zarco did, and you don't understand politics."

"Didn't I just ask you to leave?" Drew moaned.

Stasha smiled. "I'm not one of your advisors. I'm your sister. Aren't you even worried about Zarco a little?"

"No," Drew said quite truthfully.

She picked up a beer and took one long sip, then she took the can from her lips and looked at it.

"Did anyone ever find the human?"

Van Gar laughed and shook his head. "What the hell has that got to do with anything? You didn't even like him, and I bet you ask about him twenty times a day."

"Well, I just think it's curious, that's all. I mean he just sort of vanished. It doesn't make any sense. So every time I try to clear my mind of all the bull shit, red tape, and paper pushers around here, my mind says, so whatever happened to that earth man?" Drew shrugged and Van Gar laughed.

After a moment Stasha joined the laughter. Then she looked at Drew and stood up. "I think I'm going to try and get some sleep."

"Well, good luck with the dissident choir singing just outside." Drew threw her half-full beer can out the window. It hit the laser proof glass and rattled to the floor, spewing beer everywhere. Drew and Van Gar both started laughing.

"That's the second time you've done that today," Van Gar laughed.

"They keep it so fucking clean that I keep forgetting it's glass."

"Margot, take a memo." Margot was at her shoulder immediately with pad and paper. "To the household staff: Don't wash the damn windows."

"For real?" Margot questioned. It seemed to her that half the time the Queen gave an order, it was just a joke. Then, just when she was sure the Queen was just joking, it turned out that she wasn't, as was the case now.

"Of course for real, Margot," Drew said in a very Queenly tone.

Stasha turned in the doorway and smiled at Drew. "You know, Drew, if you aren't very careful, you're going to wind up liking this 'Queen thing' as you call it. And you might even be good at running the palace, providing you don't drive all the staff crazy first. Good night."

"Good night, Stasha." Drew watched her go.

"Margot?"

"Yes, Drew?"

"Why don't you cash in your chips for tonight?"

"Excuse me?"

"Why don't you go to bed?"

"You sure you won't be needing me?" She looked at Van Gar. She had a feeling there was something going on there, but she didn't want to jump to conclusions. And it would be improper to leave her Queen alone with a man other than the King, without at least offering to stay.

"Don't be silly, Margot," Drew drawled out. "You know we can't have sex till you leave."

Margot blushed brightly, bowed low and left.

"She's such a nice girl. I don't know why you have to do things like that to her. She remembers you as being the sweet, mild-mannered sovereign. You don't have to go out of your way to shatter her memories."

"Oh, give me a big break." Drew got up and went to the window to stare out at the screaming masses. "She likes me better this way. They all do, even Fuckto, though he'd never admit it. These people have no life of their own. They all stand around and live vicariously through the King and Queen. So they're happy when they're not boring."

She turned away from the window and went about scouring the room for some half-full beer she may not have finished.

"You're really twisted," Van Gar laughed. But it must have sounded as hollow to Drew as it did to him. She spun around as if he had dropped something, and tried looking into his eyes. He avoided her gaze, and turned away.

"OK, what's wrong?" Drew demanded.

"Nothing."

"Oh, don't give me that shit. What do you think that I did, that I of course did not do, because I am perfect in every way?"

"It's nothing...really."

"That bad." She made a face and slumped into her chair. "I'm getting a refrigerator unit put in here," she mumbled, "not a damn beer in the place."

"Why don't you just call for one of your lackeys?"

"Is that what's eaten ya? All this Queen shit?" She shook her head. "Damn it, Van, we're making a small fortune here, and building a Salvaging empire of our own. Right under these fat bastard's faces. Do I have to remind you that we've very cleverly conned an entire nation into doing what we want?"

"You are completely absorbed in this whole power trip, Drew. Making laws and ordering people around." Van Gar looked at her hard then. "Where is this all going, Drew? Just exactly what is it that you're striving for? What is your hoped-for end product?" He shook his head at the blank expression on her face. "You don't know, do you, Drew? There never was any real plan here."

"Whatever happens, we'll be a hell of a lot better off than we were."

"We. What's that mean, Drew? We. The way I see it, it looks like you're going to be too into being Taralin Zarco to ever go back to being Drewcila Qwah."

Drew jumped out of her chair. "Don't ever say that! I don't like this Queen shit. It's just a means to an end."

"But what end, Qwah? Where do I fit in?" He paused for a moment, then continued. "I've got news for ya, Drew, I'm not going to stand around playing pet alien for much longer. You've got me waiting here for you to figure out just what you're going to do about your new life; who you can use, and how you want to use them. But you're not going to use me. I'll hang out for awhile because I've got no place better to be. I know this must all be a bit much to swallow, and I can't say I wouldn't act the same way in your place, but sooner or later you're going to have to make some choices. How you want to live your life. Who you want to be. Stuff like that. When that happens, if I happen to fit into those plans, well, that's fine, but if I don't...I'm not going to let you make me into something that fits what you want. You know what I'm saying, Drew?"

She grinned. "You won't be my Chitzky boy toy?"

"Can't you be serious for even a minute?" Van Gar chided.

"No. Because I'm not Taralin Zarco, I'm Drewcila Qwah. And to prove it, let's take the Royal limo and go bar hopping." She skipped across the room, took his hand and started pulling him towards the door.

"We can't do that, Drew."

"Bull shit, Van. I am the Queen. I can do anything I like."

"Drew, it's not safe."

"So. It never was safe."

"There is a riot in the street. You're not supposed to leave the palace grounds without an armed escort."

She stopped, let go of his hand and turned to face him, hands on her hips. "So, you coming or not?"

"I wouldn't dream of missing it."

Chapter 13

Van Gar had traveled through space with Drewcila
Qwah for the better part of five years, and still the woman's
utter audacity never ceased to amaze him. Wanting to go in-
cognito, she dragged him off to the King's room where they
plundered through his wardrobe till they found something Drew
deemed appropriate. Then she had ripped this off, and added
that, till the two of them looked like something straight out of
one of those sleazy magazines Drew was always picking up at
the Salvager stops.

Then she went to the garage and picked out the most expensive limo in the fleet, and asked one of the guards to drive it.

"But my Queen, surely a full convoy is in order. With
the riots..." the guard had tried to protest as they went out the
front gates.

"Riots, shmiots, open this fucking roof and stop the car."
He complied. As the angry mob ran towards the car, Drew popped
up and fired a clip out of the projectile weapon she had taken to
wearing into the air and the crowd immediately parted to allow
them to pass through.

Drew flopped onto the seat beside Van Gar. "Ah, the
people's love for their Queen."

"Where to, my Queen?" The guard asked.

"The shopping plaza? The opera? Maybe we'll take in a
play...Nah, fuck it, take us to the nearest bar."

The nearest bar went well. No one recognized her, and
they were run out for throwing food at the other patrons. The
second bar was pretty good. They got into a fist fight there, and
beat up three men. It was only when the police tried to arrest
them that she told them that she was the Queen. After she proved

it, they left the bar to a chorus of Long Live the Queen, and "come back anytime."

It was in the third bar that all the trouble started. A few men were playing battle ball (a game which consisted of trying to knock your opponent's wooden ball down a hole with your wooden ball before he could knock your ball down the hole) in a far corner. They were also talking politics, and the problems the system was causing them. That was when Van lost Drew. She pretended to want to play battle ball, but then it started, and three hours later it was still going on.

"So, let me get this straight," Drew was saying. "This guy murders this person, is convicted and sentenced, and then they tax the people to feed, clothe and house him?"

"Exactly right," one man answered.

"Well, that's without a doubt the stupidest thing I have ever heard," Drew shook her head and took a long sip of her drink. "No wonder people are rioting outside the palace."

Van Gar sat in a corner drinking, for all intents and purposes forgotten. For a little while he had been sure that he had been over reacting. That Drew was, after all, the same old Drew she'd always been. But as the night wore on, it was obvious that she was more interested in politics than she was in getting stumbling drunk and kicking some butts. More interested in these people's problems than she was in having a good time, and that was just not the Drewcila Qwah he knew.

An hour later she decided it was time to go home. She didn't even stagger when she got in the car. Van Gar's shoulders sagged sadly. Drew wasn't even drunk. Instead of laughing and screaming, she was solemn and quiet. When they got to the palace, she bid him a quick good night and went off to get some sleep—alone. Leaving Van Gar standing, staring at her closed door. He had been hoping that tonight would be different. That tonight she would want him. But tonight was just like every other night for the past three weeks. She was too busy, or too tired, or too something. At any rate she hadn't come searching him out to fill her animal desires. He started to walk to his own room.

"Van," He turned around and saw Drew standing in her door way, wearing nothing but a smile. "Wanna screw?"

"You make me feel so cheap," Van said, batting his eyelashes.

"Only if you're lucky, baby. Only if you're lucky."

He walked into her room and the door closed.

He had been waiting for the Queen to return, but as the minutes had turned to hours, he began to realize just what a huge fool he was. She wanted to turn their country into a festering dung heap, where nothing Regal could flourish. He had clung to the hope that she could be changed, at least enough to fit in, but now he realized that would never happen. He had been wrestling for hours about what his course of action should be, and had come to the conclusion that the only thing he could do was talk to her. When he heard that she had returned, he made his way directly to her sleeping chambers, determined to have his say before he lost his nerve. He arrived just in time to see her entice that beast into her room. Shocked and confused, he ducked into the shadows to wait. The beast did not emerge, and he decided that there was only one course of action left. The abomination which inhabited Taralin's body must be killed before she made a laughing stock of the kingdom and its King.

Drew slept all of four hours, then she got up and went to her office. One quick call brought Margot, who came bustling into the room, obviously still dressing.

"Margot?"

"Yes, my...Drew?"

Drew smiled at her sleepy attendant. "Get me all the data that was gathered through the letter-writing campaign." She looked to make sure Margot had pen and paper in hand. When she saw her making notes, she continued. "Get me kingdom law books and books on social programs. Get me everything you can find on current affairs and prison reforms. Get me records on hospital costs and who's getting care, life expectancies, etc., etc., etc. By the end of the week, I want to have some answers that will shut

those screamers up. After all happy people are productive people
and productive people make me more money."

By late afternoon, her office was so full of paperwork and
books that there was hardly room for people. Drew shook her
head. "I should have had it put on the computer."

She was going through yet another pile of papers on hospital costs and adjustments. "Most fucking places would have all
of this on computer. Backwards fucking bung hole." Outside,
the noise seemed to grow in pitch, and at the moment that it seemed
to reach its crescendo, Stasha ran into the room.

"Drewcila, Mother and Father have just arrived!"

"Oh, damn, and just when I was quite sure that I had offended them so badly that they would never return. Guess I'll
have to work up a good vomit for the occasion. Have the cooks
prepare that spiced meat dish that I absolutely can not stand."

Drew kept on looking at her papers.

"Mother is quite miffed," Stasha said hotly. "It seems
you've turned the ranch they gave you as a wedding present into
a bar, grill, and space-port for your Salvager friends. Including a
sex-for-hire parlor." Stasha's face glowed pink.

"Hey!" Drew screamed. "Those girls have got to make a
living, too!" Van Gar laughed, and she smiled at him.

"Some people just don't want economic progress."

"Drew, that ranch has been in our family for ten generations..." Their father and mother stormed past the guards then,
and their father finished Stasha's sentence for her. "...and you've
turned it into a den for the perversions of Salvagers."

"Well, they've got to do their perversions some place. I
figured they were better off way out there away from the general
public." She didn't look up from the papers in her hand.

"Oh, I see. You don't want the people to find out the true
nature of these scum you've got running the country," Lillith screamed.

"In a nutshell, yes." Drew tried once more to concen-
trate on the papers in her hand. "By the way, I am trying to run
the country here. I don't have time to worry about any of this
petty family crap."

"Drew, our ancestors homesteaded that land. They built their first homes there out of hand-cut wood and stone," Stasha said appealingly.

"I'm not going to let a bunch of stiffs dictate where I put my space port," Drew said in disbelief.

Lillith walked across the room and slapped Drew across the face. The entire room fell silent. As Drew looked up from the papers, she stared with cold hatred at her mother, and ran her hand over her face where she had been slapped.

"I don't have to justify myself to you, or anyone else," she looked unblinkingly into her mother's eyes. "I am Queen. I am in control now. Not you, and not anyone else. Just me. I have good reasons for everything I do. I don't give a flying fuck if you've got your shorts in a wad because you don't like the way I chose to use our ancestral home. Just get over it. Now, I have just about had it with screaming peasants," she swept an arm towards the window, "and bitching advisors," she waved a hand at Facto and Fitz. "And you have been here all of three minutes, and I've had it up to my dirty ass with you. I am Queen, and this is my party. I don't know you; either of you. I look at you screaming at me, demanding things of me, trying to tell me how to think, act, and feel, and I'm sure that even if I did know you, I wouldn't like you. So get the hell out of my house, before I have you thrown out."

They started to protest.

"Get out, or I swear, I'll have you kicked out on your lily white asses."

"If you do this, I swear you'll never see me again," Lillith swore.

"Ah, so soon?" Drew hissed. She motioned towards one of the guards, and her parents left.

"Facto, Fitz, if I need you, I'll call for you."

"By Royal Law…" Facto started.

Drew hit the arm of her chair hard. "I AM Royal Law, Facto. If you haven't taught me anything else, you've taught me that. Now, get the fuck out! I need time to work on all this shit."

Van Gar looked at her. He knew her well enough to know that she was on the verge of throwing a hissing shit fit.

As if on cue, the screaming in the street got louder. She jumped out of her chair and pulled her pistol from its scabbard. She ran to the balcony door and opened it so fast that Van didn't have the time to stop her. She walked out onto the balcony and started firing. She didn't stop till she was out of bullets. The crowd below murmured and rattled around.

"Shut the fuck up! Do you fucking assholes hear me? Shut the fuck up!" Below, the crowd was silent. "I just got the latest reports: unemployment is down to fifteen percent. That was the main problem, and I tackled it. Now I'm working on the others. Or at least I'm trying to, but you assholes won't fucking shut up. Instead of screaming all day, why don't you go look for work? There is some now. Of course, if honest work is too good for you, I have another alternative for ya. I'm passing a new law. It's called the Taralin don' want no dead-beats screaming on her lawn Law. You've got ten minutes to get the fuck out ah here, or I call in the army and tell them to start shooting. That's not the palace guard, which, by the way is now double what it was before the King's abduction. We're talking tanks and big shit here, assholes. So, clear out, or clear things up with your Gods, because one way or another I am going to have some peace and quiet."

She turned to walk in, and that's when the shot rang out. She immediately hit the ground and something landed on top of her. There was a pain in her right arm.

"Up there on the roof," Van Gar screamed, at which point she realized that it was he who had landed on top of her.

The guards opened fire for what seemed like ten minutes.

"Hey, I think that forty-sixth hit killed him," Van Gar announced dryly.

They quickly hustled the Queen inside and the doors were closed. They sat Drew in her chair. She looked at Van, and he smiled.

"It's not bad."

"Well, it's not good," Drew held her arm. "Thanks, Van."

Margot ran in with the doctor.

"You know, we would save Margot about a hundred miles a day if we would just put in an intercom system."

The doctor pulled her hand away and she winced.

"Be gentle with me, it's my first time."

"Ah, she says that to all the guys," Van Gar said lightly.

Stasha looked at him. She saw his trembling hands and the sweat on his forehead. He was putting on an act. He didn't want any one to know how scared he'd been or still was. She had seen him launch himself at the door even before the shot rang out. Somehow, he had felt that Drew was in danger, and had acted accordingly. And she knew in that instant that Van Gar loved her sister, loved her more than Zarco ever had or ever could. He had flung himself at her without fear of personal injury. All he cared about was Drew. If Van Gar had been King, the country could have gone to hell in a hand basket while he went after his Queen. Stasha knew now why Drewcila would never forgive Zarco, and she understood her sister a little bit better. She looked at the blood the doctor was wiping up, and with the realization that it wasn't bad at all something else hit her.

"Drew, someone tried to kill you."

"Duh, ya think so?" Drew looked dumbfounded, then screamed at her sister. "What was you first clue, the hole in my arm?"

"My Queen," one of the guards ran in and knelt at her feet. "They have identified the body of the sniper."

"Are you going to tell me, or do I have to guess?" Drew said sharply.

The guard seemed reluctant. "It was Lord Greyston."

"Lord Greyston," Stasha gasped, "but he was one of Zarco's oldest and dearest friends!"

"Maybe that's the point," Facto said. "It's obvious that Drew has no intention of running the country the way the King did, nor does she seem to be in any hurry to locate him and have him returned to power. For the obvious reason that she is getting a charge out of running things. To someone like Lord Greyston, in fact to anyone with a Royal title, it's going to seem that your actions are…well, traitorous to your class."

"Charge out of it?" Drew said with raised eyebrows.

"A term I've hear you use many times," Facto said defensively.

Drew nodded.

"I wouldn't suggest a stroll outside, or on the balcony until we can be sure that Lord Greyston acted alone."

Drew nodded again, then looked at Facto and smiled. "I thought I told you to get lost."

"I wasn't quite through the door when the shots rang out. I thought I'd better stay close."

"Is that loyalty I hear in your voice, Fatso?" Drew asked.

"Not at all. If something had happened to you, I would be in charge." He bowed low and departed.

Drew laughed after him.

The doctor had finished dressing her wound. "I put J-16 on it. It should be healed by nightfall."

"Thank you very much."

The doctor started to go.

"Wait! Hold on there a minute, doctor. What do you think about the health care problem?"

"Drew," Van protested, "someone just tried to kill you."

"You're acting like it's the first time that ever happened," Drew laughed.

"Margot, get me a cigar and a beer."

"So, Doc. Let me hear it. What do you think can be done about the health care problem?"

Van Gar threw up his hands. He guessed he'd have to check this thing out himself. He looked around for Fitz, but he was nowhere to be found. Obviously, he had followed orders and left. Van Gar left the office and started looking for Fitz. He found him some ten minutes later talking to one of the palace guards.

He looked at Van Gar and nodded. "And remember, Varge, double security at the doors and gates." The guard nodded and went off. "I heard about the attempt on the Queen's life, and was just fortifying the palace."

Van Gar nodded.

"Do they know who the would-be assassin was yet?"

"Lord Grey...something."

"Greyston?"

"Yep, that was it."

Fitz drew in a deep breath and shook his head. "I guess the lack of protocol was just more that he could stand." Fitz shook his head and sighed. He was obviously shaken by what this man had done.

"You stupid sucks would kill someone over protocol?" Van Gar asked in disbelief.

"I know it doesn't mean anything to you, or for that matter to our Queen. But to certain people, especially those of noble birth, protocol is very important. They're very proud of their heritage. And, let's face it, Drewcila is making a mockery of everything they stand for. Lord Greyston was a member of the advisory council, as was his father and his grandfather before him. She's messing with generations of tradition, and it's obvious that some people don't appreciate it."

"People like you, Fitz?" Van Gar asked softly.

Fitz smiled and nodded. "That's no secret. I've tried to get Drewcila to act in a more queenly manner, but you see how much progress I've made. If she would just give in a little. For instance, since her return she has not made any attempt to hold a ball or a banquet for the nobles of the kingdom. Such a simple thing would show them that she respects them."

"But you and I both know that she doesn't. She thinks they are a lot of fat, rich fuckers, resting on their titles."

Fitz smiled and nodded. "Yes, we know it, but there is no reason that they must. And if she would hold a banquet and get to know them again, who knows? Maybe she might even like them. If she didn't, she could at least pretend."

"I'll see what I can do about talking her into it. Meanwhile, there's something bothering me. Something that Facto said."

"Facto? What did he say?"

"He said that if anything happened to Drew, he would be in charge. It that true?"

"Yes, it's true. Why do you ask? Certainly you don't think Facto had anything to do with the attempt on Drew's life?"

"You tell me. Power of that kind is a pretty good motive for murder," Van Gar suggested.

"You can put that right out of your mind. Facto may not approve of Drew. And, yes, it's true that he tried to get Zarco to leave her where she was, but he's just not capable of such a plot."

"I'll tell you something, Fitz. If this little excursion to your planet has taught me anything, it's that you never know anyone as well as you think you do. If it's all the same to you, I think I'll just keep an eye on old Facto."

Chapter 14

Zarco stared at the wall. He had lost track of time. Day turned into night, and night into day, and it had all lost meaning as he sat in his tiny cell waiting for his release. He had just about given up hope. Taralin seemed more that happy to let him rot here, and it seemed from the news casts that no one even remembered they had a King, much less were in any hurry to see him returned to power. He saw Marcus pushing the screen over.

"The Queen's making a speech. I thought you'd like to see it." He turned the TV on, and Taralin's face filled the screen.

"As you all know, unemployment is at an all-time low, but that is not the only problem our country faces, nor am I pretending that it is. In the last few weeks, with the help of my staff and from concerned citizens out there who took the time to write about what they saw as problems—as well as the possible solutions to those problems. I believe I have come up with some answers—real answers. Not a bandage on a cut, as has been suggested by my advisors, but a cure.

"I will start with health care, as that seems to be the number one bitch, and I will work my way down the list. Right now, the government has a policy concerning health care which I simply do not understand. It seems that if you do not work, or are unable to work, or are too old to work, you can get any sort of health care—free. In other words, if you contribute nothing to society, and don't pay any taxes, we—the government—take care of you. Once again, let's look at the country like a business. One, Two and Three are hard workers. Four never lifts his hand to work, Five has no hands, so he might as well not be there, and Six is so old that he works too slowly to be effective—he might as well stay home. One day, there is an explosion in the plant, and all six employees are injured.

As the employer, I can afford to send three workers to the hospital. Obviously, I send One, Two, and Three, right? Wrong. According to current policy, I send Four, Five and Six—leaving One, Two and Three to fend for themselves. Except that they can't afford medical care, because it is hideously high, so they go without. One dies, Two suffers injuries so bad that he can no longer work, and Three is permanently disabled so that he can only do half the work he used to do. So, now I have gone from having three out of six employees being unproductive to six out of six. That is the cost of our current health care program. People are punished for being healthy and productive.

"This is my proposal. Under the new law, anyone currently paying taxes will receive emergency medical care free—emergency to include life-threatening illnesses. All children under the age of majority will also receive free medical care. Anyone else must pay for such care. According to my calculations, the government can save billions of Gildoltars in revenue each year simply by taking these unproductive members of our community off the health care programs, and placing tax-paying, productive members on it.

"Now, before you start calling me a cold, calculating bitch and accuse me of being uncompassionate, let me say this. Right now, only one in twenty can afford health care. Under my new program, only one in twenty won't be able to. I also have a parts two and three to this program. They will all tie in, so please let me continue before you stop listening.

"Part 2: No one shall be unemployable simply because of their age, nor shall their age be an excuse to stop working. Under the new law, all employers will find a suitable position for the aged employee—his or her work day not to exceed five hours, four days a week, with no cut in hourly rates. Such employees will then receive the same medical benefits that all tax-paying individuals receive. Because the government will not be paying old-age pensions, and because the elderly employed will still be paying taxes, not only will they save the country several million Gildoltars, but I have to believe that the resulting feeling of productivity should reduce the now high rate of suicide among our elderly.

"Part 3: No one shall be considered too handicapped to work. Employers accommodating a handicapped worker shall receive tax cuts matching the wages paid to these people. Citizens too debilitated to leave their homes shall be given the chance to do piece-work from their homes, or other home-based work, depending upon their skills. In this manner, all handicapped persons can be covered under the national health plan. And again, because we would not be paying these persons for their disability, and because they will be paying taxes, this will once again save the country millions."

She paused long enough to drink half a can of beer, and to wink at the camera man, and then she continued.

"Second problem: The indigent—people who are unproductive for no other reason than it's become a way of life. Because of our free medical to the 'poor' they have bred like flies. Why? Because we give them more money for each child they have. Well, the days of the hand-out are over, boys and girls. Our country's roads, parks and space-ports are in bad need of repair. All people now receiving free rent, free utilities, grocery allotments, and/or large sums of money for sitting on their asses will be put to work. You will be moved to government housing and given food of our choosing. While you are working, a government staff will keep under-age children. A government staff will also clean quarters. All such government staff members will be drawn from those presently indigent persons who are living off the government. Since we are already supporting these people, this program will cost the government nothing, and hopefully we can teach these people—or at least their children—a little pride, as well as cleaning up our roads and other much needed work. Since taxes would be taken from their wages, they would then fall under the medical program.

"Third problem: The outrageous cost of medical care. These costs brought my attention to the fact that there are a whole lot of people out there making outrageous wages who don't work any harder, if as hard, as the rest of us. These people are systematically raping our population. Extravagantly high wages were a big part of our employment problem. It also caused a huge gap between the so-called classes that had nothing at all to do with the real productivity of a worker. This problem was the most easily solved. There is already a minimum wage. I will also make a maximum wage, under which no one will be allowed to make over a certain amount of money per hour. This law covers everyone from the factory worker to the doctor and the guy who owns the pharmaceutical company. This in itself should bring the cost of health care, cars, textiles, etc., down. For those of you who think you can not get rich under this program, please take some time and figure it out. In an economy where a man can't make less than one Gildoltar an hour or more than twenty, any man who makes eighteen is rich. He's just not filthy stupid fucking rich.

"Fourth problem." She finished her beer. "Crime." She laughed and shook her head in disbelief. "The way we handle crime in this country is nothing short of ludicrous. When a criminal is convicted of a crime they take him to a special hotel where he is given free room and board, an athletic training area, free higher education, and free medical. In short, they live better than most tax payers—at a high cost to the government."

She leaned forward and her expression suddenly got very dark. "Solution: Trenches are now being dug. Tomorrow, every person now in prison having been convicted of a violent crime-violent crimes being murder, attempted murder, rape, attempted rape, and child abuse in any form—shall be shot and buried. From this day forward, such crimes shall be punishable by death upon conviction without appeal."

She sat back, and some of the tension left her face. "All other prisoners shall be released. All those newly-released prisoners convicted of robbery or other 'non-violent' crimes, and all who have a previous conviction of any type on their record, shall be shot without appeal upon conviction of the next offense of any type. First-time non-violent offenders will spend five years in jail upon conviction without appeal. In other words, get caught the first time committing a non-violent crime, and you rot in jail doing hard labor without pay. First-time violent offenders and second-time non-violent offenders will rot in the ground."

Drew took a deep breath, smiled and shrugged.

"Obviously, this program will save us countless billions. Not just in care and feeding, but we will only need one in five of our present prison facilities. So, what do we do with the other buildings? You should all know me too well by now to believe that I don't have a plan to re-use them." She grinned again, widely this time. "Well, the soon-to-be-empty buildings will be used to house those people in the new government work program—remember the second problem? Their first job will be to make these former prisons into decent housing. The housing they are now using—mostly rental property—should give affordable housing to the tens of thousands of working people who desperately need it.

"That leaves us with problem number five." She started a new beer. "The plight of our country's farmers. The only problem they seem to have is that they had a good year, and so did everyone else. Their store-houses are full of Rash. Next year, they'll know to diversify. In the mean time, they're all going to go broke unless we help them—but they're also going to help us. As most of you know, Rash is the one grain known to be a complete diet. So, the people on the new work program will be eating a lot of Rash. In the future, whatever the product, the government will buy the farmer's surplus to feed the people on the work program." She downed the beer. "So, that's about got it. Any questions?"

Everyone started shouting at once, and she held up her had. "Yo! One at a time, or you can forget it. I haven't really slept in two weeks, and I'm on the rag, so don't push it."

One man held his hand up higher than anyone else, and she nodded in his direction. He was so surprised that she had called on him, that it took him several seconds to remember what he had wanted to ask. "My Queen, your new crime program seems a little harsh. Do you really think it will work?"

"Dead people don't commit crimes," Drew laughed and nodded at another reporter.

"Don't you think the 'poor' will revolt? I mean, talk about harsh. Where is your compassion?" A young woman asked.

"If the 'poor' revolt, we will have no other recourse than to shoot them in the street. As for compassion—two things. One, my compassion is for the people whose backs the unproductive have been riding on too damn long. And two, I am offering these people a chance to be productive, live in decent housing and eat wholesome food. Plus, no one has said that they *must* enter the work program—just don't expect a check from us. Next," she nodded at an older man.

"What about those of us that have been looking forward to our retirement?"

"I'm not telling you that you can't retire. All I'm saying is that we're not going to pay for it. Many shops have retirement programs—save part of your earnings towards the goal of retirement."

"Many of us have paid into the government program…"

"Yes, a whole fifth of what most of you would have drawn out under the old plan. All the money will be paid back through income tax reductions to those who paid in, up to the amount they paid in, less any government support they may have received—over the next five years. Next." She pointed to a young male reporter.

"I very much approve of the idea that all can work, but do you really believe that?"

"You bet I do. If a man has no arms and no legs, he can sit at the end of an assembly line and look for defects. If he's blind, too, he can sing a happy tune for his co-workers, and if he's also mute, they can use him to hold a door open. My idea is that working makes people feel good. Knowing that you have a purpose, some place important to be every day, is worth a whole lot. Enough questions."

Drew rose and left the conference room. Her retinue followed, and Marcus turned off the TV.

Zarco sat back hard in his chair, and the cheap thing almost went over with him.

"Now, there is someone who understands the needs of the people…"

"Marcus! Taralin just put the poor in prison…"

"So?" Marcus said hotly. "You've kept us all in economic prison for years. We couldn't hope for better jobs, better homes, and hospitalization. The Queen is right. It's our turn for some compassion. We at least have worked for it."

"And what about bringing back the death penalty? We haven't had one for a hundred years! It has no place in a polite society. And a mass execution and burial—it's barbaric!"

"What's barbaric is making the victims of a crime and their families pay to keep the perpetrator alive. And just how polite is a society where hundreds of violent crimes take place every day?"

Zarco looked at Marcus then. Marcus understood what Taralin was doing. He understood Zarco's wife better than Zarco did, and Taralin understood the people better than he, their King. He might not approve of the way she was ruling, but the people did. He walked over to his cot, lay down, and stared at the ceiling.

He had already begun to believe that he had failed as a man and husband when he let the Lockhedes not only take, but also keep, his wife. But it wasn't until his wife started to run his country that he realized that he had also failed as a King. He had been too involved with the war and his hatred of the Lockhedes to notice the ills of the people he was supposed to be serving. It was easy to say "feed the poor" when the bread didn't come off your table. Easy to forgive a killer when he hadn't killed your loved one in your home. He thought about how he had gone after the Lockhedes with such vengeance, how he had wanted them all dead because they had taken Taralin. How their actions and his inability to act had made him feel helpless and impotent…the way commoners must feel all the time. How many men's wives had been killed while he warred with the Lockhedes, wanting revenge upon them for what they had taken from him?

Had he found the men that took Taralin, he would have killed them without a second thought. Yet he had deemed it cruel for the common man to enjoy such justice.

He hadn't even known that so many of them had no medical care, or for that matter that it was so costly. And when did the farmers start growing Rash? He had failed his wife, because he refused to put his own needs above those of the people. And then he had failed the people because he refused to put their needs above his own.

"Are you all right, Sire?" Marcus asked with concern.

Zarco looked at the young guard. He now saw him as he truly was; not a traitor at all, but a good man driven to this deed by Zarco's neglect. "How long did she ask you to keep me here?"

Marcus looked startled. "It wasn't her idea…!"

"But it was convenient for her. How long?"

"Three months. She wouldn't meet our initial demands. I said we'd kill you, but she didn't believe us. She said if we kept you out of the picture for awhile, she could fix things…"

"How long have I been here?"

"Eight weeks."

"Couldn't you let me go now? I mean, she's changed everything, and you seem pleased…"

Marcus shook his head. "Give her programs a chance to get under way. Right now, you could ruin everything. I figure if her ideas work, you're not going to be so gung-ho to run in and change things. No matter how much flack you get from your blue-blooded kin."

After the press conference, Drew dismissed everyone, went straight to her room and flopped on her bed without even bothering to turn down the covers. Margot would be livid. She was so exhausted that she couldn't go to sleep—naturally. She stared at the ceiling and wondered why she couldn't turn her brain off.

"Maybe it's the thought of all those convicts I've just ordered put to death. Maybe I feel guilty in some way." She spoke out loud and thought about it. "Nah."

She moved to a more comfortable position, and something moved at the foot of her bed. She must have been closer to sleep than she thought, because it took her several minutes to realize that there shouldn't be anything in her bed but her.

"Van, I'm tired," she mumbled, half asleep. There was no answer, but she felt something move again. Suddenly wide awake, she jumped out of bed and quickly threw back the covers. Squirming at the foot of the bed, right where her feet would have been if she had jumped between the sheets, was a hideous slug-looking thing. It was about two feet long and two inches around. She grabbed the gun off the bedside table, and shot it twice.

Instantly, the guards outside her door were in her room. Not far behind them was first Van Gar and then Stasha.

Drew laughed. "Quick, someone call the Royal exterminator and have the palace sprayed for slugs at once."

"Drew, do you know what that is?" Stasha asked, pale and shaken.

"The ugliest mother fucker I've ever seen," Drew answered.

"It's a brain slug."

Stasha turned to the guards. "Don't just stand there, check the room."

They started searching.

"They come from the swamps of Dildot. If it was in here, someone put it here."

"Dildot's a long ways off, then?" Drew asked.

"Several hundred miles," Stasha said, gently chiding her sister's geographical ignorance.

"So, someone put an ugly slug in my bed. It's not the first time I've slept with a slug, and it probably won't be the last."

"It could have been," Stasha said, still shaken. "Brain slugs get their names because they crawl into the ear of their victims, eat part of their brains, and lay their eggs in the still-living body."

Drew made a face and then smiled. "I wouldn't have been a whole meal, then. I decree that from this day forward we call them Lockhede slugs…"

"It's not funny, Drew," Van Gar said hotly.

"Certainly not. I don't have enough brains left to spare."

"You could have been killed," Stasha warned.

"But I wasn't. So, why don't you two just lighten up?"

"The room is clean," one guard said.

"Then you'd better do something quick, because it wasn't a minute ago," Drew said with a laugh.

It was funny. Drew hadn't acted like Drew in weeks, and now that she was, all Van wanted to do was stuff a sock in her mouth.

"Go back to your post. In the future, you will check the room before my sister enters it. Including the bed," Stasha ordered.

"I've got a better idea. You boys just climb right in bed with me, and don't let any long skinny things crawl in me."

"You are the biggest asshole in the fucking galaxy," Van Gar screamed.

"Then you must be my son, because you're the biggest pile of shit I've ever seen."

Drew didn't even try to keep the smile off her face. She turned to the guards. "Go back to your posts."

"How can you make jokes?" Stasha wanted to know. "Someone is trying to kill you."

"You know, Stasha, you seem to have a real talent for stating the obvious," Drew shrugged. "Of course someone's trying to kill me, but they're going about it in really lame ways. So excuse me if I don't wet myself. I'm too damn tired to worry about someone trying to kill me. If I don't get some sleep soon I won't even know when they do it. So, go on and let me go to bed."

Van Gar started to follow Stasha out. "Not you, Van," she smiled appealingly at him. "I'm afraid to sleep by myself now."

He smiled in spite of himself, and shook his head. "You know, Drew, you really are a piece of work."

"Well I'm a piece anyway."

"I really can't believe you, Drew," Stasha screamed. "Zarco is who knows where, and you're carrying one with this alien right under the nose of everyone in the palace!"

"So, do you have a point Stasha?"

Stasha turned on her heel and stomped from the room.

Chapter 15

"No, no. Like this," she stuck her thumb in the guy's ribs and twisted. He doubled up in pain and fell to the floor.

"Ooops, sorry," she smiled apologetically and helped him to his feet. Drew turned to the group of guards. "What is the first principle of Trigade?"

"Anything goes," they repeated.

"Very good. What is the second principle of Trigade?"

"Use your anger," they repeated.

She smiled and nodded. "What is the third and most important principle of Trigade?"

"Save yourself."

"Why?"

"Because you can't hold your post if you're dead."

"And?"

"Being dead sucks."

"Very good. Now, I'm going to show you a couple of more moves, and then we'll break."

She was half-way through the first exercise when someone screamed, "What are you doing now?"

Drew smiled and wiped her face on the towel that Margot attentively handed her. "Take over for me, would you, Van?"

She went over to Facto. "What are you doing down here? Slumming?" She asked.

"Please tell me that you were not teaching the King's Royal Guard Trigade," Facto intoned heavily.

"I was not teaching the King's Royal Guard Trigade," she said.

"Good," Facto sighed with relief. "Some urgent business needs your attention."

"What?" She obviously didn't really care.

Facto shrugged. "All I was told was that it was urgent."

"What is the fourth rule of Trigade?" Van Gar bellowed.

"There is no such thing as safety in numbers," the guards bellowed back. Facto gave Drew a hard look.

Drew shrugged and smiled. "You wrote the script."

"So, when did you start listening to me?" Facto shook his head and started following the Queen and her servant as they started back for the palace. "Do you really think it's proper to teach the King's Guard a fighting style which teaches self-preservation over all else?"

"Someone's trying to kill me, Facto," she said in a whisper. As if it were something only she, and now he, knew. The truth was that it had been splattered in the news all through the last week. "Trigade teaches you to be aware of every sound around you, a change in the breeze, a different scent. To run and get help if you sense danger, rather than to stand by your post, die, and leave a hole in the defense of what you are supposed to be guarding. To sound the alarm at the first sound instead of the first shot. Trigade is the fighting style of a country which has lived with war for twenty generations. The fighting style of a people under siege. I think the King's guard will benefit from the teachings of Trigade. And I, for one, will feel safer."

"It is, of course, your decision," Facto's tone was resigned.

"Excuse me," a voice called out. They both turned. A young page was running up behind them, obviously out of breath. "Councilor Facto, there is a problem in the household. The head butler has just had a terrible row with the cook, and they are both threatening to resign."

"If you'll excuse me, my Queen," Facto bowed low and at Drew's nod, he took off after the boy.

"I thought he'd never go," Drew said. Margot laughed.

"You really shouldn't go out of your way to anger him. He can be a rather pleasant man when things are going his way." Margot said. "Now that's odd."

"Yes, well that does seem to be the way it is with men. What's odd?"

"I thought I saw…" she laughed, "but that's not likely." She shrugged and they continued their trek to the palace. As they walked under one of the three archways leading to the castle from the guard house, Drew heard a sound from above them like the crack of a pistol, and she looked up just in time to see the keystone splinter and start to fall. "Margot look out!" She pushed the girl one way, and jumped the other, rolling as she hit the ground. When she looked back at the spot where they had been standing a second before, she saw the huge keystone crash into the flagstones below, splintering both. The debris splattered all around her like a hard rain, and then the remains of the archway started to rock. She jumped up and ran, only aware of having done so when the stone arch crashed just behind her. She looked down at the rubble for a minute before she saw the body tangled in the wreckage.

"Margot—no!" Drew scrambled through the stones and pulled the stones off the woman. "Margot, can you hear me? Help! We need a doctor over here!"

"Margot, can you hear me?"

"My…Queen…are you all right?" Margot coughed out.

"I'm too fucking mean to die. Listen, kid, you're going to be all right. You're not going to be dancing in the near future, but you're going to be fine. Just lay very still."

The guards ran up, lead by Van Gar. "Turj, go for the Doctor. The rest of you, scour the grounds. Leave no stone unturned. I want to know how this happened, and who did it. Van, stay here and protect my butt."

"I came running as soon as I heard the explosion," he pulled his laser and scanned the whole area. Then looked back at her. "Your cheek is bleeding a little. Are you all right?"

"I'm fine," she brushed the dust off Margot's face. "Where the hell are they with the doctor? Margot, can you hear me?"

This time, she didn't even groan, and Drew quickly checked her pulse. "Hang on, kid."

She saw the doctor and his staff run out of the palace then. "Hurry, man," the doctor got there first and immediately started to check Drew out. She jerked her face out of his hands. "I'm fine, take care of Margot." The doctor knelt beside the fallen woman and was soon surrounded by his staff.

"Who would want to hurt Margot? They had to know she'd be with me…Hell she's always with me."

"I hate to say this, Drew, but…Whoever wants you dead doesn't seems to care who goes down with you."

"Then maybe you shouldn't stand so close," Drew said in a harsh whisper.

"There's a chance that Margot is the assassin. That having had her last attempt foiled she was willing to go down with you."

"You're fucking out of your tiny little mind!"

"Who else has access to your room?"

"You, my sister, and probably most of the cleaning staff. Margot is my friend!"

"Margot is Taralin Zarco's friend. She might well think of you as the person who murdered her."

"You are really grasping at straws. I tell you, Margot is no killer."

"How is she, Doctor?" Drew saw that Margot had been loaded on to a stretcher.

"I won't know till I can get her X-rayed. I think there is some internal bleeding. The thing that worries me most right now is the head trauma. OK, boys, get her to the infirmary. Now, about your injury, my Queen…"

"Fuck it. I can put on my own bandage. You just take care of Margot."

She looked hard at Van Gar and whispered. "I think Margot saw who did it."

They watched them carry her inside.

"Why do you think that?" Van asked curiously.

"She said something…she thought she saw something or someone just before the fucking arch blew up in our faces."

"Well, whoever it is, we know one thing. He or she is in here with us."

"How comforting. It could be anyone." She saw the look on his face. "Anyone but Margot. I've got to get up to the palace. There was some urgent shit I had to attend to there. Either that, or someone was just setting me up. Either way, I think I had better go check it out."

Van Gar followed her closely, his weapon in his hand. He didn't really think Margot was the assassin. But since she wasn't, that meant that the assassin was healthy and getting pretty frustrated. A desperate man was more likely to start taking risks, stop worrying about getting caught, and worry only about his objective-killing Drew.

The only person in Drew's office was Stasha. "So, what's so damned important?" Drew flopped into her desk chair as her sister vacated it.

"What's all the hubbub in the yard?" Stasha retorted.

"Oh, nothing. Just your normal, every day assassination attempt," Drew drawled out. "By the way are you surprised to see me?"

"What are you saying…You think I would…"

"Nah, but I love that little hissing sound you get in your voice when you get pissed off."

"Your face is bleeding! Has the doctor looked you over yet?"

"I'm fine. Margot is hurt pretty badly, though."

"How badly?"

Drew shrugged, and Stasha shook her head.

"So, what's so damned urgent?"

It was Stasha's turn to shrug. "What do you mean?"

"Facto said there was urgent business here. He didn't say what. I just assumed you knew."

Stasha shrugged again. "There were a couple of calls from the Salvager centers, but nothing I couldn't handle."

Van Gar headed for the door.

"Where are you going?" Drew asked.

"I thought I'd go check on Margot and bring you a report."

Drew nodded, and he was gone.

He stopped at the door and addressed the two guards on duty there. "No one is to go in this office unless I say. Do you understand?"

"You're not authorized..." one guard began. Van Gar stuck his head back inside Drew's office.

"Drew, am I authorized to tell these knuckle heads what to do?" Van yelled.

"Yeah, yeah, sure," Drew said with a wave of her hand.

Van Gar drew his head out of the office looked at the two guards and smiled. "No one. Do you understand? No one!"

"What about the high councilors?" asked the talkative one.

Van grabbed him by the neck of his uniform and held him up in front of the other one. "Would you explain to this gentleman what 'no one' means."

The guard looked into the other guard's strained, pleading face and cleared his throat. "No one. Not the high councilors. Not visiting dignitaries, no one."

Van Gar turned the man he held to face him. "Do you understand?" He asked slowly, as if speaking to the mentally impaired. The man nodded as much as the hold on his collar allowed, and Van Gar put him down, straightened his collar and smiled, baring most of his impressive teeth. Then he set off down the hall.

Chapter 16

After Drew had finished making a list of everyone on the staff that she had offended or screamed at, there was no one left but herself and the head gardener.

"Quick! Run out and tell the gardener that I said his roses look like shit, then we won't have to leave him off the suspect list."

She glared across the table at Fitz, whose idea it was to make the list in the first place. "It's ridiculous to think the head cook would want to kill me because I bitched about her cooking, or that the steward would want to crush my head in with masonry because I ordered a beer keg to be delivered to each room in the palace."

"Some people do not take their duties lightly, my Queen," Fitz said. "They are very proud, and…"

"If Margot did it…" Van Gar started.

"Margot has been in a coma for three days now," Drew hissed. "I don't want to hear you accuse her one more time while she is unable to defend herself."

"The accusation is absurd anyway," Facto mumbled.

"You're my number one suspect, Facto. You have the most to gain. We all know that you don't like or approve of Drew, and it was you that delivered the message that she was needed at the palace. Then, as fate would have it, someone came and pulled you away just seconds before the archway blew up."

"Except there was no business here," Stasha said accusingly.

"Obviously, someone wanted to shift blame to me, and they did a good job." Facto looked at Drew. "I don't believe that Margot had anything to do with it, but I didn't either. We questioned both the page that gave me the first message, and the one that delivered the second. As you know, neither would divulge who had sent them."

"Which only means you might have sent them yourself," Van Gar said, and Stasha nodded.

"Which means we should put our prisoners to the torture." Drew said grabbing her thumb and making a twisting motion.

Van Gar looked at Fitz. "You're awful quiet, Fitz."

"I don't want to believe that any of us would want to harm the Queen. Let's not forget that Lord Greyston made the first attempt. Those persons of Royal Blood have made no bones about the way they feel about Drewcila. Why, just last night on the view screen, Lady Damest was saying that you had committed High Treason by dismissing the advisory council, and that you should be dethroned. Daily, I hear complaints from those of the nobility that feel that you have closed yourself off from them completely."

"None of them are in the Palace, Fitz," Drew said skeptically.

"No, but many of the staff, as well as the guards owe them loyalty for one reason or another. In fact, most are distantly related, and have noble blood themselves."

"Great, so I am surrounded by people who hate me because I have offended or cussed them, and who owe loyalty to people who want me dead." She lit a cigar and puffed on it madly until it got going. "Some days being ruler of all you survey is just not what it's cracked up to be." She thought for a minute, and then smiled. "So, we fire each and every one of them and bring in Salvagers to take their places."

"Oh, yeah," Van Gar scoffed. "I can just see Benny the Can Opener as court herald, or Jackie Skin as head cook, or..."

"I get the picture, Van. Any better ideas?"

"I think it's that guy with the little eyes and no nose who puts towels in the bathrooms," Van said, nodding his head. "He's always sneaking around, staring at me."

"You know, Van. You're going to have to stop jumping around, here. First Margot, did it, then Facto. Then they did it together. Now it's that poor deformed boy that delivers towels to the bathrooms," Drew grinned and shook her head.

"He's always staring at me," Van Gar said.

"I hate to bring this up, Van Gar," Stasha said, "but you happen to be the only alien most of them have seen."

"Which brings me to my own theory," Facto said. "It's no great secret that you would like to have Drew to yourself, or that you think she made a mistake coming here. I'm not the only person who has seen you make those late-night trips to the Queen's chambers, nor am I naive enough to think that these rendezvous are innocent. Eventually, Zarco will be returned, and I would imagine you find that thought distressing…"

"First off, you are reading things into mine and Drew's relationship that simply are not there. Our meetings, I can assure you, are quite innocent."

Drew didn't add credence to his words when she nearly choked to death on the cigar smoke that went down the wrong way when she laughed.

Van Gar ignored her. "But let's say, for the sake of argument, that you are right about us. Why would I try to kill her?"

"Oh, you're not," Facto said with a sly smile. "You're just trying to scare her into thinking someone's trying to kill her, so that she'll get scared and go away with you. You put the slug in her bed—we all know you have access. You rigged the keystone to break away, knowing that she'd hear the explosion and move. I don't think you planned on Margot's being hurt, or the arch coming all the way down, but I'm sure you did it. Who else would have reason to try and frame me? You probably got the idea after Lord Greyston's failed attempt…"

"You're just trying to pull the blame off yourself," Van Gar screamed.

"Ridiculously, I might add," Stasha said.

"Really, well what about you, Stasha?" Facto said hotly. "You were in the office when Drew got here. You could have ordered the pages to give me those messages, and I doubt they would betray you."

"I don't know anything about explosives…"

"No, but any of the guards do, and again, it would have been easy for you to gain their aid…"

"What reason would I have to kill my sister?"

"Do you really want me to answer that?" Facto asked sadistically. Stasha's face went scarlet. Drew looked at her then rocketed to her feet.

"You fucked my husband!" Drew screamed in disbelief. "After all the rot you fed me about his being true to me, and his great love. Damn he's an even bigger creep then I thought he was. All the servants and courtiers and he has to screw my sister." She glared at Stasha. "All the shit you gave me about fucking Van Gar and you were boffing my husband while I was having my brains sucked out of my head."

"It only happened once," Stasha cried.

Facto laughed loudly.

"He was so lonely, and…"

"You fucked my husband!" Drew shook her head in disbelief.

"So, you can see Stasha's motive," Facto said with a smile.

"My sister may be a whore, but she's not a murderer." Drew defended shaking a finger in the air. Stasha bawled loudly and ran from the room.

Drew looked at Van Gar, who was laughing loudly. "I don't think it's funny," she said.

"The King had no way of knowing whether you were alive or dead," Fitz said in the King's defense.

"So he balls my baby sister," Drew hissed.

"They were both devastated by your abduction. They were comforting each other…"

"What? Kind of a 'let me cry on your shoulder—take off your clothes' sort of thing?" Drew screamed.

"With all due respect, my Queen. I hardly think that you are in a position to hold a grudge about infidelity…"

"I didn't even know who I was, much less that I was married…what's his great excuse? His fucking winky was lonely!"

"I think we are wasting our time pointing our fingers at each other," Fitz said. "As much as I hate to say it, I fear we are dealing with a conspiracy buried deeply within the nobility of this kingdom. It's the only thing that makes sense. They're the only ones that command the kind of loyalty that would have those pages go to prison rather than divulge who they were working for. As I have said before, the nobility does not approve of the way you are running either the palace or the kingdom..."

"So, what's the answer? Order them all shot?"

"No, no, no," Fitz said quickly. He laughed nervously. "Just show them that you haven't forgotten them completely. That you still value their input..."

"But I don't," Drew said. "I think they are a lot of fat, gluttonous pigs, living off the backs of the working class."

"How could a little pretense hurt you, my Queen? A banquet, a chance to re-acquaint yourself with your own class."

"You know, they're just shallow enough that it might work. OK, Fitz. Arrange it. The sooner the better."

"How about a week from tomorrow? That should give us time to get the invitations out." Fitz seemed elated. "I'll get on it right away. If I may be excused?"

"You may." She watched him go, then she looked at Facto. "Do you think he's right?"

Facto shrugged. "It would seem to tie in with the Lord Greyston thing," he shrugged again. "He's right about one thing. Only a noble could command that kind of loyalty."

"But what about this banquet? Do you really think it will make a difference?" Drew asked.

"Actually, it might. But only if you act Queenly. If you walk in there dressed like a Salvager and tell them that you think they are a bunch of fat bloated pigs...Well, I don't really think that's going to help."

"I think I'd rather be shot." Drew made a face. "I suppose I could kiss their blue-blooded asses for one night."

"You might also reinstate the advisory council."

"That bunch of incompetent idiots?"

"I didn't say you had to take their advice," Facto said with a smile. "For that matter, you could call it the advisory council, and have them work on your letter-reading campaign. As long as they get to call themselves advisors, they're not going to care."

"I like your thinking." Drew nodded her head.

"If you're through with me, I think I'll turn in now," Facto said.

"No problem, sleep well."

"Thank you." He got up and walked to the door, but he stopped half-way through it and turned around. "Please believe me, Drew. I don't want you dead." He left.

"Drew, that man is trying to kill you…" Van started.

"Yeah, and the butcher and the baker and the candlestick maker." She smiled, and then frowned. "I can't believe Stasha. My own sister…how could she sleep with my husband?"

"I can't believe that you're making a big fucking deal out of it. Why should you care?"

"Why should I care?" Drew echoed in disbelief. "Let me spell this out for you. This husband who is supposed to have this undying love for me, consoled himself in my absence by doing my sister…"

"And again I say…So fucking what?" Van Gar felt the anger welling up inside himself long before he identified it. "You wouldn't give a shit if you didn't have feelings for him. You know something, Drew? I'm beginning to agree with ole Zarco. You've got to be remembering something. Feeling something for him. Or why would you care what he and Stasha did, especially since you were halfway across the galaxy boffing everything that moved…"

"You fucking dick head!" She threw a paper weight at him, and he dodged it with the ease of much practice. "I was never a fucking space tramp, and you by damn well know it!"

"Kicker, Sloat, Jackson, Dreake, Terlon, me. And those are only the ones I know about."

"Six men does not a slut make. Why don't we talk about all the space hags you've banged…"

"Because I'm not the one throwing a fit because my sister slept with my husband."

"Because you don't have either a sister or a husband," Drew spat back.

Van Gar got up and took a deep breath. "You know something, Drew? That was a really low blow." He stomped out of the office.

She threw a book at his departing figure, then ran to the door and screamed after him. "Fuck you, Van Gar!"

"Yeah, and half of space!" he shouted back, and marched out of sight.

Drew looked at the two guards and smiled nervously. "Ah, could you pick up that book I...dropped?"

"Yes, my Queen," the guard said with a smile.

"And wipe that damned grin off your face."

After the guards checked her room, she went in and lay down, hoping to escape from the day's troubles with a few hours sleep. She hadn't been in bed ten minutes when there was a knock on the door. "Eat shit, Van Gar!" She screamed, having learned her lesson about saying fuck you.

"It's me. Stasha."

"Why don't you go find Van Gar? I think he needs to be consoled," Drew spat out hatefully.

"Please, Drew, let me try to explain. It's not like you think."

"Oh, let her in!" Drew screamed. "I suppose she won't shut up until you do."

Stasha walked in slowly. It was obvious that she had been crying. As the door closed, she sat on the foot of Drew's bed.

"So, what do you want, tramp?" Drew spat.

Stasha started crying loudly. "What do you want me to do, Drew? Grovel? Beg your forgiveness? You can't imagine the hell I've put myself through. The hell Zarco went through. I know it sounds cliché, but it really did just happen."

Drew took in a deep breath and realized that she was being ridiculous. "Calm down, Stasha. It's funny. You know, I'm not mad a Zarco at all—he doesn't mean anything to me. But you…Well, you I trust."

"I'm sorry, Drew. I never meant to hurt you. But I thought you were dead, everyone did but Zarco, and…" She stopped there.

"And you love him, don't you?"

"I'm so s-sorry!" Her body was racked with sobs.

Drew took her in her arms and patted her back.

"I d-didn't mean to fall in love with him. All I was doing was helping him run the palace—the day-to-day business. But he's so sweet, and so kind, and so wise, and one night I threw myself on him…I'm sorry. When we heard that you'd been found, I was happy, but at the same time I felt cheated. You should have seen the look on Zarco's face. It was obvious that in his mind, he had never slept with me—he was always faithful to you."

"Oh, please," Drew drawled. "In his mind he was always faithful to you…Please! What a lot of fucking hooey."

"I had hoped you would never find out."

"You must really love him," Drew said softly. "To be willing to let him go on with his life with me and pretend like nothing ever happened between you. To even be happy for him, and he's such a shit."

"It helped that I was glad to have my sister back. But then you didn't have all your brain, and someone kidnapped Zarco, and everything is just so messed up!" Her crying raised in pitch. "You have no idea what it's like to love someone who doesn't love you."

"Yea, I think I do," Drew said heavily.

"But he does love you," Stasha dried her eyes.

"I wasn't talking about Zarco. That cheating bastard doesn't flip my bacon."

"I wasn't talking about Zarco, either. I was talking about Van Gar."

"Van Gar doesn't love anybody but himself," Drew scoffed.

"He wouldn't stay here if he didn't love you."

"You don't know Van like I do. Right now, he doesn't have a ship. Erik's gone, and I'm not running ships. All of his contacts are through me. If I gave him a ship and someone to work with, he'd be gone tomorrow."

"I think you're wrong, Drew. He risked being shot to save you..."

"I didn't say Van wasn't a good friend. I said he didn't love me. What's funniest about that is that until recently, I didn't think I wanted anyone to love me. But now I want him to, and he won't, and it's really starting to piss me off."

"I know what you mean." Stasha sniffed. "Do you forgive me?"

"Yeah, I suppose so...I'm such a push over. You won't say anything to the walking talking ego, will ya?"

"No."

"Good. Now, let's celebrate making up the way normal sisters would."

"How's that?"

"Let's get sloshed and talk about what dicks men are."

Marcus sat down carefully in the seat across from the Queen.

"Marcus, do you know why I've called you here?" Drew asked solemnly.

Marcus swallowed hard. He looked from the Queen to her sister, to the alien and swallowed again. He very much feared a double cross. He shook his head no.

"Here's what we want you to do."

Marcus sighed with relief and listened.

Chapter 17

Drewcila watched the newscast happily. Everything was going as planned, and without a hitch. There hadn't been an assassination attempt in a week, and all the preparations for the banquet seemed to be going smoothly. The only dark cloud on the horizon was that Margot was still in a coma.

"I wonder whatever happened to that human?" Drew asked.

"Wow! That's the first time you've asked about him in awhile," Van Gar said. "You know, Drew...I've been thinking,"

"Well, don't hurt yourself."

"Drew, this is kind of serious. Zarco will be back soon, and...Well, maybe it would be better if I wasn't here when he got back. Give me a ship and I can start working. Then, when and if you decide you're tired of playing Queen..."

"I've got a ship in dock for you now, but it won't be done before Zarco gets back," she said stiffly.

Van Gar took a deep breath. "I think it's best. Don't you?"

"I suppose..."

Stasha ran in. "Drew! Margot just came to!"

"Finally," Drew pushed away from her desk. "I was beginning to think I was going to have to put in that intercom system." She followed her sister to the infirmary, but as they got there, crash carts came around the corner at a run, heading for Margot's room. "What the hell?"

"Someone tried to smother her by holding a plastic bag across her face," the palace Doctor answered.

"Did anyone see who it was?"

"No, my Queen. The person wore a mask, and I'm afraid they escaped capture."

"You fucking morons!" Drew pulled at her hair. "Will she be all right?"

"We think so, but I'm afraid she's lapsed back into a coma."

"Damn! Well, keep me appraised of her condition." She turned to one of her personal guards. "You stay here. I'll send a replacement. I want a twenty-four hour guard put on this door."

"Yes, your Majesty."

"Kind of like shutting the hanger after the rats get in. Come on, Stasha. Let's get back to the office. I want to know where every fucking person in this palace was."

"Why would anyone try to kill Margot?" Stasha asked.

"Because she saw the assassin."

Zarco sat in his cell. His days seemed endless. His life had no meaning or purpose. He felt unloved and unwanted. He watched the screen in front of him and listened to the reporter.

"A few weeks ago the Queen asked to be called Drewcila Qwah, the name that she used in her five years away from us."

Zarco grimaced.

"The Queen's popularity among the working class is phenomenal. Most people now refer to their queen as Queen Qwah. Behind me is a beauty salon. As you can see, the sign in the window says they now do the 'Drewcila Do'. With me today is Bartis, a stylist at the Beauty Wave Salon. So tell us, Bartis, what is the 'Drewcila Do'?"

The man smiled for the camera and waved big, before he spoke. "It's the fabulous cut that our marvelous Queen Qwah is sporting. It's simple, dramatic and easy to care for. The perfect do for the busy working woman on the go."

"Thanks, Bartis. We'll now join Yarta down at the Rags clothing store. Yarta?"

The picture switched to a middle aged woman in a "Drewcila Do". She was standing at a counter in the clothing store. "Thanks, Jar."

"Hello! I'm Yarta, and I'm here in the Rags store on the corner of Rock and Stone, speaking to Bobit who owns the Store. Bobit, tell us what has become your number one selling item."

The man held up a palace guard's uniform. "These. I can't keep them in stock. They sell as fast as I get them. Everyone wants to look like the Queen."

"And what do you think of the Queen, Bobit?"

The man smiled broadly. "Long live the Queen! She's an absolute doll, and not bad looking, either. Now remember, we have all sizes in stock, and best of all, these uniforms are made of fifty percent recycled materials."

"Thanks, Bobit." The reporter walked away from the counter. "And that's not all. There is a Drewcila doll. A board game called Salvagers' Paradise. And you can get Queen Qwah trading cards, or a T shirt featuring either the Queen, her sister Stasha, members of the palace guard, or the queen's alien body guard, Van Gar. To top it all off, the Queen has opened her own brewery, and soon you'll be able to go to the store and pick up a six pack of Salvager's Grog. This is the very same beer that they serve in the palace, and the Queen's picture will be on every totally recycled can."

"Marcus!" Zarco screamed. Marcus ran in. "Turn it off! Turn it off!" Marcus turned the set off, and looked with concern into Zarco's crazed eyes.

"You OK?"

"Can't you see, boy? It's too late now! Too late! There's no going back!"

Drew looked at the fancy frocks paraded in front of her, and made a face. She was tired of trying to find something suitable to wear to this banquet thing.

"Enough!" She waved her hand in a dismissive manner. "Call Lulu the leather lady."

"Drew, the point was to show the nobles that you can act with regal grace and dignity!" Facto protested.

"Let me tell you something, Facto," Drew said. Then she took a sip of the smoking drink she held in her hand, smiled with appreciation, and went on. "Class has nothing to do with how you dress, or how you act, or how you carry yourself, or even the way you talk."

"Heaven help us," Fitz mumbled.

"What's that?" Drew asked.

"Ah...I was just saying that whatever you choose will be heavenly," Fitz stammered, his face scarlet.

Drew laughed, and shook her head. "Stasha, call Lulu. I must have something suitable..."

"Just for one night, couldn't you...well, wear something tasteful?" Stasha pleaded.

"Leather is tasteful, and it's certainly not cheap."

She thought for a minute, and then turned to Van Gar. "Van, get me Jack Knife."

"The arms dealer? But he's a..."

"...very charming business man. I know. You'll find his code in the files."

"What do I tell him when I reach him?"

"Tell him that Taralin Zarco, Queen of all Gildart, wishes to do business with him. But quickly. What I need, I need within four days."

"Can't you just order it over the computer direct from him?"

Drew looked at Van Gar in disbelief. "No, I can't."

She cut a quick glance at Facto.

"Oh. Oh!" Van nodded his head in understanding. After all, it would be very easy for any member of the staff to access the computer and extract information. There were three common terminals in the building, and Facto, Fitz, and several other upper level staff had their own terminals. With this antiquated system, anyone could link into anyone else's terminal.

Till now there had never been any real need for secrecy within the palace walls. Back in the "good old days," everyone was to be trusted. But that was before Marcus abducted the King and someone tried to kill first Drew and then Margot. Whatever happened, Van Gar had a feeling that trust like that would never again be part of life in the palace. He was shaken from his train of thought by raised voices.

"You still have not explained why you can't deal with an arms dealer from our own country. Or for that matter go through the military." Facto was obviously hot under the collar. "Why would you rather give kingdom funds to some alien instead of your own people!"

"Don't get uppity with me, Fucktoad. I could still have your ass beheaded." She laughed loudly. "Behead your ass, that's funny."

"Perhaps if we knew what it was that you wanted…"

"Shut the fuck up, Fatso! You're getting on my nerves, besides which I'm not at all sure that you're not the asshole who keeps trying to kill me, so why the hell would I tell you anything of importance? You are all dismissed. And for the record, I don't mean that in a 'kindly leave so I can get some work done' sort of way. I mean that in a 'you're pestering the shit out of me, get the hell out of my face' way. Stasha, get me Lulu the leather lady. Van Gar, put in that call to Jack Knife."

They started to file out; Fitz stopped in the doorway.

"I just wanted to report that all seems to be going as planned as concerns the banquet."

"You're a good man, Fitz." She started to go through the papers on her desk, but realized that he was still there. "Is there anything else, Fitz?"

"I was just wondering if you have heard anything this morning concerning Margot."

"I'm afraid there's been no change. The doctor says it could be hours, or it could be months."

"I'm sorry to hear that. Margot was simply in the wrong place at the wrong time. It's a shame."

He walked away, and Drew went back to her rat killing. She looked at the papers regarding the ship she was preparing. Decision time was just around the corner, and she still had no idea what she was going to do. Since they had argued the other night, Van Gar had kept his distance, and Drew could feel a rift growing between them. She also felt a growing attachment to the country she was running, and she liked the power. She liked watching the newscasts and realizing that she was making the news. She liked the giant salvaging empire she was building. But Zarco would be back soon, and what then? The only way she could keep all this power was to keep Zarco gone, or make him dead. But Stasha loved Zarco, and she couldn't do that to her only sister. If she went back to Salvaging…she just didn't know if she could now. Go back to a hard life where nothing she did really seemed to matter, and the only important things in life were keeping your ship running, getting a good load, and getting shit-faced drunk.

She had become far too accustomed to snapping her fingers and having the world change to suit her needs and her dreams. It would be very hard to go back to food processors which spit out brown goop three times a day, and re-cycled water. But what could she realistically expect here? The people loved her, but the nobles hated her. Recent public opinion polls showed that ninety percent of the population was happy with the way she was running things. Zarco would have to listen to her.

Zarco. He was a major problem. He said he loved her, but she didn't love him. Stasha loved Zarco, and he didn't love her. And Drew absolutely refused to love Van Gar as long as he wouldn't love her. Someone hated her enough to kill her, and that damn Earth man was still missing. Sometimes it seemed to her that it was a hell of a lot easier to deal with the problems of an entire country than it was to tackle a single one of her personal problems.

When Fitz woke up on the morning of the day of the banquet, it was to the sound of power tools running and workers screaming. He threw on his robe and ran in the direction of the noise. When he walked into the banquet room, there were ladders and scaffolds everywhere, and twenty to thirty aliens of all descriptions were running around the room with their hands full of wire.

"What's going on?" he screamed.

"The Queen wants new lights put in for the banquet." A worker explained as he approached Fitz.

"Are you aware that the banquet takes place tonight?"

"Hang onto your hat, pops. We'll be outtah here in a couple of hours."

"Just make sure that you are." Fitz stormed off towards the Queen's office. The guards stopped him at the door and checked him with the objects detector. "What the hell…"

"By the Queen's orders, everyone entering her presence must be checked."

Fitz stormed into Drew's office. She stood in the middle of the room, modeling a black leather loin-cloth and vest. The vest was covered in gold chains. She looked at Fitz.

"Don't you really think you should be dressed?" he asked.

She spun around. "So, what do you think?"

Fitz threw his hands up in the air and stormed right back out of the office again.

"Maybe he's right. OK, Lulu. I'll take the black pants with the silver studs down the side and the red wrap-around shirt."

"Good choice," the leather lady said. "Anything else?"

"Ah, what the hell. I'll take this outfit, too."

The alien workers got out of the banquet room barely in time for the staff to get the room decorated and prepared for their guests. In fact, it had been so close that the finishing touches were being done as the first guests arrived. But now the guests were all present. Everything was right on schedule, and the Queen and her retinue stood poised, waiting for the last of the guests to be seated.

"This is stupid," Drew mumbled.

"Just this once, Drew," Stasha begged.

"They all have to be seated so that we can walk in and make them stand up again. That is just the stupidest fucking thing I've ever heard."

Facto stood in the very back, and tried to shut the Queen's latest tirade out. He felt a tapping on his shoulder, and turned to face a young page.

"What is it, boy?"

"It's Margot, sir. She's just come to, and she says it's urgent that she speak to the Queen."

"The Queen is preparing to meet the nobles of the country. I'll go receive the message, and give it to the Queen."

The page nodded and was off.

Facto tapped on Fitz's shoulder. "I've got to go. Go on without me. I'll be back as soon as I can." Fitz made a face. "With any luck I'll be back before we go in. But it is urgent." Fitz nodded and Facto was off.

Facto ran all the way to the infirmary. The guards stopped him only briefly. He went to Margot's bedside. "My Lady?"

"Facto, where's the Queen?"

"She's getting ready to address the nobles of…"

"I know who's trying to kill the Queen."

The band played the Royal anthem, the huge doors opened, and the Queen entered the room followed by her retinue.

"Nice touch," she whispered to Stasha, speaking of the band.

"Harlot!" A woman in the crowd screamed and stood up. "What right have you got running our country? You're not even one of us!"

"Guards," Drew said calmly and with a smile. "Get this bitch out of my palace." The guards ran in and seized her, but she put up a fight. Then the door burst open and Facto ran in, gasping for breath.

"Stop him!" Facto screamed and pointed his finger—at whom, no one was quite sure. There was a loud hissing noise and the Queen fell to the ground. The assassin was now obvious, and having lost all hope of going undetected, he started to fire another shot at his target. Facto ran across the room and tackled him, and his weapon went spinning across the floor.

Drew lay still on the ground. Stasha leaned over her, shaking her and crying.

"Drew, Drew can you hear me?"

Drewcila coughed, "I see a light, a bright light and some one is calling me." She coughed again.

"What are they saying?" Stasha asked through her tears.

"They're saying…" She coughed, and her body was racked with spasms. "They're saying 'come into the light, Drew, join us.'"

"Don't listen, Drew," Stasha cried. "Don't go into the light."

Van Gar made a face. "Give it a rest, won't ya?"

"My sister's dying, you beast!" Stasha screamed back.

"I wasn't talking to you." He kicked Drew. "Come on, asshole, get up."

Drew sat bolt upright, and Stasha grabbed at her chest and gasped in shock. Drew leaned over and kissed Stasha on the cheek. In response, Stasha slapped Drew on the shoulder so hard that she rocked backwards.

"Geeze! Learn to take a joke, sis…So, who was it?" Drew asked.

"Fitz," Van Gar said in disbelief. He looked at Facto. "I really owe you an apology."

Facto shrugged.

"Why?" Drew asked Fitz. "I thought you liked me."

"You're destroying the dignity and beauty of our kingdom. You've turned this country into a festering heap of dung, where pageantry and honor have no place…"

"I disagree." Zarco walked into the room.

"Oh, Honey, you're home!" Drew skipped up to him and hugged his neck. He hugged her back, tightly. "So, can we eat now?"

Later, they all stood around Margot's bed.

"So, why did he try to kill Margot?" Stasha asked.

"I thought I saw him walk out of the archway, but I immediately dismissed it because Fitz rarely goes into the courtyard. He has violent allergies," Margot said.

"He knew Drew hadn't seen him, but he couldn't be sure that Margot hadn't, and he couldn't take any chances," Facto said.

"He must have known I'd seen him," Margot said, shaking. "I'll never forget his expression when he held that bag over my face. He looked more scared than hateful."

"Well, I for one refuse to feel sorry for him." Zarco gave Drew's shoulders a squeeze.

"Please don't misunderstand, but I want to know why the laser shot didn't hit you. He couldn't have fired it from more than six inches away." Facto said.

"Oh, it hit me. At least it would have, but I figured there would be an attempt at the banquet. Too many people were pulling for it besides Fitz—including yourself. And since everyone kept insisting that the force behind the assassin must be a member of the nobility, I figured that walking into a room full of them unprotected would have launched me right into the stupid category. That's where my old friend Jack Knife came in. As you undoubtedly know, sometimes the best offense is a good defense. Jack has weapons of all types—even the defensive ones. I had him hook up a system keyed to my body chemistry. As long as I was in the banquet room, I was protected by my own personal force field."

"The workmen Fitz was so excited about! The lights…"

"There never were any new lights. It was all part of the security system," Drew said.

"My King," Facto said. "It is good to have you back. And may I say that you look none the worse for wear."

"My captors were very good to me," he said.

"Do you have any idea who they were?" Facto asked.

"No, I never saw their faces. They weren't a bad lot, they just wanted change. I guess Taralin gave them something I couldn't."

Van Gar crept quietly from the room. He started down the long hall, feeling very much like a fifth wheel.

Drew looked around and noticed Van Gar was gone. She pushed away from Zarco and started for the door.

"Where are you going?" Zarco asked.

"Give me a break. I've got to go to the can, if that's all right with you."

"The bathroom," Facto interpreted.

Drew nodded and was gone.

"I think we'd all better leave and let Margot get some rest," Stasha said.

"I've been asleep for weeks," Margot protested. "I think I've had enough rest."

"Even so, I have to agree with Stasha," Zarco said. "Come on, we can talk in my office."

"About your office, Sire." Facto began yet another explanation.

Drew caught up with Van Gar.

"Van!" He stopped and turned to face her. "Where are you going?"

"I don't know, Drew. Why don't you tell me?"

"Boy, you're in a mood."

"Give me a ship, Drew. I think you owe me that for putting up with all this palace shit and being your step and fetchem boy."

Drew had an angry retort poised on the tip of her tongue, but swallowed it. "I got you a ship," she bit out.

"One that flies—now. I'm tired of being a pawn in your waiting game."

"The ship is ready for take-off, and the pilot is on board."

"Why didn't you say so?"

"I was hoping you'd want to stay here with me."

"Why? For what reason?" Van Gar looked at her in disbelief.

"I was hoping that you could answer that."

"There is nothing for me here, Drew," Van Gar said. "I just want to go."

"Vista Port, dock 19." She hugged him and stood back. "Good luck."

"You, too...Taralin." He hugged her tight, then let her go and walked toward the exit.

Zarco looked around his office and made a face. Beer stains on the walls and carpet. Cigar burns in all the furniture. Papers stacked haphazardly everywhere. He sat down in his chair and stretched. "There's no place like home."

"It's good to have you back...but...well, I hope I'm not out of line, Sire, and don't tell Drew I said this, but...well, the country's healthy. I don't approve of her methods. But while she would never admit to it, she has a genuine care for the people, and she knows how to get things done. I hope you'll listen carefully to her council in future."

"Facto, if I have learned anything from my experience, it is not to take anything lightly. Drew got the job done because she didn't care whose toes she stepped on to do it."

Zarco looked up as Drewcila walked into the room. "What's wrong?"

"Van Gar left. I'm gonna hit the sack. It's been a long day," Drew left, and Zarco felt his heart sink. She had let him stay in a cell for three months, and life had gone on. But the alien was leaving and she looked as if she had been crushed.

"Well, I'm looking forward to my own bed." Zarco tried to keep the disappointment from his voice. "I think I'll get a shower and turn in as well. It's good to see you all again. Good night."

Zarco went to his room. After showering and shaving he lay down on his bed—alone. He stared at the ceiling, hoping against hope that Taralin would want to spend this night with him. Just as he was prepared to give up, the adjoining door opened, and she walked in—still in the black pants and red shirt she'd worn to the banquet. She turned the lights down.

"You know something, Zarco? I wish I did remember you. Your love is the purest thing I've ever known. I've never had anything like that in my life." She walked seductively over to him and wrapped her arms around his neck. "Show me, Zarco. Show me how to love. Make me remember what it was like."

She had watched her sister walk through the adjoining door, and knew it was time for her to go. She walked out the door and started down the hall with her bag in her hand.

"Stasha," a voice called after her. She turned around to face Facto, and he took a step back. "Where...Where are you going?"

"I think it would be best...well, if I wasn't around for awhile."

Facto nodded. "Perhaps. Well, I, for one, will miss you."

"And I shall miss you, my friend. Take care of them for me. They deserve some happiness."

"Good-bye, and good journey."

Chapter 18

The drive to the spaceport had been a real bitch. He traveled through a hundred miles of boring countryside and into the congested streets of the spaceport at midnight. It had taken him three hours to get ten miles.

During that three hours, he decided that nothing could be worse then that drive.

Then he got lost at the spaceport. He'd been wandering around for half an hour and still hadn't found Dock 19. Everything looked exactly the same. Every hall. Every water fountain. Every spaceport bar, restaurant, or rest room.

All exactly, boringly the same.

"Want a flower?" a man in a white robe and ponytail pushed a flower in Van Gar's face.

"No, I don' wan' no damn flower!" Van Gar pushed the man's hand away with a growl. The man ran after him.

"Want a flower?"

"I said, I don't want no dam flower!" He spun around and glared at the man, fully intending to take his anger out on the man's face. Then he took a closer look at him. "Monkey boy?"

"Van Gar!" Tim grabbed Van Gar's hand and started pumping it up and down.

"Tim, what the hell are you doing?"

"I've found the place where I belong," he said throwing his arms out in an all-encompassing sweeping motion. "I am the Universe, and the Universe is me. All of nature is my brother, Van Gar. I feel so complete. So whole…want a flower?"

"No, Tim, I don't want a fucking flower. What I want is Dock 19."

"It's down that way." Tim pointed, then he held up a book. "This is a book by our prophet. For a mere two Iggys you can find the inner peace that has encompassed my soul…"

"If I buy the book, will you leave me alone, Tim?"

"Well…if that's what you want," Tim said.

"If you'll leave me alone that's well worth two Iggys. I had really forgotten what an irritating little fucker you are."

Tim held the book out one hand while holding his other hand out. Van Gar put the money in Tim's open hand and grabbed the book, grumbling.

"Good to see you again, Van Gar. May the Great Bubba watch over you on your way." Tim was stepping out of Van Gar's way when a ship landed. It shook the whole station.

The Earthman passed out cold.

Van Gar step over Tim's prone body and made his way to Dock 19. He couldn't miss it. He stopped, struck dumb. There in the dock rested the *Garbage Scow*, looking better than the day she had rolled off the assembly line.

"Well, I'll be damned."

The hatch was open, and he walked into the ship. It was then that he started to wonder if it wasn't just a new ship of the same model. Everything was perfect. Everything was clean. He walked onto the bridge and flopped down in his old chair. He looked around and then frowned.

"Only one thing missing," he whispered into the emptiness of the ship.

"Yeah, they haven't had time to install the whirlpool."

Van spun around in his chair, his jaw dropped and he stared in disbelief.

"Well, maybe next time we dock. Right now we've got a load of tank tracks needin' to go to Ganis."

"Drew…I…" Jumping up, he ran to her and embraced her. "I never thought I'd see you again!"

"Ah, I knew you'd miss me," Drew said with a crooked smile. She pushed away from him a little, looking up at him. "You'd mope around and be all moody and wouldn't be worth a shit for moving salvage. Besides I was getting bored. Being treated like a tiny god gets tedious after awhile."

Drew sat down in her command chair and Van Gar sat back down beside her. Drew grabbed a beer out of the cooler she had stocked and waiting for her. She popped the bottle cap off on the console then leaned back in her chair and flopped her feet up on the console.

"Yeah, like the humans say, 'There's no place like home, Dorothy.'"

"What's a Dorothy?" Van asked with a smile.

Drew shrugged. "Damned if I know."

She turned to look at him. "I have learned a very valuable lesson, Van Gar."

"That friendship is more important than power and money?" Van Gar suggested.

"No."

"That it's better to help others than to get rich yourself?"

"Have you been sitting out in the desert eating sun-cooked Hurtelas? No, no, none of that meaningless drivel. What I learned was...If you have enough money, you can get anything done. I had the *Scow* retrieved about two months ago when I learned that the sands of the Galdart desert are only fifty feet deep, and they've been working on it ever since. I've put equipment on this fucker you wouldn't find on the best salvaging rig in the quadrant. Fancy shit right off of royal yachts."

"How did you beat..."

"You here? Did you not hear what I just said about un-limited material resources? I took the Royal Jet."

"But Drew...you can't just take off. You're the Queen. Don't you think there's a chance they'll miss you?"

"One night Stasha and I got really drunk and bashed men. We were farting around, and we noticed that with just a little makeup, a hair cut, and a wardrobe change, we could easily pass for each other. We even fooled the household staff, with a little help from a wig...We even fooled you."

"Up close you wouldn't have and you won't fool Zarco either. He'll figure you out."

"By the time he does, it won't matter. Zarco wants a Queen who will behave the way he wants her to behave. Stasha can do that, she wants to. Zarco can claim that undying love shit all he wants, but you and I both know that he has got to be tired of my hot little ass by now."

"So, you're going to give up being Queen just like that?" Van Gar said in disbelief.

"It wasn't *just like that*. It wasn't an easy decision. But eventually I got tired of having everything my way. Maybe it's not right for any one person to have so much power for an extended period of time. I would miss the brown stuff three times a day, and the re-cycled water—and I'd miss you. Even though you are a pain in the ass."

"I don't know what I would have done without you, Drew..."

"Probably rot in some worm hole," Drew said looking at her nails.

After a moment, Van Gar looked up and asked suspiciously, "So, what do you get out of all this?"

"What do you mean?" Drew said defensively. "I get that good feeling you get from knowing that you have done the right thing."

"Oh, come on, Drew. I know you better than that. There has to be an angle. With you there is always an *angle*. You wouldn't have done all of that. You wouldn't have held all that power and all that wealth in your hand and walked off to come back to the same ship, same crew, same life. So...what did you get?"

Drew grinned. "Why, Van, I'm ashamed of you! What do you mean, *what did I get out of it*? Why, I got to see who I was; where I came from. I got to help a struggling country get on it's feet."

Van Gar stared at her in disbelief.

She grinned widely. "All right, all right...While I was Queen I put myself in sole control of the country's Salvaging operation. My name is on all the Salvaging contracts. I personally own all the salvaging ports, and the brewery, too."

"And what do I get?" Van Gar asked with a laugh.

"Why, you get the privilege of basking in my presence." Drew looked at Van Gar and smiled triumphantly. "I built a Salvaging Empire...the largest salvaging operation in the galaxy. And it's *mine*, all *mine*." She laughed and held her hands above her head. "And now, I am Drewcila Qwah, Queen of the Salvagers."

Selina Rosen biography

Selina Rosen lives in rural Arkansas with her partner of 7 years and her 18 year-old son. Her work has appeared in several magazines and anthologies including a story that will be coming out in *Sword and Sorceress 16*.

Selina's hobbies include gardening, sword fighting, and hanging out in bars. She's not much of a gardener, mediocre at sword fighting however rumor has it that she is actually quite good at hanging out in bars.

She believes in researching her work in every detail. *Queen of Denial* is the end product of a life time of drinking, working in the trash collection business, and getting into fist fights over petty crap.

Selina is currently editor and chief of *Yard Dog Comics*, and is working on several writing projects including a sequel to *Queen of Denial*, tentatively titled *Recycled*.

Don Maitz biography

The work of Don Maitz is quite literally fantastic. For some twenty years, he has created paintings containing elements of fantasy, exaggerated fact, and imaginative fiction. His work began appearing from New York City based book publishers and continues to evolve in that market. He has received wide exposure as the original artist of the Captain Morgan Spiced Rum pirate character that appears on bottles, billboards, and magazines through national advertising campaigns. Joseph Seagrams & Sons, National Geographic Society, Kodak, Bell Telephone, Bantam Doubleday Dell, Warner Books, Ballantine Del Rey, Penguin USA, and Harper Collins Publishers are some of his clients. His work has been produced for the limited edition print market with images released by Mill Pond Press, and a poster with the Greenwich Workshop.

He has illustrated books and stories by such authors as; Isaac Asimov, Ray Bradbury, C. J. Cherryh, L. Sprague De Camp, Raymond Feist, Eric Lustbader, Stephen King, his wife, author/artist Janny Wurts, and Roger Zelazny.

His works are internationally recognized and acclaimed. He has twice been presented the world science fiction's premier accolade, the Hugo award in the Best Artist category. Also, a special Hugo award for Best Artwork in 1989. He has earned a Howard award from the World Fantasy Convention, a Silver Medal of Excellence and Certificate of Merit from the Society of Illustrators in New York City where his work has been included in four of their prestigious annual exhibitions. He has received ten Chesley awards from his peers in the Association of Science Fiction and Fantasy Artists. His paintings have been featured in exhibitions at NASA's 25th Anniversary presentation in Cleveland, Ohio, the New Britain Museum of American Art, at the Park Avenue Atrium, and the Hayden Planetarium in New York City. They were also featured at two separate shows at the Delaware and the Canton Art Museums, the Discovery Museum in Bridgeport, CT, and in the Orlando Science Center, Florida. His works are included in the permanent collections of the Delaware Art Museum and the New Britain Museum of American Art.

Born in Bristol, Connecticut, Don grew up in the adjacent town of Plainville where he proceeded through the school system. Existing in the mundane environment this town suggests, an active imagination was a Godsend. Drawing became an adventurous escape. School art classes, an art correspondence course, and evening figure drawing classes at the University of Hartford led to enrollment at the Paier School of Art from 1971-75. He graduated top of the class, receiving instruction from Ken Davies—one of America's foremost still life and trompe l'oeil painters, Rudolf Zallinger—Pulitzer prize winning muralist and Time Life Books illustrator, Leonard E. Fisher—Pulitzer prize winning fine artist, book illustrator and author, and Deane Keller—portrait and figure painter affiliated with Yale University. These are just a few of the talented and actively working professors that provided instruction. Four of his professors authored and published art instruction books.

Don Maitz's work has enhanced various published formats including: books, magazines, cards, a record album, posters, limited edition prints, puzzles, and computer screen saver programs. Two art books collections of his color paintings have been published. They are *First Maitz* and *Dreamquests*, both are now sold out. He illustrated a signed, limited edition of Stephen King's novel, *Desperation*. Best selling screensaver software entitles *Magical Encounters* and *Magical Encounters II* compile a variety of his work with the works of his talented wife Janny Wurts.

Don Maitz spent the 1985 school year as guest instructor of illustration, drawing, and multi-media at the Ringling School of Art and Design in Florida. Some time later, he married Janny Wurts and together they moved their combined studio and residence to Florida.

Plan B is now in effect!   This is not a test!

Plan B

The new Laiden Novel by
Sharon Lee and Steve Miller

ISBN 1-892065-00-2 $14.00 Soft cover trade 336 pages

From the authors of *Agent of Change, Conflict of Honors,* and
Carpe Diem.

"You've done it again! That was one
marvelous read!"—Anne McCaffrey

"It comes to life when one turns the pages."
—Andre Norton

What Ho, Magic!

Tanya Huff

ISBN: 1-892065-04-5 Price: $16.00
Soft cover trade 384 pages

What Ho, Magic! is a collection of fifteen short stories by Tanya
Huff the acclaimed writer of the Blood and Kigh series. Included
in this collection are the three earlier short stories of Vicky, Michael,
and Henry from her Blood series and a brand new never before
published novella of Vicky and Michael.

"Well done, with truly likeable and interesting characters…"
—*Locus*

"Huff's adventure is great fun to read."—*Publishers Weekly*

Come check out our web site for details on these Meisha Merlin authors!

Kevin J. Anderson
Storm Constantine
Sylvia Engdahl
Jim Grimsley
Keith Hartman
Beth Hilgartner
Tanya Huff
Janet Kagan
Caitlin R. Kiernan
Lee Killough
Lee Martindale
Sharon Lee & Steve Miller
Jim Moore
Adam Niswander
Selina Rosen
Kristine Kathryn Rusch
S. P. Somtow
Allen Steele
Michael Scott

http://www.angelfire.com/biz/MeishaMerlin

If you would like a free copy of
Meisha Merlin Publishing, Inc.'s new cataloge,
please send a self addressed stamped envelope to:

Meisha Merlin Publishing, Inc.
P. O. Box 7
Decatur, GA 30031